The Hawks of Hawk-Hollow
A Tradition of Pennsylavania
Vol. I

by

Robert Montgomery Bird

The Hawks of Hawk-Hollow
A Tradition of Pennsylavania
Vol. I
by Robert Montgomery Bird

Copyright © 2024

All Rights reserved.

No part of this publication may be reproduced, stored in a retrieval system, or transmitted in any form or by any means, electronic, mechanical, photocopying or Otherwise, without the written permission of the publisher.
The author/editor asserts the moral right to be identified as the author/editor of this work.

ISBN: 978-93-62201-34-8

Published by

DOUBLE 9 BOOKS
2/13-B, Ansari Road
Daryaganj, New Delhi – 110002
info@double9books.com
www.double9books.com
Tel. 011-40042856

This book is under public domain

ABOUT THE AUTHOR

Robert Montgomery Bird was an American author, playwright, and doctor. He was born on February 5, 1806, and died on January 23, 1854. Bird was born on February 5, 1806, in New Castle, Delaware. He was born into a family of pioneers. His father was a wealthy partner in the firm of Navy agents Bird and Riddle. When Bird was four years old, his father died. His mother and brothers moved to Philadelphia, but his rich uncle, Nicholas Van Dyke, took him in. Then Bird went to New Castle Academy, where he was encouraged to get better at music. He later wrote that school was not fun for him. After going to the New Castle Academy and the Germantown Academy, he got his degree in 1824 from the University of Pennsylvania. Bird began to write about Latin, American, and English literature, especially the playwrights of the Elizabethan era. Then, while he was in medical school, he began to write short poems and stories. He wasn't very interested in medicine. By 1827, he had written for the Philadelphia Monthly Magazine and written two comedies, 'Twas All for the Best and News of the Night. After he graduated from medical school, he tried to start his own medical practice, but after a year, he gave up and went into writing instead.

CONTENTS

INTRODUCTION 7
CHAPTER I 10
CHAPTER II 17
CHAPTER III 33
CHAPTER IV 41
CHAPTER V 48
CHAPTER VI 54
CHAPTER VII 69
CHAPTER VIII 74
CHAPTER IX 84
CHAPTER X 94
CHAPTER XI 103
CHAPTER XII 114
CHAPTER XIII 122
CHAPTER XIV 136
CHAPTER XV 147
CHAPTER XVI 153
CHAPTER XVII 161
CHAPTER XVIII 168
CHAPTER XIX 174
CHAPTER XX 185

INTRODUCTION

"Escúchame, y no me creas
Despues de haberme escuchado"—

"Hear me, but don't believe me, after you have heard"—says Calderon, the Spanish dramatic poet, with a droll spirit of honesty, only equalled by the English Burton, who concludes the tale of the Prebend, in his Anatomy of Melancholy, by exclaiming, "You have heard my tale; but, alas! it is but a tale,—a mere fiction: 'twas never so, never like to be,—and so let it rest." We might imitate the frankness of these ancient worthies, in regard to the degree of credit which should be accorded to our tradition; but it would be at an expense of greater space and tediousness than we care to bestow upon the reader. We could not declare, in the same wholesale way, that the following narrative is a mere fabrication, for such it is not; while to let the reader into the secret, and point out the different facts (for facts there are) that are interwoven with the long gossamer web of fiction, would be a work of both time and labour.

We have always held the Delaware to be the finest and noblest river in the world,—not, indeed, that it *is* so, but because that was a cardinal item in our creed of childhood; and to all such points of belief we hold as strongly as we can, philosophy and experience to the contrary notwithstanding. They are holy and useful, though flimsy, ties—little pieces of rose-coloured packthread that keep sorted together whole bundles of pleasant reminiscences, and therefore as precious in our esteem as shreds of gold and silver. In consequence of this persuasion, we have learned to attach importance to every little legend of adventure, in any way associated with the Ganga of our affections; and of such it has been our custom, time out of mind, to construct, at least in imagination, little fairy edifices, in which golden blocks of truth were united with a cement of fancy. A novel is, at best, a piece of Mosaic-work, of which the materials have been scraped up here and there, sometimes in an un-chronicled corner of the world itself, sometimes from the forgotten tablets of a predecessor, sometimes from the decaying pillars of history, sometimes from the little mine of precious stones that is found in the human brain—at least as often as the pearl in the toad's head, of which John Bunyan discourses so poetically, in the Apology for his

Pilgrim's Progress. Of some of the pebbles that we have picked up along the banks of the Delaware, the following story has been constructed; but at what precise place they were gathered we do not think it needful to say. The torrent of fashionable summer rustication has already sent off a few little rills of visitation towards different corners of Pennsylvania, and one has begun to flow up the channel of the Delaware. In a few years— — *Eheu! fugaces, Posthume, Posthume!*— —this one will increase to a flood, all of men, women, and children, rolling on towards the Water-Gap; and *then* some curious individual will discover the nook into which we have been prying; and perhaps, if he chooses, come off with prizes still more valuable. At all events, he will discover—and that we hold to be something worth recording—that his eyes have seldom looked upon a more enchanting series of landscapes than stretches along this river, in one long and varied line of beauty, from New Hope and the Nockamixon Rocks, almost to its sources.

The story, such as it is, is rather a domestic tale, treating of incidents and characters common to the whole world, than one of which these components can be considered *peculiarly* American. This is, perhaps, unfortunate,—the tendency of the public taste seeming to require of American authors that they should confine themselves to what is, in subject, event, and character, indigenous to their own hemisphere; although such a requisition would end in reducing their materials to such a stock as might be carried about in a nut-shell. America is a part of the great world, and, like other parts, has little (that is, suited to the purposes of fiction) which it can call exclusively its own; and how far that little has been already *used up*, any one may tell, who is conversant with our domestic literature. Some little, however, of that little yet remains; and, by and by, we will perhaps ourselves join in the general scramble after it.

To conclude our Prolegomena—we recommend to all Philadelphians, who thirst for the breath of the mountains, and are willing to breathe it within the limits of their own noble State, to repair to the Delaware Water-Gap, sit them down in the porch of our friend Snyder, (or Schneider— we forget whether he yet sticks to the *Vaterländisch* orthography or not,) discourse with him concerning trout, deer, and rattlesnakes, and make themselves at home with him for a week. They will find themselves in one of the boldest mountain-passes in the United States, in the heart of a scene comprising crags, forests, and a river sprinkled with numerous islands, all striking, harmonious, and romantic. There, indeed, is neither a Round-Top nor a Mount Washington, with ladders on which to climb to heaven; but there are certain mountain ridges hard by, from whose tops he who is hardy enough to mount them, can well believe he *looks down* on heaven, so broad, so fair, so elysian are the prospects that stretch below. There, also, our friends will find such lime-trees as will cause them to rejoice that they have planted scions of the same noble and fragrant race at their own doors; and such a glorious display of rosebays, or *rhododendrons*, the noblest of American flowering shrubs, as may perhaps teach them the wisdom of transferring a few to their own gardens.

But we have not space to mention one-half the charms that await them in the Gap. If they have eyes to distinguish between the flutter of wings and loose hanging mosses, they may behold, at evening, the national bald-eagle soaring among his native cliffs, and winging to his perch on the far-up old hemlock, where they may see his reverend white head gleaming like a snow-flake among the leaves, until the wail of the whippoorwill calls the shadows of night over the whole mountain. Besides all this, and the other charms too tedious to mention, if they commend themselves to the favour of mine host, they will be roused up in the morning by the roar of a waterfall under their very pillows, and then, leaping into a boat, and rowing into the river, they may survey it at their ease,—as lovely a sheet of foam, rushing over a cliff an hundred and forty feet high, as was ever stolen from its bed of beauty to drive——*'Eheu! eheu conditionem hujus temporis!'*——the machinery of—a saw-mill.

CHAPTER I

> What man that sees the ever-whirling wheele
>   Of Change, the which all mortall thing doth sway,
> But that thereby doth find, and plainly feele,
>   How Mutability in them doth play
>   Her cruel sports to many men's decay
>
> SPENSER—Faerie Queene.

America is especially the land of change. From the moment of discovery, its history has been a record of convulsions, such as necessarily attend a transition from barbarism to civilization; and to the end of time, it will witness those revolutions in society, which arise in a community unshackled by the restraints of prerogative. As no law of primogeniture can ever entail the distinctions meritoriously won, or the wealth painfully amassed, by a single individual, upon a line of descendants, the mutations in the condition of families will be perpetual. The Dives of to-day will be the Diogenes of to-morrow; and the 'man of the tub' will often live to see his children change place with those of the palace-builder. As it has been, so will it be,—

"Now up, now doun, as boket in a well;"

and the honoured and admired of one generation will be forgotten among the moth-lived luminaries of the next.

That American labours under a melancholy infatuation, who hopes, in the persons of his progeny, to preserve the state and consideration he has acquired for himself. He cannot bequeath, along with lands and houses, the wisdom and good fortune which obtained them; nor can he devise preventives against the natural consequences of folly and waste. His edifice of pride must crumble to dust, when both corner-stone and hypogeum are based upon the contingencies of expectation; and the funeral-stone and the elm of his family mausoleum will vanish, in course of time, before the axe and plough of a new proprietor.

This is the ordinance of Nature, who, if she scatters her good gifts of talents with a somewhat despotic capriciousness, is well content that men should employ them in republican and equal rivalry.

In a little valley bordering upon the Delaware, there stood, fifty years since, a fair dwelling, within an ample domain, which a few years of vicissitude had seen transferred from its founder to a stranger, although wealth and a family of seven sons, the boldest and strongest in the land, might have seemed to insure its possession to them during at least two generations. The vale lies upon the right bank of the river, imbosomed among those swelling hills that skirt the south-eastern foot of the Alleghanies, (using that term in the broad, generic sense given it by geographers,) the principal ridge of which,—the Ka-katch-la-na-min, or Kittatinny, or, as it is commonly called, the Blue Mountain,—is so near at hand, that, upon a clear day, the eye can count the pines bristling over its gray and hazy crags. It stretches, indeed, like some military rampart of the Titans, from the right hand to the left, farther than the eye can reach, broken only by the gaps that, for the most part, give passage to rivers; and but for these, it would be entirely impassable.

The original proprietor of the estate was an English emigrant of humble degree, and, at first, of painfully contracted circumstances; but having fallen heir to a considerable property in his own land, and events of a very peculiar nature altering the resolution he had formed to enjoy it within the limits of the chalk-cliffs of Albin, he sat himself down in good earnest to improve the windfall at home. The little farm which he had cultivated with his own hands, was speedily swelled into an extensive manor; and deserting the hovel of logs which had first contented his wants, he built a dwelling-house of stone, so spacious, and of a style of structure so irregular and fantastic, that it had, at a distance, the air rather of a hamlet than a single villa, and indeed looked not unlike a nest of dove-cots stuck together on the hill-side. Without possessing one single feature of architectural elegance, it had yet a romantic appearance, derived in part from the scenery around, from the beauty of the groves and clumps of trees that environed it, and the vines and trailing flowers that were made, in summer at least, to conceal many of its deformities. It was exceedingly sequestered also; for except the log hovel, into which Mr. Gilbert (for that was his name) had inducted a poor widow, befriended out of gratitude for kindness shown him, when their respective conditions were not so unequal, there was not another habitation to be seen from his house, though it commanded an extensive prospect even beyond the river. The highway to the neighbouring Water-Gap, indeed, ran through the estate; the broad river below often echoed to the cries of boatmen and raftsmen, floating merrily onward to their market; and the village dignified with the title of County-town, was not above seven or eight miles distant; so that the valley was not always invested with a Sabbath-day silence; and, besides, his protegée, the widow, had, with Mr. Gilbert's consent, converted her hovel into a house of entertainment, which sometimes seduced a wayfarer to sojourn for a period in the valley. Mr. Gilbert himself did all he could to add life and bustle to his possessions, by doing honour to such well behaved villagers, or even strangers, as he could induce to ruralize with him; for having built and planted, and torn down and transplanted, until he knew not well what to do with himself, he hit upon that expedient for driving away ennui which passes for hospitality,—namely, converting into guests all proper, and indeed improper, persons from whom he could derive amusement, and who could assist him to kill time. To this shift he was driven, in great part, by the undomestic character of his children; who, so soon as they arrived at an age for handling the rifle, individually and infallibly ran off into the woods, until, as the passion for hunting grew with their growth, they might be said almost to live in them. It was this wild propensity, acting upon a disposition unusually self-willed and inflexible, in the case of his eldest boy, Oran, that defeated his scheme of spending the remainder of his days in England. He actually crossed the sea, with his whole family, and remained in the neighbourhood of Bristol, his native town, for the space of a year; but in that time, Oran, a boy only twelve years old, 'heartily sick,' as he said, 'of a land where there were no woods, and no place where he could get by himself,' finding remonstrance and entreaty fail to move his father's heart to his purpose, took the desperate resolution of returning to America alone; which he did, having concealed himself in the hold of a vessel, until she was out of the Channel. His sufferings were great, but he endured them with incredible fortitude; and finally after many remarkable adventures, he found himself again in his happy valley, in the charge or protection, if it could be so called, of the good widow Bell,—for that was the name of the poor woman befriended by his father. In a few months, his father followed him, perhaps instigated by affection, (for Oran, being the worst, was therefore the most favoured of his children,) by the murmurs of the others, or by the discovery he undoubtedly made, that his wealth would secure him, if not equal comfort, at least superior consideration, in the New World.

Consideration indeed he obtained, and increase of wealth; but the wild manners and habits of his children greatly afflicted him; and having married a second wife, he was induced, in the hope of 'making a gentleman,' as he called it, of the boy she bore him, (none of the others having that ambition,) to commit him to the protection of a sister, the widow of a Jamaica planter, who had divided with him the bequest that had made his fortune, and being childless herself, desired to adopt him as her heir.

Thus much of the early history of Mr. Gilbert was recollected with certainty, so late as the year 1782, by the villagers of Hillborough, the county-town already mentioned, who had so often shared his hospitality; but long before that time, he had vanished, with all his family, from the quiet, beautiful, and well-beloved valley. They were wont to speak with satisfaction of the good dinners they had eaten, the rare wines they had drunk, the merry frolics they had shared, in the Hawk's Hollow,—for so they perversely insisted upon calling what Mr. Gilbert, in right of possession, chose to designate as Avon-dale, in memory, or in honour of his own buxom river of Somerset; they related, too, to youthful listeners, the prophetic sagacity with which they had predicted violent ends to the young Hawks of Hawk-Hollow, (so they called the young Gilberts,) for their disobedience to father and mother, and their unusual passion for a life of adventure; and, finally, they shook their heads with suspicion and regret, when they spoke of Jessie, Gilbert's only daughter, of her early and mysterious death, and still more, to them, unaccountable burial. All that could be gathered in relation to this unhappy maiden, was dark and unsatisfactory: her death had seemingly, in some way, produced the destruction of the family and the alienation of the estate. It was an event of more than twenty years back; and from that period, until the time of his own sudden flight, Mr. Gilbert's doors were no longer open, and his sons were no more seen associated with the young men of the county. The maiden had died suddenly, and been interred in a private place on the estate.

In connexion with this event, some, more garrulous than others, were wont to speak of Colonel Falconer, the present proprietor of Hawk-Hollow, as having had some agency in the catastrophe; but what it was, they either knew not, or they feared to speak. Evil suspicions, however, gathered about this gentleman's name; and as he was seldom, if ever, seen in Hawk-Hollow in person, but had committed the stewardship of the property to the hands of a distant relative, who resided on it, the young felt themselves at liberty to fill up from imagination, the sketch left imperfect by the old; and accordingly, the Colonel, in time, came to be considered by those who had never seen him, as one of the darkest-hearted and most dangerous of his species. He was very rich; the station he occupied in the eyes of his country was lofty, and might have been esteemed noble; for he had shed his blood in the great and fearful battle of rights that was now approaching to a close; and after being disabled by severe and honourable wounds, he had changed the sphere of his exertions, and was now as ardent and devoted a patriot in the senate as he had been before in the field. Yet in this distant quarter, these recommendations to favour were forgotten; it was said, if he had done good deeds, there were evil ones enough to bury them as in a mountain, and if he had fought well for his country, he had struggled still more devotedly to aggrandize himself. In a word, he was called a hard, avaricious, rapacious man, whose chief business was to enrich himself at the cost of the less patriotic, and who had got the mastery of more sequestrated estates than an honest man could have come by. It was a sin of an unpardonable nature, that he had succeeded in getting possession of Hawk-Hollow, when there were so many others in the county who had set their hearts upon it.

His representative on the estate was a certain Captain John Loring, who, with all the patriotism of his connexion, and perhaps a great deal more, had never been able to turn it to any account. On the contrary, beginning the world with an ample patrimony, at the time when Mr. Falconer commenced as an adventurer, he had descended in fortune with a rapidity only to be compared with that of his friend's exaltation. The love of glory had early driven him from his peaceful farm on the Brandywine; and after distinguishing himself as a volunteer in the Indo-Gallic wars of Western Pennsylvania, it was his hard fate to bring his career of effective service to a close on what he was always pleased to call the Fatal Field of Braddock. From that bloody encounter he came off with more honour than profit, and with a body so mangled and a constitution so shattered, that a quarter of a century had scarce served to repair the dilapidation of his animal man. But the Captain had lost neither his spirit nor his love of glory. At the first trump of the Revolution, he donned the panoply of valour; he snatched up the pistols he had taken from a dead Canadian at the Fatal Field of Braddock, strapped upon his thigh the sword he had received for his services in storming certain Indian forts on the Alleghany river, clapped into his pocket the commission which the colonial government had granted him in reward of that gallant exploit, and reported himself, among a crowd of younger patriots, as ready to do and die for his country. The Commissioners looked at his gray hairs and shattered leg, (the latter of which had once been as full of musket-bullets as was ever a cartouche-box,) commended his virtue and enthusiasm, and divided the honours of command among those who were better fitted to do the state service. The Captain retired to his patrimonial estate, and there contented himself as well as he could, until the current of conflict, diverted from one bloody channel into another, came surging at last into the pastoral haunts of the Brandywine. At that time, his home was blessed with two children, a gallant boy of eighteen, and a merry little maiden of twelve. But one morning, he heard a trumpet pealing over the hills and a cannon roaring hard by, behind the woods. He looked at the face of his son, and the eye of the boy reflected back the fire of his father's spirit. Their horses were saddled in the stalls, and the spurs were already on young Tom Loring's heels. It was enough—the Captain carried his son to the grave.—But, to his own dying day, he rejoiced over the young man's fall. On this subject, the Captain was commonly considered by his neighbours to be crack-brained.

After this, came other misfortunes; and the Captain was a ruined man, landless, homeless, and childless, save that his little Catherine was still left to share his poverty, and, like a lamp in a cavern, to exaggerate rather than enlighten the gloom of his desolation. At this critical juncture, he found a firm and prudent friend in Colonel Falconer, by whom he was installed into the privileges, if not the actual possession of Hawk-Hollow, in the supervision and improvement of which he seemed now likely to pass the remainder of his days. How far the kindly feelings of relationship, or how far the influence of his daughter's growing beauty, had contributed to secure him the benevolence of this friend in need, was a question frequently agitated by the curious villagers. It was settled among them, that there was a wedding in the wind; but whether the young lady was to share the lot of her distinguished patron, or to be given to his gay and somewhat wild-brained son, was a point on which busy bodies were long coming at a conclusion. The Captain, though frank enough in his way, was not exactly the individual whom one would think of troubling with impertinent questions; and Miss Loring, however hospitable and courteous, had not yet selected a confidante from among the blooming nymphs of Hillborough. She was, however, the theme of as much admiration as curiosity; and being very beautiful, and of manners always gentle, and at times irresistibly engaging, the village poet immortalized her in rhyme, and the village belles forgave the eulogium.

It remains but to say a word more of the Gilberts, as a necessary introduction to a record, designed to rescue the story of their fate from the uncertain and unfaithful lips of tradition. After mingling in all the border wars, both Indian and civil, that, from the time of Braddock's defeat to the dispersion of the Connecticut settlers, distracted the unhappy Susquehanna settlements, they deserted the cause of their countrymen at the beginning of the Revolution, and appeared in the guise of destroying demons, at Wyoming, on that occasion of massacre, which has given to the spot a celebrity so mournful. In other words they were traitors and refugees; and however dreadful the reputation they obtained as bold and successful depredators, their fate was such as might have been, and perhaps was, anticipated by themselves. One after another, they were cut off, some by the rifle and tomahawk, one even by the halter, and all who did perish, by deaths of violence. It was indeed, at the time we speak of, confidently believed that Oran, the eldest of all, and the last survivor, had fallen within the space of a year, at a conflict on the banks of the Mohawk, along with other refugees of the neighbouring commonwealth, with whom he had associated himself. Great were the rejoicings in consequence with all who dwelt among the scenes of his earlier exploits; though some professed to have their doubts on the subject, and swore, that Oran Gilbert was not to be trusted, dead or alive, until his scalp was seen nailed on the county court-house door.

CHAPTER II

> Come here, my good hostess, pray how do you do?
> Where is Cicely so cleanly, and Prudence, and Sue?
> And where is the widow that dwelt here?— —
> PRIOR.

The year 1782 was distinguished on the western continent as the close of the great contest, which obtained for America the name and privileges of a free nation. The harbingers of peace came flitting into the land, with the swallows of spring; and before the autumn had withered into winter, so little doubt prevailed of a speedy reconciliation taking place between Great Britain and the United States, founded upon a full recognition by the former of all the claims of the latter, that the Continental Congress passed a resolve for the reduction of its army, to take effect on the first day of the coming year. War was no longer waged upon any scale of magnitude; such hostilities as continued, were conducted almost solely by the desperate and lawless of both parties, and consisted of predatory incursions, occasionally attempted in the wilder parts of the country, by some skulking band of refugees, and of expeditions of vengeance, planned and executed in a moment of wrath, by the excited sufferers. At this period, the only portion of the States, north of the Potomac, in the hands of the British, was the city of New York, with its dependencies; and around these narrow possessions the lines of the Continental army were drawn, extending from the Highlands of New York to the plains of Monmouth in New Jersey. Military posts therefore existed at no great distance from the Hawk's Valley; and although the wild and mountainous country on either bank of the Delaware offered the strongest retreats to men of desperate character, it had been very long since the inhabitants had apprehended any danger from the presence of enemies. In the earlier part of the year, at least, they had no cause for alarm; and accordingly they mingled, without alloy, their raptures at the prospect of returning peace with their rejoicings over the death of Oran Gilbert, the most dreaded and detested of the Hawks of Hawk-Hollow.

One atrocity had indeed been committed, in a neighbouring state, which, besides exciting the fiercest indignation, had taught the occupants of the valley how little their security was owing to any relenting of spirit, or want of military daring, on the part of the refugees, whom the general success of the republican arms had driven in great numbers into the city of New York. A certain Captain Joshua, or Jonathan, Huddy, of the New Jersey state troops, having been captured, after a gallant resistance, at one of the posts in Monmouth county of that state, by a party of loyalists from New York, was for a while immured in prison, then carried back to his native state, and finally hanged by his captors, without trial, sentence, or any authority whatever, except what was derived from the verbal orders of a body of men calling themselves the Board of Directors of the Associated Loyalists. The result of this wanton and brutal murder, and of the failure of the British authorities to bring the chief perpetrator to justice, was an instant order on the part of the American Commander-in-chief, to retaliate upon a British prisoner of equal rank; and before the month of May was over, young Asgill of the British Guards, whose story is familiar to all readers of American history, was conducted to the lines at Morristown, to await, in painful uncertainty, the fate that now depended, or seemed to depend, upon the movements of his countrymen in relation to the true criminal.

Late in the spring of this year, Hawk-Hollow received a new addition to its society, in the person of a stranger, who, one pleasant evening, rode up to the hovel, which, as was before mentioned, Dame Alice, or as she was more familiarly called, Elsie Bell, had, so many years before, converted into a house of entertainment. But the credit of the poor woman, now aged, infirm, and almost friendless, had long since departed; and the tongues of the ignorant and foolish, in an age when the most ridiculous superstitions were not wholly confined to the brains of children, had invested her habitation with a character which repelled alike the curious and the weary. Her age, her poverty, her loneliness, her unsocial character, and perhaps also her attachment to the memory of a family all others had learned to detest, had brought her into bad odour; and some thoughtless or malicious persons having persuaded themselves that a certain famous mortality among their cattle could have been caused by nothing short of witchcraft, it was soon determined that old Elsie had stronger claims to the character of a broom-rider than any other person in the county. It was fortunate for her that the imputation fell upon her in a land, which once, in the case of an old woman brought before a jury under the same charge, had rendered the wise and humane verdict, that they found her "guilty, not of being a witch, but of being *suspected*." It never once occurred to any individual to prosecute, or even persecute, poor Elsie; nor is it supposed that any sane man ever seriously believed a charge so cruel and absurd; yet the stain rested upon the unfortunate creature, and was the cause of her losing all the little custom of her house, and being, at one period, reduced to great straits.

Her house had a very lonely appearance, especially dreadful, at nightfall, in the eyes of the passing urchin. It was in a hollow place on the road-side, the head of a gully, which, expanding into a wide, though broken and winding ravine, ran down to the river, half a mile distant, receiving, before it had yet reached it, the waters of a foaming rivulet coming from another quarter. A little enclosure, or yard, serving as an approach to the house, was surrounded by oak-trees. Its surface was broken, and on one side was a rough and jagged rock, almost a crag, sprinkled with sumach and other wild plants, that hid one half of the lowly fabric, while the other peeped insidiously from under the boughs of an antique, spectral-looking sycamore, springing from the side of the ravine, which was, in part, overlooked by the hovel. A little runnel crossed the road immediately before the house; and flowing through the yard, and making its way among the naked roots of the sycamore, it fell, with a gurgling sound, into the ravine. The murmurs of this little cascade, affected variously by drought and rain, and by the echoes of the hollow, sent many a superstitious thrill to the heart of the countryman whom any unlucky accident compelled to pass by the cabin at midnight.

Of a silent, reserved, and even saturnine temper, there was perhaps enough in Elsie's cold welcome to repel visitation, even without the addition of imputed witchcraft; and long before that heavy charge had fallen upon her, it was esteemed a misfortune to be obliged to tarry above an hour at the Traveller's Rest, as the inn had been called in its days of credit. To crown all, about the time when men and boys were beginning to talk ominously about the rot and murrain, a rival establishment was set up, a few miles farther down the river, which offered the attractions of good liquors, lounging idlers, and a talkative host, who made it his business to be always well provided with news from the market, the army, and Congress. The last resource of the Traveller's Rest gave way before such a rival, and never more (at least for many years) was there seen a guest quaffing his cider, or smoking his pipe, in the shadow of Elsie's porch, except occasionally, when some stranger passed by, who boldly disregarded, or was entirely unacquainted with the popular superstition in relation to the hostess.

The privations suffered by the poor old woman, in consequence of this failure of her ordinary means of subsistence, were very great,—greater, indeed, than was suspected; for she uttered no complaint, and sought no relief. A few acres of ground had been added to the hovel, given to her by the elder Gilbert. The title was not, indeed, thought to be very strong, and as it lay in the very centre of Colonel Falconer's domains, a true *regnum in regno*, it was sometimes wondered he made no attempt to dispossess her, and thus complete her ruin. From these worn-out fields, had she been able to retain any one about her to cultivate them, she might have gleaned a scanty yet sufficient subsistence. But neither son nor kinsman of any degree, had the poor widow left in the wide world; and when men began to doubt, suspect, and shun her, she was no longer able to procure the assistance even of hirelings; and her fields lay fallow and overgrown with brambles. Her situation grew hopelessly distressed and desolate; in vain she exposed her slender stores of gingerbread in the window, and her bottles of spruce-beer in the cool brook, to tempt the wayfarer to turn aside for such refreshments. If the stranger did feel for a moment urged to exchange the scorching road, on a July day, for the shadowy porch, he cast his eye upon the garden, at the road-side, now the last dependence of the miserable widow, and beholding her uninviting and squalid appearance, passed on, without thinking how much real charity might have been conferred by the disbursement of a few pence at that abode of poverty.

Such was the condition of this poor solitary creature, when Captain Loring was installed into the manor house; and such it might have continued, had not his daughter, shocked at the discovery of her distresses, and interested doubly when she found in her a tone of mind and manners worthy of a better fate, came immediately, like an angel, to her aid, and restored her again to a state of comfort. Not satisfied with rendering this assistance, she rested not day or night, until she had procured a labourer to till the neglected fields, and had even obtained a little negro wench to dwell with Elsie as a domestic; and perceiving how much her sufferings were really owing to the ridiculous fears and prejudices of the country people, she made it a point frequently to visit her house in person, dragging along with her, when she could, the beaux and belles of the village, in the hope that others would soon follow the example, and thus restore the Traveller's Rest to its ancient reputation. She even prevailed upon her father to honour the house with his patronage, at least so far as to visit it, when riding by; and, though there was nothing in the tempers of the two to make any intercourse between them very friendly and agreeable, the Captain had humoured his daughter so long in that way, that it grew to be one of his habits; and he seldom passed by, without stopping for a moment, to bestow a few civilities upon the widow. Notwithstanding all these benevolent exertions of Miss Loring, however, the Traveller's Rest never recovered its reputation or custom; and when the traveller spoken of before, rode up to the porch, and announced his intention of entering, and even sleeping, under her roof, the poor widow herself regarded him with a species of amazement.

"How is it, good mother?" said he, observing her hesitation: "They told me, in the village, you could give me both meat and lodging. Do not fear I shall prove a fault-finder;—a crust of bread and a cup of milk, or, if need be, of water, will satisfy me; and as for a bed, why a sack of straw,—or the floor and my saddle-bags,—will be a couch for a king. Can you not receive me?"

As he spoke, he took note of her countenance and appearance. The former was withered and furrowed, for she was very old; her hairs were gray and thin, and one of her hands shook with a paralytic affection. Yet she bore her years bravely, and when she had shaken off the abstraction of mind, which had become almost habitual from her long life of solitude, and lifted her eyes, he saw that they shone with any thing but the gleams of dotage. He observed, too, as she rose from the wheel she had been plying on the porch, and approached to its verge, that her step was firm, and even, as it afterwards appeared, agile. Her dress was of the humblest texture, and none of the newest, but studiously clean and neat, and the muslin coif on her head was white as snow.

"If your wants be indeed so humble," she said, with a manner that surprised him, and a voice almost without the quaver of age, "I can receive you into my poor house, and bid you welcome. But, good young sir, here have I no one to help you, and to take your horse. My man Dancy, is in the field, and the girl Margery"——

"Say not a word about them," said the traveller, leaping from his horse, "I am my own groom and lackey of the chamber; and with your consent, I will find my way to the stable, which I see behind the rock; and Long-legs here will follow me."

He was as good as his word, and stabled his steed without farther preliminary; and thus, by showing himself ready to adapt his manners to his circumstances, he won the good will of Elsie immediately. Indeed, as if to convince her of his sincerity, he told her at once his name, and his objects in coming to her house. His name, he said, was Hunter,—Herman Hunter,— his country South Carolina; he was a painter,—or so professed himself; and his only motive for intruding upon the solitude of Hawk-Hollow, was to improve himself in his art, by devoting some weeks to study, among the neighbouring cliffs and mountains. It had been his intention, he avowed, to take up his quarters some miles farther on, in the heart of the neighbouring gorge; 'but he liked the neatness and privacy of the Traveller's Rest so well, he thought he could do nothing better than remain where he was; at least, he would remain a few days,—perhaps, he might stay two or three weeks,— he did not know, but he thought Hawk-Hollow exceedingly pretty.'

There were two circumstances which recommended him to the poor widow's regard, even more strongly than his affable and conformable behaviour. In the first place, it appeared that his name Herman, had been borne by some deceased son or relative, and its familiar sound brought a mournful pleasure to her ears,—in the second, his appearance was highly prepossessing. He could not have been above four or five and twenty years old; his figure, though somewhat beneath the middle size, was good, and his limbs well knit and active; his face was decidedly handsome, with a very dark complexion,—his eyes black and sparkling, and his mouth, which disclosed at every laugh, a set of the finest teeth in the world, expressive of good-humour and a mirthful spirit. As for the ornaments of his outward man, they consisted of under-clothes of some white summer-stuff, a frock of blue cloth, a grass hat, short boots and gloves; and to show that he was somewhat of a coxcomb withal, he wore a laced scarlet vest, an embroidered neckcloth, and a huge gold ring on his finger, glistering with a sapphire, or some cerulean substitute. He had a good roan horse, too, and saddlebags of enviable capacity; besides which, he made his first appearance with a carbine slung to his back, and a leathern portfolio under his arm; so that he looked like one who visited the retreat, with a resolution to make the most of its advantages.

Having taken a second look around the hovel, he saw no reason to abate his satisfaction. Though poverty was apparent on the naked walls and uncarpeted floors, yet every thing was clean and well ordered. The hands of the widow had eked out the lack of more costly decorations, by sticking in the fire-place and windows, and over the mantel and table-tops, green laurel boughs and sprigs of flowers, such as abounded on the neighbouring hills, or were cultivated in her little garden, and such as were pleasant enough at this season. Besides, a grape-vine had been encouraged to trail over one corner of the porch, and the other supported festoons of nasturtions and morning-glories. His evening meal, though simple and humble enough, he was pleased to commend; and if his bed was hard, and the sheets somewhat coarser than were wont to encircle his limbs, a happy temperament and a heart at ease made them endurable, and even pleasant. If he found Dancy, the farmer, when he returned from the fields, to be taciturn and even stupid, still he liked his honest face; and the little negro wench, Margery, ugly, awkward, and a thousand times more stupid than Dancy himself, he soon discovered, would prove a source of unfailing amusement.

Being of this happy mood, and persuading himself that his quarters were exactly to his desire, he prepared, the day after his arrival, to approve his zeal and skill, by sketching some one or other of the pretty prospects presented from the Traveller's Rest. He rose with the dawn and trudged down the ravine, until he reached the river; wherein, after looking about him with much satisfaction, at the hills sleeping in morning mist, he plunged, and amused himself with a bather's enthusiasm, now swimming luxuriously in the limpid and serene flood of the Delaware, and now trying his strength against the ruder current, that came dashing from the rivulet. This bore the patronymical title of Hawk-Hollow Run. And here we may as well observe, that upon a promontory at its mouth, he discovered the origin of that name, which, notwithstanding the efforts of Mr. Gilbert to christen it anew, his neighbours had so obstinately continued to give the valley. Upon a tall and conspicuous oak-tree, dead, barkless, and well nigh branchless, a pair of antique fishing-hawks screamed over their eyry; and here they had preserved it from immemorial ages. The dead tree and the nest of sticks being conspicuous objects, even from a distance on the river, the earlier navigators had soon learned to designate the whole valley after the majestic birds that seemed its monarchs.

After this, he set himself to work with paper and pencil, but with no good effect, not being in the mood, or because he discovered there were divers obstacles in his way. First, the sun did not shine from the right place, and secondly, it shone in the wrong one; then there was no way of getting a rock converted into a chair, at the precise place where he wanted it, though there were so many thousands where he did not; and, in fine, he found himself, when all was ready, waxing eager for breakfast.

After breakfast, he had as many difficulties to encounter; and in short, after making divers essays, he beheld the afternoon sun sink low towards the west, without having accomplished any thing worthy of being deposited in the port-folio. "But never mind," said he, with a philosophical disregard of his indolence and fickleness, "we shall have the fit more strongly upon us on the morrow."

He sat down in the porch and cast his eyes towards the manor house, which was commonly known by the title, so little flattering to the founder's memory, of Gilbert's Folly. At this distance, and from this spot, it had an impressive and even charming appearance. It lay upon the slope of a hill, perhaps a mile or more from the Traveller's Rest; and, as it faced very nearly towards the east, he had remarked it, in the morning, when illuminated by the first beams of the day-spring, shining, with a sort of aristocratic pomp and pride, at its lowly neighbour, from the midst of green woods and airy hills. At the present moment, the front being entirely in shade, it had a somewhat sullen and melancholy look, resulting in part from the sombre hue of the stone of which it was built; and though slanting rays of sunshine, here and there striking on the sides of chimneys, gables, and other elevations, gave it a picturesque relief, it still preserved an air of soberness and gloom. It seemed to lie in the heart of a mighty paddock, once, however, termed a park, that was circumscribed by a line of pollards, sweeping over the hill-side, and here and there broken by groves of unchecked growth. In one or two places on the grounds, were rows of Italian poplars, stretching along in military rank and file, and adding that peculiar *palisaded* beauty to the landscape, which is seen to the greatest advantage in a hilly country. Here, too, was another exotic stranger, the weeping-willow, drooping in the moist hollow, and shaking its boughs in the pool. The principal trees, however, were the natives of the valley, most of them perhaps left standing in their original places, when the grounds were laid out in the forest. The picture is complete, when it is added that the slopes of the hills were carpeted with the rich embellishments of agriculture: the wheat-fields and maize-plantations, waving like lakes of verdure, in the breeze, were certainly not the least of the charms of Hawk-Hollow, except perhaps, at that moment, to the anti-utilitarian painter.

He regarded the prospect for a long time in silence, and then muttered his thoughts aloud, half to himself, and half to his ancient hostess, who had drawn her wheel up to her favourite seat on the porch, and added its drowsy murmur to the sound of the oak-boughs, rustling together in the breeze:

"This, then," he exclaimed, "is the little elysium, from which wrong, and the revenge of wrong, drove a once happy and honoured family, to wander exiles and outlaws in the land? And not one permitted even to lay his bones in the loam of his birth-place! and no friend left to avenge or lament! '*Quis sit laturus in aras thura?*'"

The wheel of Alice revolved with increased velocity, but she betrayed no inclination to yield to the prattling infirmity of age; though she, doubtless, of all persons in the country, was best informed on the subject now uppermost in the mind of the painter. He was in the mood, however, for extracting such information as he could; and after a moment's silence, he resumed, with a direct question,

"That is Avondale Hall, is it not, good mother?"

"It is Gilbert's Folly," replied the hostess, drily. "We know no other name.—There are some call it Falconer's Trump-card—but that is nothing."

"Perhaps not," said the young man: "but who can tell better than yourself? Good mother Elsie—you must forgive me for being so familiar; but, in truth, I love the name—it was the name of my nurse, the first I learned to utter:—I have a great curiosity about these poor Gilberts; and, I was told, no one could inform me about them so well as yourself."

"And why should you ask about them?" demanded the hostess, who, as Herman had long since observed, conversed in language that would scarce have been anticipated from her appearance. "They can have done you no harm, and certainly they never did you good. You cannot fear them, for they are dead; and you yourself said, they left none to lament them."

"But they left many to curse," said Herman; "and it is this that makes me curious to know the truth about them. I have not heard any men pronounce the name, without accompanying it with maledictions; which were just so many proofs that they were unsafe informants."

"It is better then that they should be forgotten," muttered Elsie: "If they did wrong, bitterly have they been punished; if they provoked men to curses, the curses have been heavy on their heads, and are now even heaped upon their graves. Yet you speak of them not like others—how comes it that *you* pronounce their name without a curse?"

"Simply because, never having received any hurt at their hands, and having nothing of the hound about me, I feel no impulse to join in the cry of the pack, until I know what beast they are baying. I saw, in the village, an old man begging; I was told, his house had been burned down, and his wife and children in it, by 'the accursed Gilberts;' I saw also, a miserable idiot, or madman, I know not which, dancing along the road-side, and inviting me to a wedding: I asked about him, and was informed he dwelt of yore in the Wyoming Valley, and was set upon by the Hawks of Hawk-Hollow, in the hour of his marriage, and he alone saved of all the bridal party—I saw"— —

"It is enough—God has judged them," said the old woman, with a voice both solemn and reproachful. "All these things have they done, and many more as dreadful and cruel. These are the fruits of civil war; for men are then changed to beasts. I knew a man of Wyoming, who was killed by his own brother—shot through the head, while he knelt down, begging for quarter of his mother's son! God has judged these acts, for they who did them are gone; and God will yet judge the men that drove them into their madness."

"They had cause, then, for what they did?" asked Herman, with interest. "It was not in cold blood, and upon deliberate choice, that they sided with the tories against their countrymen?"

"Perhaps it was, perhaps it was not," said Mrs. Bell, mournfully. "A plough-furrow on the hill-side may grow at last into the bed of a torrent; and what is but a cause for light anger, may, in time, work the brain into a frenzy. But ask me not of these things now: it was in a season like this, twenty-four years since—but it is foolish to remember me of it,—perhaps sinful. Some time, perhaps, I may speak of these unhappy people to you; but I cannot now. Trust, at least, that if the Hawks of Hawk-Hollow, as you called them, did much wrong, they also endured it,—and that, too, when they had not provoked it."

Finding that his curiosity could obtain no farther gratification at the present moment, Herman Hunter again cast his eyes upon the mansion, and being greatly charmed by an effect made by the striking of the sunshine on certain parts, while others lay in the broadest and deepest shadow, he was seized with a fit of artist-like enthusiasm, and arranging his drawing materials upon a little table, which he drew into the porch for the purpose, he was straightway immersed in the business of sketching. While he was dotting down chimneys and windows with great haste and satisfaction, he was struck with a new and unexpected effect in the picture. A scarlet mantle, beside which glittered another of snowy white, suddenly blazed out like a star from a clump of shadowy trees in the paddock, and he became aware that two females on horseback were issuing from the park, and riding down the road. But losing sight of them again, as they ambled into a hollow, and being now really engrossed in his employment, he thought no more of them, until they suddenly re-appeared from behind a thicket no great distance off, galloping forward with an impetuosity and violence that would have done honour to veteran dragoons.

Somewhat astonished at such an unexpected display of spirit, he dropped his pencil, and for an instant supposed that their ponies were running away with these damsels errant. They were not attired for the saddle, and seemed rather to have sprung upon their palfreys from some sudden whim and spirit of frolic than with a purpose of leaving the park, in which he had first caught sight of them. They were arrayed merely in simple walking-dresses of white, over which one had flung a light scarlet shawl; and instead of caps or round hats, they had low and broad-brimmed hats of thin felt, without veils, much better fitted for rambling in, over sunny meads, than for displaying to the winds on horseback.

His suspicion that their ponies had taken the matter into their own hands,—or rather the bits into their own teeth, was of short duration; and as they advanced with increased rapidity, he saw plainly, by the mirthful rivalry displayed in all their actions and gestures, that they were positively running a race, the scarlet mantle being the winner,—or, so far, at least, as a full length would go, in full prospect of winning.

Not a little diverted at the spectacle, and the merry cries with which they encouraged their steeds, he rose from the table, to take a better view of the fair jockeys, as they should brush by; when, to his great surprise, no sooner had they reached the little oak-yard that conducted to the Traveller's Rest, than they made a rapid wheel, and came dashing up to the porch in a style worthy of a race-course.

It happened, either because he was in part concealed by the veil of nasturtions that grew near to where he had placed his table, or because they were too much engaged in their frolic to raise their eyes, that the young painter was seen by neither of the ladies, until they were within six yards of the porch; when the headmost, suddenly observing him, drew up in such confusion that she had well nigh jerked her pony over on his back. He perceived at once, that *his* appearance at the Traveller's Rest was wholly unexpected, and was any thing but welcome to the adventurous pair. Indeed, it was manifest that the consciousness of having been detected by a stranger engaged in such jockey-like amusement, had greatly disconcerted them both.

All this the young man observed in a moment, and could scarce suppress the smile that gathered over his visage, even when he saw that the confusion of the foremost damsel had discomposed her palfrey. However, as he looked into her face, florid at once with exercise and shame, he beheld a pair of such radiant black eyes, flashing with mingled mirth and vexation, and withal a countenance of such haughty and decidedly aristocratic character, as instantly put him upon his best behaviour. He took off his hat, like a well-bred gentleman, and advancing from the porch, would have taken her pony by the rein, had she not instantly recovered herself, and turned the animal aside, with an empress-like "I thank you, sir!" He thought the refusal of assistance, so respectfully offered, was somewhat ungrateful, and even rude; but she looked so beautiful, he could do nothing less than testify his admiration by another bow.

Meanwhile the second maiden, whose confusion seemed, at first, even greater than her companion's, and who blushed at the sight of him with even painful embarrassment, recovering herself more quickly, (for her filly was not so restiff as the other,) rode up to the porch, and saluting the ancient widow, who had risen to receive her, exclaimed, though with a flurried voice,

"You must pardon us, good Elsie—we came to visit you—but we knew not you had guests with you." Then turning to Herman, just as her friend had rejected his proffered assistance, she said, with the sweetest voice in the world, as if to make amends for the rudeness, "We are much obliged to you, sir—but the horses are very gentle." She then turned again to Dame Bell, and, as if resolved to explain away as much of the cause of visitation as possible, said,

"We are looking for my father, Elsie; and we thought, that, instead of waiting for him in the park, we would ride by your house, and ask you how you did. We will not intrude upon you longer.—Good by, my dear Mrs. Bell."

With these hurried expressions, and having inclined her head courteously to the painter, she rode out of the yard, followed by her companion; when having hesitated a moment, as if uncertain whether to continue upon the road or not, they suddenly came to a decision, and rode back towards the paddock, though at a much more moderate pace than before.

So great was the admiration with which Herman Hunter regarded the beauty of the red shawl, that he had scarce bestowed two glances upon her friend. He had noticed indeed, that a profusion of gold-shadowed locks and eyes of extreme gentleness and sweetness, gave a very agreeable expression to a countenance at least two years younger than the other's; but as there was none of the spirit of fire breaking out at a glance from those loop-holes of the soul, to make an instant impression on his imagination, as had been the case with the other, he lost the opportunity of satisfying himself by another look, how well her charms might endure a comparison with those of her companion. His admiration was doubly unfortunate; since, little as it deserved such a return, it laid the foundation for a spirit of hostility, little short of absolute hatred, in the bosom of the lady, as will be seen in the sequel of this tradition.

As the gay but disconcerted pair rode away together, he could scarce content himself until they got beyond earshot, before he exclaimed, with the most emphatic delight,

"I vow to heaven, my dear mother Elsie, she is the most beautiful creature I ever laid my eyes on!"

Alice responded with a faint sigh and a yet fainter smile; but her countenance immediately darkened, while she muttered,

"I pity her, poor child. The storm is coming upon her that she dreams not of; the curse will swallow up all that are, and shall be, of his house; and she in whom there is no wrong, and who was born no child of an unjust father, will share the penalty with his children. Yes, yes," she added, straining her eyes, after the maidens, "I shall see *her* bright eyes dimmed with tears, and then closed,—*her* yellow locks parted over a forehead of stone and death,— and perhaps help to lay her in the earth out of men's sight, as I have helped with one who was as young and as fair!"

"I vow, mother Elsie," said the young man, surprised at the prophetic sadness and emphasis of her speech, but still more at the mention of "yellow locks," while his own thoughts were musing upon ringlets of raven. "I vow, you have mistaken me altogether. I meant the other lady, the black-eyed, angelic creature, who tossed her head at me with such disdain,—and, hang it, incivility, too; for it cannot be denied, she was uncivil."

"I thought you were speaking of the Captain's daughter," said the widow, coldly.

"I know no more about the Captain's daughter than my grandmother," said the youth, irreverently; "nor do I care half so much. But tell me Elsie,— who is that black-eyed creature? I never beheld any body to compare with her!"

"She is the daughter of Colonel Richard Falconer," said the hostess, resuming her labours at the wheel, yet apparently disposed to reply to any farther interrogatories the young man might propose. But the painter seemed satisfied with what he had heard. He exclaimed at once, with a look of strong disgust,

"Why then may the fiends seize the fancy, and my fool's head along with it! Hark'e, good dame Bell, did you ever hear of the old heathen *Lamiæ?* the *Lemures*, as they were sometimes called?"

"I have heard of some such beasts of Peru," said the complaisant hostess; "and I believe they are a kind of camels."

"Oh, that's the *llama*, the pretty little llama," said the young man, with the good-humour that became an instructor. "The Lamiæ were monsters and sorceresses of Africa, with the face and bust of women, and the body of a serpent,—a sort of land mermaids. (By the by, do you know, I saw a mermaid once? Some time, I will tell you all about her; but, just now, all I can say is, that she was monstrous ugly.) These Lamiæ often bewitched men, who looked them in the face: if you looked there first, you were so blinded, you could not perceive their true deformity, until assisted by the counter-spell of some benevolent magician. Now, Elsie, this is my thought: I hold Miss Falconer to be a Lamia; and the sound of her father's name was the spell that opened my eyes to her true ugliness. Pho!" continued the youth, observing the incredulity and wonder of his auditor; "the image is a bad one after all, for it conveys an improper impression. I should say, that *I* am like the Lamia's lover, not Miss Falconer like the Lamia. To tell you the truth, I have heard so many ill things said of the father, that I feel myself heartily inclined to hate the daughter. A vixen, I warrant me!"

The old woman regarded him earnestly, and then replied,

"Little cause have I to love Colonel Falconer, or to speak well of him and his; yet why should a stranger like you, assume the post of the judge, and visit the father's faults upon the head of his offspring? But you do not speak seriously. I know no evil of Miss Falconer, and I have heard none. This is the first time I have ever seen her so near to my threshold: and I know not what strange fancy could have brought her hither. As for Miss Catherine, the Captain's daughter, she often comes to inquire about me. Poor child! she fears not the 'old witch,' for she has done no harm to me nor to any other mortal; she does not hate 'wicked old Elsie,' for hatred dwells not in her nature; but she looks with respect and pity upon the miseries of age and penury. And many a good deed she has done me, when others passed me by with scorn and hate. Would that I might go down to the grave in her place! were it but in memory of her goodness. But when the bolt is aimed at the little willow, even the withered old oak cannot arrest it."

With such expressions as these the old woman, if she did not re-inspire Herman Hunter with admiration for Miss Falconer, succeeded at least in awakening some interest for the younger lady; which was greatly increased, when he came to suspect, from some expressions Elsie let fall, that the miseries she seemed so confidently to predict as being in store for the maiden, were predicated upon the knowledge of a contemplated union between her and the brother of her friend. It was plain, from what Elsie said, that this was to be a marriage of convenience, in which Catherine's affections were to be sacrificed, or disregarded. It is true, that Elsie did not directly affirm this to be the case; but the inference from her expressions was consequential and inevitable; and Herman only wondered that the young lady, whom he now pictured to himself as dying of a broken heart, should have looked so rosy and happy.

In the meanwhile, the maidens rode on, returning towards the park, until they reached the grove in the hollow, where they were sheltered from view. Here they paused, and the Captain's daughter gave at once the flattest contradiction to all Elsie's piteous allusions to the state of her feelings, by looking archly into her companion's face, and then bursting into an uncontrollable fit of laughter.

"Well, what now, dear Hal?" she cried, while tears of genuine merriment swam in her eyes and rolled on her cheeks; "what do you think of your race *now*? Shall we try it over again?"

"Upon my word, Miss Loring"——

"Kate! call me Kate, or never look to see me laugh more," exclaimed the Captain's daughter. "Now pray, cousin Hal, do you not think we have exhibited our horsemanship somewhat too advantageously to-day? Fy, Harriet, I will never forgive you! To think we should go galloping in this manner, almost into the arms of a young fellow with a scarlet waistcoat! It is *too* ridiculous!"

"So much for dragging me along after you, to the old witch's!" said Miss Falconer, pettishly.

"*After* me?" cried the other, with increased mirth; "why, you were leading—you had beaten me by full a length and a half, as the jockeys call it:—so much for not starting fair! And as for dragging you there, Harriet, pray do me justice; you know it was your own wicked suggestion altogether that carried you thither, and my frailty that made me follow. It is all a punishment on you, for breaking the commandment, and running after the forbidden fruit. Oh, curiosity! curiosity! when shall we poor women shuffle the little tempter from our bosoms? But pray, cousin, what made you treat the young man so rudely? Sure, he was very handsome and well-behaved; and sure, young gentlemen, handsome and well-behaved, are not so plentiful in Hawk-Hollow! I think we will get pa to invite him to dinner."

"Well, Catherine," said the other, "you are merry to-day; but it happens so seldom, and I am so glad of it, that I pardon you, although your mirth is all at my expense."

"You are angry with me, Harriet?" said the Captain's daughter, riding up to her friend, and stretching forth her hand. Her frolicsome spirits vanished in a moment, and the change on her countenance and in her whole manner, from extreme gayety to impetuous emotion, was inexpressibly striking and touching.

"Angry? by no means," said Miss Falconer, as Catherine flung her arm round her neck and kissed her. "Poor wayward Kate! I would you could laugh at me for ever. Why do you cry, mouse? You are certainly the most extraordinary mad creature in the world!"

"Yes, I am," said Miss Loring, smiling through her tears; "I can't abide being talked stiffly to. But what shall we do? Shall we ride up to the park? Shall we sit down here, and play long-straws for sweethearts? Shall we take heart of grace, and ride on in search of papa? Or shall we play termagant again, whip, cut and spur, whoop and halloo, and call Monsieur Red-Jacket to stand up for umpire? Any thing, dear Hal, to kill time, and find you amusement."

"Was Monsieur Red-Jacket so handsome, after all?" demanded Miss Falconer.

"I don't know," said Catherine: "He kept his eyes so fixed upon your own face, I could not half see him. But, really, he seemed to admire you very much—I suppose, because you were first in! I don't see how you could have the heart to treat him so uncivilly, when his admiration was so manifest, and his bearing so respectful?"

"Was it, indeed?" said the other, shaking her head, as if regretfully. "Young, handsome, well bred, and an admirer—and yet, I know, I shall never abide the sight of him. What! see me riding in full race, with whoop and halloo, and all that, as you say, like a grazier's daughter!—poh, it is intolerable: it can never be forgiven!"

"Why, he saw me, too," said Miss Loring; "and I am sure, *I* forgive him! And it is no such great matter, after all."

"No great matter, to be sure; but small ones govern the world. No one can forgive being made ridiculous, especially a woman of spirit. Come, we will gallop back to the park, and leave the Captain to find his own way."

With these words, they returned to the paddock.

In the confession of a weak and capricious prepossession, which was perhaps more than half serious, Miss Falconer showed an almost prophetic sense of what would be the future temper of her mind towards the unlucky Herman. Neither the manifest folly nor injustice of the sentiment, even when gratitude should have expelled it from her bosom for ever, could prevent it ripening into jealousy and final dislike; and unfortunately circumstances of an accidental nature soon arose to give a double impulse to these unamiable feelings.

CHAPTER III

A man of blood, being brought up in the wars
And cruel executions.
BEAUMONT AND FLETCHER.

— — —A very foolish, fond old man,
Four-score and upwards; and, to deal plainly,
I fear, he is not in his proper mind.
KING LEAR.

The painter, still keeping his eyes upon the pair, pondered over that propensity of our nature, which urges even the coldest and demurest of mortals into acts of extravagance, when removed a moment from artificial restraints. The whole system of social federation is a state of enthrallment and captivity, although undoubtedly a wholesome one; and he who publicly rejects its fetters, though he may personally enjoy his independence, violates that compact which separates the refined from the primitive and uncivilized states of existence, and encourages others to rush back upon the savage freedom of the latter. The preservation of a certain share of dignity is incumbent upon men, not merely as a means of holding caste, but of preventing a downslide in manners and mind. The hero may properly play at bo-peep with his children, though not at the head of his army; and, by the same rule, a fair lady may shoot and drive, play the fiddle, and race horses, to her heart's content, so long as the amusement is confined to the proper circle. For our own part, we think there is no more delightful spectacle in the world than is afforded by a troop of grown-up hoydens, released from the heavy trammels of etiquette, and yielding, in all the confidence of privacy, to the wild extravagancies of freedom; though a public display of the kind would, undoubtedly, be any thing but agreeable. Such were the sentiments of the painter; and however much the young ladies may have been mortified at an introduction made in a way so boisterous and masculine, it is questionable whether any other could have caused them to produce a stronger, or even more favourable, impression on his imagination. Being of a joyous temperament himself, he rejoiced at the manifestation of similar spirit in others; and only regretted that the parentage of the most admired (for his prejudice against the name of Falconer had been strongly avowed,) should have so soon driven away the visions of amusement and delight, that, at the glance of her brilliant eyes, came rushing through his brain.

He had scarce lost sight of them in the park, before the road again echoed with the sound of hoofs; and looking round, he beheld three young men, very genteely dressed, ride by, and make their way to the park gate. As they passed the cottage, they turned their faces towards it, saluting the widow by name, and acknowledging the presence of the stranger by courteous nods. He perceived, however, that they were somewhat surprised, and not a little diverted, by his appearance at such a place; for they exchanged smiles, and by and by, when they had got a little beyond the brook, they were heard laughing together.

"Well done, ye vagabonds," muttered the good-humoured youth to himself: "never trust me, if I do not make you more in love with my lodgings than your own empty skulls, before we are many days older. There *is* some life in Hawk-Hollow, after all."

He had just succeeded in recalling his attention to his unfinished sketch, when it was distracted for the third time by the sudden appearance of a carriage, somewhat old-fashioned and grim, that rolled up to the inn at an unusual speed, and was in the act of passing it, when an old gentleman, whose head was thrust from the window, caught sight of Herman, and immediately diverted it from its course, by roaring out to the coachman, a venerable negro,—

"Holla, you Dick! right about wheel,—turn,—halt!" and the coach, guided with ready skill, stopped at the porch-step, almost before the last word had been pronounced.

Open flew the door, for it was evident the old gentleman was too impatient to await the tardy assistance of his servant, and out flew the steps, unfolding at a kick of his foot, which immediately followed them. As he thrust himself thus hurriedly from the vehicle, Herman observed, that besides his aged appearance, he had another claim to such duties as a young man could render, in a second foot, which, instead of displaying any of the strength and agility of the former, was battered out of shape by some ancient injury, and was pendent to a leg unquestionably infirm and halt. Seeing this, the young painter instantly stepped forward, and assisted him to descend; a courtesy that was acknowledged by a hearty gripe of the hand, and the exclamation,

"Surrender, you dog, or I'll blow your brains out!"—And to complete the astonishment of the young man, he perceived, at the same moment, a great horse-pistol, which the old gentleman had whipped out of the vehicle, presented within three inches of his ear.

Astounded at such an unexpected mode of salutation, the painter could do little more than express his alarm and confusion, by echoing the word, "Surrender?" when Elsie interfered in his behalf, crying out, "For Heaven's sake, Captain Loring! what are you doing? Do the young gentleman no harm!"

"*Gentleman!*" cried the Captain, somewhat staggered himself. "Adzooks! do you say so?—a gentleman? What! and no cut-throat Gilbert, hah? By the lord, I thought I had him! Why, you vagabond young fellow, give an account of yourself.—Who are you? what are you? and how did you come here? You are a gentleman, hah? and you have not killed Colonel Falconer, hah? and you profess yourself to be an honest man, hah! Why, what will the world come to!"

As he spoke, in these abrupt and startling phrases, Herman had leisure, notwithstanding his surprise, to observe that he was a comely, eccentric-looking old man, with a bottle-shaped nose, gray eyes, and huge beetle-brows, his whole countenance puckered into wrinkles, that seemed to begin at the tip of his nose, or on his upper lip, as a common centre, and radiate thence to all parts of his visage, though they appeared in the greatest luxuriance on the chin and forehead. His hair was clubbed, queued, and powdered; and, although he was evidently battered by time and hard service, and limped withal very uncouthly on his wounded leg, a three-cornered hat, and a half-and-half old military dress, gave him a somewhat heroic appearance. His coat was blue, his breeches buff; and he had a boot on one leg, and a shoe on the other,—or,—to speak more strictly, on the foot thereof, *that* being incapable of the more manly decoration. But at the present moment, it was scarce possible to obtain a just idea of his appearance or character, had Herman been cool enough for the attempt. The violence of his attack upon one in the act of rendering him a humane courtesy, indicated that he was somewhat beside himself; and it was equally plain, from the medley of expressions on his visage, agitated at once by suspicion, anxiety, indignation, fury, triumph, and doubt, that he was in a condition to be replied to rather with softness than anger. In truth, there was something so ridiculous in his appearance, as well as in the circumstance of his own unexpected arrest, that Herman was no sooner relieved of the fear of death, by the dropping of the pistol, which the gallant soldier removed at the remonstrance of Elsie, than he burst into a laugh, and would have indulged it freely, had not the Captain cut him short by exclaiming,

"Hark ye, ye grinning cub! is it a thing to laugh at, when a man's murdered, and you arrested on suspicion?"

"Murdered, Captain!" cried the widow, whom some of his previous ejaculations seemed to have turned into stone:—"Murdered, Captain, did you say?" she exclaimed, seizing the soldier by the arm, and wholly disregarding the presence of the painter,—"Richard Falconer murdered at last? and by a Gilbert, when all that bore the name are in the grave? Impossible!"

"Murdered, I tell you, and given over by the doctors," roared the Captain, "and by one of the cursed Hawk-Hollow Gilberts, if there's any believing words out of his own mouth: I have it by express. And hark ye, you old beldam, if you have given shelter to the villain, never trust me if I don't burn you at a stake. Adzooks! was there ever such a thing dreamed of?—Hark ye, sir, I arrest you on suspicion."

"What, sir! on suspicion of murder!" cried Hunter, who had by this time recovered his gravity, and now spoke with as much dignity as boldness: "If you have any authority to apprehend me, I am your prisoner, and will accompany you to the nearest magistrate.—This is the most extraordinary circumstance in the world; and let me tell you, sir,"—but he was interrupted by the widow; who, still grasping the Captain's arm, although he strove to cast her off, exclaimed,

"Do no rash folly with the young man. Look at him—does *he* look like a Gilbert? You are mad to think it, Captain Loring!"

Then, as if satisfied that such argument was sufficient to acquit her lodger of all suspicion, she again renewed her questions; and Herman, giving ear to the Captain, gathered from his broken and impetuous expressions, that assassination had been committed, or rather attempted, (for it did not appear that the victim was dead,) upon the body of Colonel Falconer, who had been so lately the subject of his thoughts and conversation,—that the outrage had been perpetrated at, or near, the metropolis of the State,—that suspicion had fallen upon a man long esteemed defunct,—and that Captain Loring, in the fervour of his indignation and zeal to bring the assassin to justice, being never very notorious for the wisdom of his actions, had resolved to seize upon all suspicious persons,—that is to say, all strangers,—he might light on, without much question of his right to do so, until he had caught the true offender, who, he doubted not, being a refugee and a Gilbert, would be found lurking about the Hawk's Hollow. It seemed, that the suddenness of the intelligence had overpowered the veteran's brain, and left him as incapable of distinguishing the appearances of innocence from those of guilt, as of understanding the illegal character of his proceedings; yet, being a man of impulses, excitable both in head and heart, his suspicions were as easily diverted as inflamed; and, accordingly, after having come within an ace of shooting a pistol through the painter's head, his next act was to seize upon him in the most affectionate manner in the world, crying out by way of apology,

"Harkee, younker,—adzooks, no ill blood betwixt us? When my blood's up, I'm an old fool, d'ye see. Didn't mean to insult you; and as for shooting, that's neither here nor there. But when we're after a deserter, spy, refugee, murderer, or such dogs, why quick's the word, and 'Fall in, friend,' the order of the day. Must catch the villain, and take account of all skulking fellows without the counter-sign. Here's bloody murder in the wind. The old woman says you are a gentleman: so, gentleman, as you were! Adzooks, you look no more like a Gilbert than a mud-terrapin; but all honest men answer to their names—what's *yours?*"

"Hunter,—Herman Hunter," replied the young man; "and, if need be, I can easily convince you that I am no object of suspicion."

"Don't doubt it; you've an excellent phys'nomy,—very much like my poor son Tom's," cried the soldier, now as much struck with the open and agreeable countenance of the stranger, as he had been before blinded by his own impetuosity. "I like you! You're a soldier, hah? Where do you come from?"

"From South Carolina," said Hunter, exchanging the serious mood in which he first submitted to examination, for one more characteristic of his humorous temper. He began to understand and even relish the oddities of the inquisitor; and as the Captain's questions were now put in a tone indicative of good will and admiration, and it was evident his turbulent feelings were giving way rapidly before others of a new character, he seemed disposed not only to endure but to encourage the ordeal.

"From South Carolina?" cried the Captain. "Too many tories there by half! But then you have some men there; yes, sir, some men, whom I call men! Sumpter, sir, and Marion, sir,—why I call such fellows *men*, sir! I like this swamp-fighting, too; I was brought up to it,—took my first lesson among red Delawares, and ended with Mingoes and Shawnees. A good tussle at Eutaw, too, sir, it was, by the lord!" exclaimed Captain Loring, warming into such a blaze of military ardour at the recollection, that he quite forgot the object of his delay, and the assassination of his kinsman into the bargain;— "a good tussle, (without saying any thing of my friend Morgan's rub-a-dub-dub at the Cowpens,)—a good tussle! And such glorious weather, too, when a man could fight and keep cool! Now I remember, that, at the fatal field of Braddock, ninth July, '55, it was the hottest work, what with the weather, what with the savages, what with the stupid cockney red-coats, that man ever saw,—an oven above, and a furnace all round; it was all blood and sweat, sir!—the wounded were boiled in their own gore. It was a day, sir, to make a man a man, sir,—it taught me to smell gun-powder! It was there, sir, I first looked in the face of George Washington,—a poor colonial buckskin colonel then, but now, adzooks, the greatest man the world ever saw! Harkee, sir, have you served? have you smelt powder? have you heard a trumpet? have you ever fought a battle?"

"Certainly, sir," replied the young man, with humour; "I have inflicted bloody-noses, and received them. I was quite a Hector at school; and, so long as you stop short of killing, I am a Hector yet. But I never could find any appetite in me for bullets and broad-swords; and as for a bayonet, I think it the most inhuman weapon in the world. Noble Captain, I am a non-combatant, a man of peace."

"Hah!" cried the Captain, indignantly; "and how comes that? An able-bodied man, with your bleeding country calling on you, and no fight in you? Sir, let me tell you, sir, such a pair of legs should have been devoted to the service of your country, sir! Look you, sir, my son Tom Loring was only eighteen years old, when he fought his battle on the Brandywine; and a whole year before, he was ripe for a rub, as he often told me. How comes it, sir, you have grown out of your teens, and never faced an enemy? Zounds, sir, I was beginning to have a good opinion of you!"

"There is no accounting for it, Captain, except"——

"Hark ye, Mr. What-d'ye-call-it," said the soldier, the good feelings with which he was beginning to regard the youth, giving place at once to contempt and indignation, "there is every thing in having the right sort of blood for these things, and you have no blood at all. I despise you, sir, and, adzooks, I believe you are some suspicious person after all, and very contemptible, for all of your red jacket.—Holloa, Dick, there! help me into the carriage."

And thus venting his disgust, and preparing to put the seal to his displeasure by instant departure, the young man was on the point of losing a friend so suddenly won, when, fortunately for him, the Captain's eye fell upon the little table with the drawing materials, which he had not before observed, and walking up to it, he began, without a moment's hesitation, to examine the unfinished sketch. The effect was instantaneous; the spectacle of his own dwelling, transferred, with not a little skill, to paper, though only in light lead marks, and so accurately that he instantly detected (as appeared to him wonderful enough) the windows of his own sleeping apartment, threw him into such transports, that he seemed on the point of dancing for joy, as he would perhaps have done, had it not been for the infirmity of his extremity.

"Lord bless us!" said he, "here's the Folly! the identical old Folly, with the grape-vine, the stables, the negro-houses, the locust grove, the three tulip-trees, the pot in the chimney, and the old martin-house on a pole! And here's my two negroes, Dick and Sam, at the gate, driving the cows out of the park"— —

"No, Captain," said Herman, with a painter's dignity; "those are the two young ladies; and I flatter myself, when I have done a little more to them"— —

"My girls?" cried the Captain, in a rapture; "why, so they are! And *you* did this? and you're a painter, hah?"

"A sort of one, as you see, Captain," replied the youth, with an air.

"A painter!" cried the Captain, grasping his hand, with delight. "Can you paint a soldier, hah?"

"Ay," replied the youth, "if he'll hold still long enough."

"And cannon, and horses, and smoke, and trees, and a dreadful splutter of blood and dead men, hah? Then, by the lord, you shall paint me the Fatal Field of Braddock, with the red-coats and the continentals, the savages and the Frenchmen,—and Braddock, lugged off on men's shoulders,—and George Washington rallying the colony-boys for another charge on the redskins! What a picture that will make!—I'll tell you what, Mr. Harkem Whatd'-ye-call-it, you shall come to my house, drink and be merry, and then you shall paint me that picture. You shall paint me the battle of Brandywine, too, with my poor Tom Loring bleeding to death, like a hero, as he was: and hark ye, you may bring *me* in, too, holding him on my knee,—for I did it,—and telling him to die like a man,—for an old fool, as I was, to think he could die like any thing else! And stick in my girl, too, if you can, weeping and wringing her hands, when I carried Tom Loring home that day. And remember the bugles and trumpets, blasting up for the charge of cavalry; you should have heard them sweeping by, just as Tom was dying.—It was the finest sound in nature!" continued the Captain, vehemently, and as he spoke, dashing a tear from his eye; "the finest music ever heard; as Tom acknowledged himself: 'Father!' said he, as he bled in my arms, 'it is not hard to die to such music, for I hear our own trumpets among the others!' And so died Tom Loring; he went to heaven amid thunder and trumpets; and if I had seven sons more, I should wish nothing better for them, than that they might go to heaven the same way,—I would, by the lord! For why? there's no way that's better!"

There was something in this eccentric burst of ardour, which, however ludicrous it seemed, touched some of the finer feelings of the painter, and checked the laugh which he could scarce repress, when the Captain began his energetic instructions. Not being disposed to accept a commission so capriciously proffered, or to undertake a composition, in which, it was evident, if he hoped to please his employer, he must mingle together as many different scenes and actions as would furnish subjects for a whole gallery, and desiring to temper his refusal to the peculiarities of his patron, he was puzzling himself in what way to express it, when his good-fortune sent him aid in the person of another stranger, who, as the capricious stars would have it, designed, like himself, to make trial of the accommodations of the Traveller's Rest.

CHAPTER IV

> *1st Friar.* No doubt, brother, but this proceedeth of the Spirit?
> *2d Friar.* Ay, and of a moving spirit, too; but come,
>   Let us intreat he may be entertain'd.
>   MARLOW — *The Jew of Malta.*

As the Captain concluded his eccentric oration, rather from want of breath than because he lacked the will to continue it, a sonorous voice, very manly and agreeable, save that it had a strong nasal twang, was heard pronouncing hard by, with solemn emphasis, the words from the Apocalypse, —

"'And I looked, and behold, a pale horse: and his name that sat on him was Death, and hell followed with him. And power was given unto them over the fourth part of the earth, to kill with the sword, and with hunger, and with death, and with the beasts of the earth.'"

Startled at an interruption so unexpected, both looked round at the first sound of the voice, and even Elsie Bell woke from the trance into which the Captain's news had plunged her, to gaze as eagerly as the others after the cause. As they directed their eyes towards the entrance of the little oak-shaded yard, they saw, turning into it from the road, and slowly riding towards them, an apparition that might almost have been supposed by a profane imagination to imbody the conception of the grisly terror. It was a tall man in black raiment, riding an old gray horse, very meager and raw-boned, which moved with a step so slow and drowsy, as to oppose no obstruction to the meditations of the rider, who held a book in his hand, from which he read the words that followed so ominously after the burst of the Captain. He seemed so inwrapt in his study as to be unconscious of the presence of strangers, having apparently yielded up the guidance of his course to the animal he bestrode; and as he drew nigh to the porch, still pronouncing the words, the first one of which had attracted their attention, all had an opportunity of gazing on him at leisure. He was a tall man, as has been said, being somewhat gaunt and thin in the lower part of his body, though his shoulders were broad and square. His joints were large and bony, and his hands and feet were any thing in the world but fairy-like. His neck was long and scraggy, his face of a cadaverous hue and lantern-jawed, and long locks of straight black hair, a little grizzled, fell from beneath an old cocked-hat, the brim of which was inclined to go slouching along with them, towards his shoulders. His coat was of black velvet, worn and soiled, and indeed extremely shabby, and so long, that, as he rode, the wide skirts almost concealed his saddle-bags and flapped about his heels; the collar was straight and short, and its place was supplied by a red bandanna handkerchief, which was twisted round his throat in a thong like a cable.

He continued to read aloud, until his horse suddenly paused before the porch; then lifting up his eyes, and closing the book, he bestowed a gracious stare upon the party, that had well nigh converted the painter's admiration into merriment, it was so extravagantly grave and sanctimonious. It dispelled also some of the reverence with which the soldier was beginning to regard him; and recurring suddenly to the objects which had brought him to the Traveller's Rest, Captain Loring hobbled up to the saintly apparition, advanced his hand to seize upon the bridle rein, and was just saluting him with a "Harkee, Mister, whoever you are,—being a stranger, you must give an account of yourself,"—when the worthy personage, rolling his eyes once more over the party, and then directing them to heaven, opened his mouth, and again lifted up his voice.

"Fellow sinners!" said he, with as much zeal as emphasis, seeming to consider that he had found a congregation in great need of his exhortations, "you have heard the words of the book: 'And I looked, and behold, a pale horse; and his name that sat on him was Death, and hell followed with him.' Death comes on the pale horse, and hell follows at his heels! Listen to what I have to say, and let your souls that are a-hungering, open their mouths and be satisfied. He that has ears to hear"— —

"Is an ass!" cried Captain Loring, interrupting him without ceremony. "Come, you fanatical fool, none of your babble and sermonizing here of a week-day; but answer my questions."

"Will you rail upon the Lord's anointed? will you do violence to my holy vocation?" cried the preacher, hotly. "Get thee behind me, Satan! If thou wilt not profit by the unction of truth, shut thy mouth and get thee away, that others may not backslide after thee. Anathema upon thee! anathema baranathema! If thou stoppest the flood of the sweet waters that are ready to fall upon the thirsty-spirited, I say to thee, Anathema! Lo and behold! I am sent upon a mission, and the spirit waxes strong within me, so that I will wrestle with thee and prevail. Am not I he that is sent to scatter the good seed by the way-side? and art thou not a bush of thorns, that chokes up the grain ere it reaches the soil, or the rock that has no soil to receive it? I will preach the devil out of thee, I warrant thee, thou most antique sinner; for what says the word"— —

"Harkee, friend methodist, or whatever you are," said Captain Loring, not a whit abashed by the violent zeal with which the fanatic prolonged this remonstrance, "it is not in my way to insult the cloth, all chaplains being non-combatants. But, hark ye, sir, adzooks, I don't believe you are a preacher at all, but a rogue in another man's feathers; and if you don't satisfy my mind, I will arrest you on suspicion of being a rascal, I will by the lord! and that's as true as any Scripture. And do you, you Harper What-d'ye-call-it," (turning to the painter,) "hand me my pistol, and hold him by the leg; and you, Dick! club your whip, and stand by to knock him off his horse; and you, Elsie, come forward for a witness; for I believe the dog's a Gilbert. Surrender, you villain, and give an account of yourself!"

Great was the confusion of the exhorting stranger, at finding he had lighted upon a zealot, of fire so much superior to his own, and a congregation so little disposed to bow down to his ministry; and great was the inclination of Herman Hunter to enjoy a rencounter betwixt two such antagonists, and even to add to its absurdities, by taking part with the Captain against a man who, whatever was his apparent sanctity, he was persuaded, was nothing more than a low and vulgar hypocrite. However, perceiving that the latter worthy, besides being greatly alarmed, was clubbing his bible as if weighing the propriety of employing all its arguments and exhortations together, in one fell swoop against the head of his irreligious captor, his humanity and love of peace drove the young man betwixt the eccentric pair, as a moderator and umpire.

"Stop, Captain," said he; "this mode of questioning is against the law; and you, reverend stranger, hearken to me. Being a man of religion and peace, and doubtless good sense and good manners, you can do nothing more than answer a civil question; which will save you the trouble of a ride, or drive, according to circumstances, to the nearest magistrate."

"Magistrate!" cried the preacher, blankly, "what have the servants of truth to do with a magistrate?"

"Yes, magistrate," blustered the soldier; "and then, adzooks, perhaps to the hangman afterwards."

"In a word, sir," said Herman, "there has been a murder attempted; though where, when, and how, I do not pretend to know; and this being a land where suspicion is somewhat capricious and even whimsical, you will see the necessity of doing as I myself have done but a moment before you;—that is, of declaring your name and business to this gentleman."

"Name, gentlemen! business, gentlemen!—Certainly, gentlemen,—certainly, fellow christians and sinners!" cried the preacher, recovering his equanimity, which had somewhat deserted him, and becoming ten times more nasal and sanctified than before. "I am a poor servant of the word, an expounder of the book, Nehemiah by name,—which is to say, Nehemiah Poke,—an humble labourer in the vineyard of sin—that is to say, of righteousness—and a warner and crier-out on the way-side, by the side of the great road that leadeth to the place of despair, and of wailing, and of gnashing of teeth. You put your scorns upon me, men of the world, and sons of a stiff-necked generation; you spit in my face, you strike me over the mouth, and you take me by the beard, crying, 'Get up, you bald-head.' But *he* will reckon with you, who goeth about like a roaring lion, seeking whom he may devour. Open therefore your ears, and repent you, lest he who comes on the pale horse, with hell after him, shall fall upon you in your pride, and twist your necks, as you twist off a quid of tobacco from the roll. I come to the house of the good widow, for such, say the men of the world, is the widow Bell. I design to eat and refresh me with sleep; and then crossing over the river that lies in my path, wend my way to the scorners of truth, that are thick among the men of blood in the army; for among them, Death on the pale horse is ever ramping and roaring. But I see, that wickedness is here, even here, in this 'desert idle,' as it is written: I will therefore tarry awhile, and expound to you the words of comfort, and that before I eat and sleep, lest you fall and perish before the morning. Rest a moment then, irreverent and headstrong old man, and I will wrestle with the devil that is in thee. For I forgive thee, and will arouse thee with an exhortation, strong and fiery, 'fierce as ten furies, terrible as night,' according to the expression. Listen, therefore, to the words of my text: 'And I looked, and behold.'—And behold! the sinner rolleth away in his pride, rejecting the word! But he of the pale horse runneth after, even in the dust of his chariot wheels, shaking destruction from his shoulders, even as 'dew-drops from the lion's mane,' as it is written. Young man, give me thy hand, that I may descend; and widow, peace be to thy house, and comfort in the midst of thy poverty. He who tempers the wind to the shorn lamb, as the word has it, and marks even when a sparrow falls to the ground, will not turn from thine humble tenement, when its door is open to the weary pilgrim, and its porch resounds with the cry of prayer and thanksgiving."

"Mr. Nehemiah Poke," said Herman, who gave his hand, as required, to the pilgrim, and assisted him to descend, "you perceive, that your exhortations have driven away one-third of the congregation."—Captain Loring had been fully satisfied with the explanations of Mr. Poke, or alarmed at the prospect of a sermon; and while the preacher was kindling into fervour, had suddenly slipped into the carriage, and in a moment rumbled furiously away.—"You perceive that your sanctity has driven away one auditor, and confounded another,—Mrs. Bell here being in a maze. Now know, likewise, that I, the remaining third, have no need of your edifying discourses, and request you to put an end to them."

This was said with a good-natured smile, and a knowing nod, which somewhat disconcerted the preacher. However, after staring at the youth awhile, he lifted up his eyes, hands, and voice together, saying,

"Are you a scorner of the word, then, in your early and tender youth? and will you shut your ears and harden your heart against the grace that is offered, even by my unworthy lips!"

"Even against all that can come from your unworthy lips, as you very properly term them," said the painter, with the most significant countenance in the world: "and to make you easy on that score, do me the favour to believe that I have studied Milton, Shakspeare, Sterne, and the Bible, so much more closely than yourself, that I never jumble them together, nor fail to perceive when another man does so. Do you understand me?"

"Truly not," said the preacher, with a somewhat humorous stare; "but out of the mouths of babes and sucklings we are sometimes wisely admonished. I perceive, that I have fallen among thieves—that is to say, among sinners; and that they are none the better, but much the worse, for any comfortable wisdom that is offered them. Therefore, I will hold my peace, lest the devil should be aggravated in your bosom; hoping that a better hour may be shown me, in which to warn you of the wickedness of your ways, and so pluck you as a brand out of the burning. Good woman," he continued, turning to Elsie, and speaking much better sense than before, "know, that by reason of thy poverty and widowhood, I have brought me lucre of silver and paper—that is to say, dollars both hard and soft—to reward thee for thy hospitality; and that I come, not like a thief and a man of war, to prey upon thy substance, and leave thee nothing in return; but as a guest, in the worldly sense, who will pay scot and lot, as the word is, without grumbling."

"Such as I have, you shall share," said Elsie, coldly, "whether you have gold or not, provided you will take the young gentleman's advice, and exhort no longer in my house."

"Woman," said Nehemiah, "let me not think that a devil has seized upon you, as well as the others. Shall wisdom cry aloud, not in the streets but at your house-door, and you regard it no more than the scoffers? I tell you, and I charge you to hear" — —

"Softly, Mr. Poke," said Herman. "Remember your promise to hold your peace. That scrap from Sir John, though it smacks of a better origin, is of as clear an one as the others. Read your Bible, man, for a day or two more, and learn your trade better."

"Young man," said the preacher, again somewhat abashed, but with a stern voice, "you talk like one of the ignorant" — —

"Groundlings!" said the other, laying a ludicrous stress upon the word. "'Thy face is valanced since I saw thee last!'—Does that come out of Habakkuk? If you will preach, why here fate sends you another auditor, in the form of another patron to the Traveller's Rest! As for myself, I am tired not only of your homilies, but your company; and I pray you, for our own two sakes, that you cross the river before supper. The sooner the better, I assure you; for though at present the 'rack' may 'stand still,' 'the bold wind' be

> 'Speechless, and the orb below
> As hush as death; anon the dreadful thunder
> Will rend the region,'

and scatter jackdaws, along with the owls and pigeons. Fare you well, 'Sir Topas, the Curate!'—'I am one of those gentle ones that will use the devil himself with courtesy'—I leave you to the pedler there, who may be of a better temper for conversation. '*Bonos dies*, Sir Topas!'"

And with these words, and laughing heartily, as at some jest perfectly well understood by Nehemiah, he left the porch, only looking once behind him, as the preacher stood regarding him with uplifted hands, and bursting into a second peal as he looked. He raised his eyes, nodding courteously to the new comer, whom he had justly characterized as a pedler—for so he seemed, having a pack strapped to his back, though riding a strong black horse. "Good luck for poor Elsie to-day!" he muttered to himself, as if even diverted by so slight a circumstance as the unusual windfall of patronage. "I thought I could not be mistaken in the rogue's lantern-jaws and huge hands; and I doubt me, his religion is a mere cloak, put on for a purpose; though I *have* heard of such conversions before. However, honest or not, a fool or a scoundrel, a saint or a hypocrite, it is certain he can do me no mischief; and I'll see he does none to Elsie. As for others, they must take their chances."

Thus reflecting, and amusing himself with his cogitations, he made his way, though apparently without design or object, along the road, until he had passed the park-gate of Gilbert's Folly, and reached the rivulet described before, as emptying into the river at the mouth of the ravine, on which the Traveller's Rest was built. Although shallow and of a smooth bottom, where it crossed the road, there were rocks lying in its bed both above and below; and he could hear a murmuring noise among the trees that overshadowed it above, as if it made a cascade at no great distance in that direction. He had no doubt that, by leaving the road, he was trespassing upon the manor; but having no fear of intruding upon the haunts of any of its habitants, and being moved by a painter's curiosity, he did not hesitate to clamber over the rude stone wall, and dive at once into the shadowy grove bordering the stream.

CHAPTER V

> To arched walks of twilight groves,
> And shadows brown, that Sylvan loves,
> Of pine, or monumental oak,
> Where the rude axe, with heaved stroke,
> Was never heard the nymphs to daunt,
> Or fright them from their hallow'd haunt.
> IL PENSEROSO.

Meanwhile, the fair jockeys, after being repulsed from the highway, had betaken themselves to the park, where they galloped about for awhile, expecting the Captain. As they looked back ever and anon upon the road, they caught sight of the three young men, whom Hunter had seen pass the Traveller's Rest but a short time after the ladies themselves.

"Was ever any thing more provoking!" cried Miss Falconer. "Those three rural coxcombs, the doctor and the two lawyers! Will no one have the humanity to break a leg, or his neighbour's bones, so as to afford *them* some employment, and *us* a little peace and quiet? Must we be ever afflicted with their admiration and homage? It is more than a misfortune to be a fine woman in the country, where merit, as the old villanous poet says of female attraction in general,

> 'In its narrow circle gathers,
> Nothing but chaff, and straw, and feathers.'

But we will escape them, if it be only for an hour. Down, Kate! down, ere they have seen you! Whip your filly, and I warrant me, she will find her way to the stable. We will hide in the woods, as I think we have done before from the same fellows."

Laughing heartily at a device that spoke so little in favour of the attractive qualities of the village beaux, the Captain's daughter leaped lightly from her palfrey, as Miss Falconer had done before her; and both flourishing their whips at the same time, the liberated animals fled towards the buildings, whilst their riders lost not a moment in burying themselves from sight, by plunging into a grove, from which they continued to ramble, until they had reached a little brook, as wild and merry as themselves, that gushed over a remote corner of the park, and then hid its gleaming waters in a hollow, overgrown with forest-trees.

Into this dell they made their way, following the brook, until it fell into a larger streamlet, which was indeed no other than Hawk-Hollow Run, so often mentioned before. Its banks were strown with huge masses of rock, gray and mossy, through which the waters, swollen by late rains, rushed with impetuous speed, and sometimes with great noise and fury, while its murmurs were rendered yet more impressively sonorous by the hollow reverberations of the forest. Proceeding farther, the woods, which now invested the hills on either bank, and the rocks, assumed a sterner character of wildness and grandeur. Hemlocks, and other gloomy trees, with here a rugged maple, or ghostly beech, and there a gibbous oak, springing from interstices of the rocks, seemed, with their knotted and contorted roots, to bind the fragments together; while their thick and arched boughs flung over these ruins of nature a chilly and everlasting gloom. Aloft, on the hill, the grape-vine swung its massy locks from the oak, and, in the lower depths of the ravine, for such it was, the swamp-honeysuckle shook its fragrant clusters, and green dodders rose on the stump of the decaying birch. When their path had conducted the fair wanderers beyond the immediate vicinity of the falls and rapids, these exchanged their murmurs for other sounds not less agreeable. The chattering of jays, the lonely-sounding whistle of the wood-robin, the cry of a startled dove, and now and then the sudden whir of a pheasant, starting from his lair under a fallen trunk, and bustling noisily out of sight,—the small uproar of young rabbits, bouncing out of a brier or a bush of ferns, and galloping away up the hill,—the dropping of half-eaten nuts from the paw of the retreating squirrel, and a dozen other such noises as invade the solitude of the forest, here added a double loneliness and charm to a scene long since a favourite with the maidens.

"Now are we safe," cried Miss Falconer, with exultation; "for no one having seen us take this course, our admirers, were they even spirited enough to pursue, would think of twenty more reasonable places to seek us in than this. But let us make assurance doubly sure. Don't tell me you are tired—what business has a country-wench to be tired? We will go down to the sycamore, and then rest us awhile, till the sun peeps red in the hollow. I will bring you to your confession; for, having failed in my precious designs upon the old witch there, (may Monsieur Red-jacket sleep harder to-night than he ever did before, for a Marplot!) and my curiosity being so much the more inflammable, I am resolved to learn what I can, and that without ceremony. So come along, Kate,—

'Kate of my consolation,
'Kate of Kate-hall, my super-dainty Kate,'

as the bear of Verona said of your amiable namesake; all that you have now to do, is to be, like her, 'Kate conformable.'"

Thus whiling away the fatigue of climbing over rocks and creeping through thickets, with a gay rattle of discourse, the black-eyed maiden dragged her companion along, until they reached a place where the stream was contracted by the projection, on the one bank, of a huge mass of slaty rock, and, on the other, by the protrusion of the roots of a gigantic plane-tree,—the sycamore, or buttonwood, of vulgar speech. Above them, and beyond the crag, the channel of the rivulet widened into a pool; and there was a plot of green turf betwixt the water and the hill, on the farther bank, whereon fairies, if such had ever made their way to the World of Twilight, might have loved to gambol under the light of the moon. A hill shut up the glen at its upper extremity; and it was hemmed in, on the left, by the rocky and wooded declivity, over which the maidens had already passed. Over this, and just behind a black rounded shoulder that it thrust into the glen, a broad ray from the evening sun shot across the stream, and fell, in a rich yellow flood, over the vacant plot. There was something almost Arcadian in this little solitude; and if, instead of two well-bred maidens perched upon the roots of the sycamore, on seats chosen with a due regard to the claims of their dresses, there had been a batch of country girls romping in the water, a passing Actæon might have dreamed of the piny Gargaphy, its running well,—*fons tenui perlucidus unda,*—and the bright creatures of the mythic day, that once animated the waters of that solitary grot. But the fairy and the wood-nymph are alike unknown in America. Poetic illusion has not yet consecrated her glens and fountains; her forests nod in uninvaded gloom, her rivers roll in unsanctified silence, and even her ridgy mountains lift up their blue tops in unphantomed solitude. Association sleeps, or it reverts only to the vague mysteries of speculation. Perhaps

"A restless Indian queen,
Pale Marian with the braided hair,"

may wander at night by some highly-favoured spring; perhaps some tall and tawny hunter,

"In vestments for the chase array'd,"

may yet hunt the hart over certain distinguished ridges, or urge his barken canoe over some cypress-fringed pool; but all other places are left to the fancies of the utilitarian. A Greek would have invented a god, to dwell under the watery arch of Niagara; an American is satisfied with a paper-mill, clapped just above it.

The fair ladies of Hawk-Hollow were no more troubled with the absence of poetic association in their lovely retreat, than any of their countrymen would have been; as was plainly shown by the first words pronounced by Miss Falconer, after taking possession of a sort of arm-chair among the sycamore roots.

"This is a place, my mannikin," said she, bending her head majestically towards her kinswoman, whose seat was not so elevated,—"this is a place where one may think comfortably of murdering, whooping, scalping, and such sort of matters; and its solemnity will therefore give a degree of point to the story. Come, begin; I am all ears—that is, metaphorically speaking; though a viler metaphor, to come from men of rational imagination, could not have been invented. I tell you, Kate, I am dying with curiosity about these terrible Hawks; and as I know, you know *something*, I am determined you shall resuscitate me, in lack of a better physician, with such information as you have. No excuses—I know them all by heart, you have repeated them over so often. I declare upon my jockey-like word, that here I sit, as fixed as the very roots around me, and as immoveable; and here I *will* sit, until you surrender your scruples, and open your mouth, though I should remain until washed away by the next fresh. I am positive; my will is as inflexible as the laws of the Medes and Persians."

"You have mistaken me, Harriet," said the other, bending her eyes upon the stream; "I know nothing of the matter.—That I have heard many idle whispers, hints, and innuendoes, is true; but there is neither wisdom nor propriety in repeating them, particularly to *you*.—But is not this the most charming place in the world? Do you know, I have determined upon the spot I am to be buried in? It is further up the river, where three lime-trees grow together; behind them is a rock, covered with laurels, wild roses, and columbines; and there is such an array of azaleas below, with blood-roots, and wind-flowers, and dogwood, as has half-turned my brain. Can you tell me, Hal, why I should be ever thinking of a grave, when I stumble upon such pretty places? It is always the first thought."

As Catherine spoke, she turned her eyes with much simplicity and earnestness of expression, upon her companion's face; and though it was evident, she had introduced the subject, for the purpose of diverting the conversation from the channel in which Miss Falconer desired to have it flow, it was equally plain, that it had already taken hold upon her imagination, and now occupied her mind alone. As she looked up, with such a thought at her bosom, it imparted a character of melancholy to her countenance, which, although not her natural and original expression, circumstances had made, of late, much more common than any other. Her face was the sweetest oval in the world, her features very regular and pretty, the hue of her complexion less brilliant than might have been expected in one with such light locks, but of a pleasant healthy tone, and her eyes, without being bright or striking, were so singularly earnest of expression, with a certain vague anxiety, or imploringness, mingled up with every look, as to seldom fail of interesting the feelings of the beholder in her favour. Besides, her brow, from which the hair was parted in the simplest and easiest manner, was particularly smooth and beautiful; and whatever might have been the depth of her melancholy, this noble feature lost nothing of its serenity. Indeed, when sadness dwelt upon her spirit, it seldom produced a change in any part of the countenance except the eyes; and it was in these alone, at the present moment, that emotion was betrayed by the change from the merry brightness which the events of the afternoon had thrown into them, to that appealing, anxious expression, already described. It must be added to this description that her voice was, if possible, even more strikingly expressive than her eyes. It was with her as with the Faerie Queene; always,

>"When she spake,
>Sweete wordes, like dropping honny, she did shed;
>And 'twixt the perles and rubins softly brake
>A silver sound:"

every exertion was characterized by some appropriate and harmonious change; her joyous spirits broke out with such sweet and jocund sounds as come from tinkling bells; and when sadness was at her heart, her accents were such murmurs of subdued and contagious melancholy as the wood-pigeon breathes from the depths of the forest.

"Do I know *why?*" said Miss Falconer, looking down upon her with a mischievous air, and humming instantly,

>"'The poor soul sat sying by a sycamore-tree,
>   Sing all a green willow;
>Her hand on her bosom, her head on her knee,
>   Sing willow, willow, willow.'

But pr'ythee, be comforted; this is the way with all young ladies who have hair-brained sweethearts. But I assure you, he we wot of is the best, truest, and most amiable creature in the world; and if he be a little wild, why all men are so, you know."

At these allusions, which were evidently unexpected, Miss Loring blushed, then turned very pale; and finally, while Harriet drew breath, as if to continue the subject, she said, recurring abruptly to the original topic of discourse, and in a hurried manner,

"If you insist I should tell you what I have heard, I must obey. The story is singular and melancholy,—melancholy under every aspect, but doubly so, if that be true which I know you are most anxious to learn. But, Harriet, I cannot tell you *all*. What concerns the Gilberts alone I am ready to relate; but that which involves the connexion between,—that is to say—Harriet!" cried the young lady, after pausing with embarrassment, "it does not become a daughter to listen to aspersions cast upon the good name of a parent!"

"It does not," said Miss Falconer, gravely, "when they are breathed by the lips of an enemy. But fear not, I will not eat you. I do not ask you to repeat slanders, but to inform me what slanders are repeated by others. You might have added, it did not become me to pry into my father's secrets; but as his child, his daughter—I would to heaven I could say his son!—it is fitting I should at least know from what to defend him. I tell you, Kate, I have this thing much at heart. Fear not to shock me by your relations; for, not being disposed to believe them, I shall not be grieved, except at discovering how extensive may be the malignity of our foes. I shall rest more sweetly on my pillow to-night, if I go not to sleep on suspicion. Begin, therefore, Kate, and scruple not to speak boldly."

CHAPTER VI

> For us, we do approve the Roman maxim,
> To save one citizen is a greater prize,
> Than to have killed, in war, ten enemies.
> MASSINGER—*The Guardian.*
>
> Blow, blow, thou winter wind,
> Thou art not so unkind
>   As man's ingratitude.— —
> Freeze, freeze, thou bitter sky,
> Thou dost not bite so nigh,
>   As benefits forgot.
> AS YOU LIKE IT.

"You know then, I presume," said Catherine, beginning her narrative, ominously, with a sigh,—"you know, I suppose, all about old Mr. Gilbert, and his"— —

"My dear creature," said Miss Falconer, "I know no more of Mr. Gilbert than the Grand Turk; and all that I can boast of knowledge in relation to his cut-throat children, is that they were the Hawks of Hawk-Hollow; but whether they were real kites, with claws and feathers, or only the philosopher's two-legged birds, human chanticleers, I could never yet determine. My father is not always so communicative as might be expected in a dutiful parent; and, once or twice, when I have been curious to come at some of his early exploits on the frontiers, (for they say he was a great Indian-fighter,) he has not hesitated to assume a severe countenance, and scold me in the most paternal manner imaginable. Nay, my dear, he once assured me that, as it became a woman rather to garnish the outside of her head than the interior, I would do well never to trouble myself by searching after information that could not make me a whit more handsome. I bowed my head at the reproof, and ran straightway to my brother. But Harry, poor fellow, knew no more about these matters than he cared,—that is, nothing. Ah! he is a jewel of a man, and will make the best husband in the world, having nothing of the meddler about him. I have often thought, if pa were to commit a murder, or even break his neck, Harry would not trouble himself with either wonder or lamentation; and this, not from any want of affection, but simply because he would consider the thing his father's affair, not his. A good easy temper is an excellent thing in men,—as excellent indeed as the 'voice soft, gentle, and low,' in woman. So, now, you perceive the necessity of beginning just where your story begins. Take up the father,—the grandfather, if you choose,—of this savage brood; give me their genealogy, if they have any, and if it be german to the matter; draw all sorts of parallels, make all kinds of reflections, and, in fine, do and say any thing you may think proper,—only conceal nothing. My curiosity is as capacious of appetite as the Moor's revenge, (so much for ruralizing, when one must kill time with Shakspeare!) and demands that its gratification should be as complete."

Thus adjured and instructed, Miss Loring began the narration of Gilbert's story, and the description of his family, as they have been already recorded; into both which, however, she entered in greater detail than it was thought necessary to attempt.

The first part of the history, which was without melancholy, and related chiefly to the dilemmas into which the founder of Hawk-Hollow Hall was thrown by the sudden accession of wealth, and his vain struggles to refine the character of his children, long since determined by early habits upon rude and adventurous lives, Miss Loring, naturally a merry and waggish maiden, with strong talents for mimicry, delivered in a manner that soon became humorous, and, at last, highly diverting; so that the hollow forest began to peal with the approving merriment of her companion. Her benevolence to the poor widow had so opened Elsie's heart, that she had cast aside most of the reserve with which she was accustomed to speak of the Gilberts; and, in consequence, Catherine was provided with an ample store of anecdotes, illustrative of their characters and habits, with which she now amused her friend. She related with what surprise the good Elsie, one autumn evening, (while Mr. Gilbert was yet in England with his whole family,) beheld the adventurous Oran, in ragged attire, and with a bundle at his back, come trudging up to the Traveller's Rest, looking as bold and resolute, to use her own whimsical illustrations, as a soldier marching up to the mouth of an empty cannon, or a militia-man returning from a campaign without battles; and she even mimicked, with voice, gesture, and looks, the appearance and bearing of the two friends, in the dialogue that followed as soon as the truant was recognized by the widow.

"'Heaven bless us!' said Elsie, with uplifted hands, 'is that *you*, Oran Gilbert?'"—Thus her story went on: "'What a foolish question!' muttered the hero of two lustres and a half, who had never affected much of the dulcet submissiveness of a child to any one, either in word or action; 'what a foolish question for you, goody Elsie! Here I am in Pennsylvany, and hungry, I reckon!' and with that, without waiting for invitation, he plumped himself down at the table, already set out for the widow's evening meal, and straightway fell to work with a zeal and industry that showed he had not mistaken the condition of his appetite. The widow regarded him with undiminished astonishment, crying out, for she feared lest some dreadful accident, by shipwreck or otherwise, had destroyed the rest, 'But your father and brothers, Oran,—where are *they?*' 'In Bristol,' mumbled the boy, scowling at her over a bone, but still making the most of it,—'in Bristol,—that is, the big English Bristol, and not our Pennsylvany town, down the river.' 'In Bristol,' echoed Elsie Bell; 'and what are you doing here without them?' 'Why, eating my supper, don't you see?' replied the juvenal. 'And how did you get here?' demanded Elsie. 'I came in a big ship to Philadelphy,' replied the boy, scarce intermitting his agreeable employment for a moment, 'and then, to be sure, I footed it.' 'You have run away from your father, Oran?' said Elsie. 'Yes, I have,' said the boy, grumly; 'let me eat my supper, and I'll tell you all about it.'

"The widow held her peace for awhile, until the lad had satisfied his ravenous appetite; and then, assuming a friendly and coaxing air, for well she knew nothing else would have any effect on that singular young reprobate, she drew from him a confession of his whole adventure, and the causes that led to it.

"It appeared, that, besides an extraordinary attachment to his native home among the wild woods, Oran had another cause to be discontented with his residence in England; and this he discovered in the public school, to which he was sent with his brother next in age, called Hyland. 'He sent me,' said Oran, expatiating upon the barbarity of his father, 'to a school, to learn grammar, and Latin, and reading and writing, and all that sort of thing!'— For you must know," said Catherine, speaking to her friend, "that the want of a teacher, or perhaps hard poverty, had prevented Gilbert sending his children to any school, before he fell heir to his fortune; which was the reason perhaps, that they got such wild notions and propensities among them as could never after be eradicated. 'Yes,' the urchin went on, 'he sent me to school, and Hy, too; for he has been a sort of crazy man ever since he came to his money. Well, the boys at school called me an Indian papoose, and I thumped 'em; and the man that was master he thumped *me*, and Hy also; for Hy came to help me. So, when school was out, I took Hyland along; and we went to a corner, and got a great heap of stones; and when the master came out, we pelted him!' 'You did?' cried Elsie, in alarm: 'I hit him one polt on the shin,' said Oran, warming with the recollection,—'I hit him one polt—it was what I call a sogdolloger,—that made him dance like a ducked cat; and just as he stooped down to scratch it, we blazed away again, me and Hy; and if you ever heard two hailstones rattle on a well-bucket, you may tell how his head sounded, I reckon!'

"'But your father, Oran?' said Elsie,—'you have not told me what made you leave your father?' 'Father chose to take the master's part,' said Oran, sulkily; 'he said as how I must learn to be a gentleman, now I was in England, and never behave like a young savage no more, because I was never more to come home, meaning to Pennsylvany; and so I must go back to the master, and be thumped again; for nobody could be a gentleman, without having it thumped into him. Well, Goody, you see, I couldn't stand that; I was not going to a school to be called papoose, and trounced too; and I was mighty sick of England, which is just like a big garden,—you can't turn out of the road, without treading on somebody's strawberry-patch, and having 'em holla after you with dogs, and men, and such things; and I got into a great pickle once, for killing a thumping big rabbit that I saw in a stubble. They called it a hare; I killed it with a stone; they made father pay money about it. Well, I made up my mind to come home, without making any more words about it. So I went down to the river among the docks, and there I saw a ship that was going to sail to Philadelphy next day. I told Hy about it, and he agreed we should go over. I went to the captain, and I said, "Captain, I want to go to Philadelphy," but he called me hard names, and swore at me—there was no getting any thing out of him. I looked about, and saw them putting boxes, and barrels and baskets, and all sorts of things, into the big hole below. I went ashore, and laid out the shilling father gave me to go back to school, in gingerbread. But Hy's heart failed him: I never thought he would come to much, he's too much of a coward; he began to cry, and said he would go home to father. I gave him a thumping for being such a fool; but that only made him cry harder. So I gave him half my gingerbread, and told him to go, letting him know, if he told on me, I would give him another banging. Then I clomb into the ship again, and slipped into the hole among the boxes. But before I went down, I looked back to Hy, and there he was on the wharf, eating his gingerbread and crying. I shook my fist at him, as much as to say, "If you tell, mind you!" and then I went below, and after awhile they fastened me up.'

"'It was as dark down there as the dickens,' said Oran, in reply to the piteous ejaculations of the widow; 'but there was plenty of rats—I tell you what, they scared me! They stole my gingerbread, and whenever I got to nodding, they seized me by the nose and fingers, and I thought I should have been nibbled up, like an ear of corn. But I knew I must stand 'em as long as I could; or it would be all up with me.—Well, after awhile they came to a place, I don't know where it was; but there was a great clatter on the deck, and swearing and trampling, and they opened the trap-doors, as I saw by the great flash of light. Then there was a heap of voices, and father's among them, and Hyland's too. The great villain Hy, was telling on me, for all I gave him half the gingerbread! When I catch him, I'll pay him up, I will, Goody, if I wait ten years!'—And here the young scape-gallows, as he revolved the treachery of his fellow truant, clenched his fist, and looked as fierce and savage as a young bantam in his first fit of valour.

"'Then,' continued this hopeful junior to the astonished widow, 'there was father, saying his son Oran was hid in the ship, and he would have him out, or bring the captain to the gallows for kidnapping him, meaning *me*; and there was Hy, the villain, telling him how I was to hide among the boxes; and there was the captain and the other folks, swearing that father was crazy, and ought to stay at home; though to make him easy, they had opened the traps, or the hatches, as they call them, and he might see for himself. Then father came down, and bawled out after me, and so did Hy; and Hy said, if I would come out, father would not send me to the grammar school, to be thumped no more; but he said nothing about father sending me back to Pennsylvany! no, not so much as a word! I was not to be caught by any such talking; so I laid snug and as mum as a rabbit. Then father took on as though I was dead, squeezed to pieces among the boxes, because I would not answer him—as if I was such a fool! Then he wanted the captain to take out the boxes, and the captain would not; then he went after constables; and when he was gone, they clapped down the hatches, and sailed away with all their might, and I never heard any thing more of father.'

"'Poor fellow!' said Elsie, her sympathy for the anticipated sufferings of her young protegé driving from her mind all disapprobation of the hardhearted perverseness that caused them, 'did they keep you long in that dismal, dreadful place?' 'You may say so,' replied the boy; 'they kept me down there till I was more tired of it than ever I had been of the grammarschool. I don't know how long it was, but I was mighty tired of it. Dickens, goody, but I was dry! I was in such a hurry to get down, that I forgot I should want water as well as gingerbread: I eat up all my gingerbread, but I was as dry as ever. Goody, you don't know what it is to be dry! I was always thinking and dreaming of springs, and wells, and pumps, and the big Delaware there, and even the ditches and gutters. But I held out as well as I could, till I thought we were clear of that hateful old England; and then I hollaed to 'em to let me out; but they did not hear me at all. There was a power of big baskets, that were rolled all about me; for you must know, a ship never holds still a minute at a time, but is always pitching and tumbling, now up and now down, like a cart in a corn-field; so the baskets rolled all over me; I thought they would have squeezed the life out of me, and I could not get out from among them. So there I pulled and hollaed, till I was tired of it, or fell asleep; but no good came of it. I tell you what, goody, I would have taken a thumping for a drink of water! but there was no coming at it. I bawled out, "Water! water!" and "Fire! fire!" but it was no good; nobody heard me; and it set me to crying, to think what a hard time I had of it. Well, I reckon!—I was scraping about among the baskets, and some gave way, they were so rotten. I scraped among the willow twigs, and got my hand among the straw, without so much as thinking what I was about, when, all of a sudden, I found I had hold of a glass bottle. "Oho!" said I; it was a great long-necked thing, with wax over the cork. I did not mind that; I knocked the neck off against the basket, and, good dickens! such a fizzing and spluttering as it made! It foamed all over my face, and some fell on my lips, and it tasted good, like cider—you may be sure I drained it.' 'It was wine!' cried Elsie. 'I reckon,' said the juvenal; 'and I reckon it made my head sing, too!' he exclaimed, smacking his lips over the grateful recollection; 'such stuff as that I never tasted before. It made me feel good,—all comical, and merry, and ticklish-like,—I don't know how, but all as if I was rolling up hill and down hill,—huzzy-buzzy, sleek, and grand! Then I seemed as if I was dreaming, but such merry dreams, and talking, and roaring, and laughing; and then some of them opened the traps, and dragged me out; and then I had a tussle with some of them, for I felt big enough to fight them all; and then somehow I fell fast asleep.'

"'When I came to, the captain said I was drunk, and he beat me: it was worse than the grammar-man. First, he thumped me for stealing into the ship, then for putting him to a bother, and then for drinking his cider, or champagne, as he called it.' 'He beat you, the villain!' cried Elsie; 'and you the son of Thomas Gilbert!' 'He did,' said the boy, with edifying coolness; 'he treated me like a dog, and he thumped me every day. I suppose the grammar-man could not have been harder on me than the captain of that big ship—they called her the Prince of Whales, for, you must know, a whale is a very big fish; but I could never get a peep at one. Goody! I never was so mauled in my life! If I crawled about the quarter-deck, as they call it, (because that's a place where the ship-boys never get any quarter,) why the captain cuffed me off; and it was pretty much the same with the mates, for they cuffed too, and every now and then, some one or other beat me with a rope's end, because I would not go up the ropes, or do any thing else to make myself useful. I never did believe a Christian man's son could be treated so! but that's the way they treat boys on board a ship, only that the regular ship-boys were not handled so hard. They all beat me, captain, sailors, and all; the cook boxed my ears when I went to the caboose;—and if I hid on the forecastle, as they call it, the sailors run me up a rope and plumped me into the sea; and even the ship-boys tried their hands at me, but I reckon *they* got as much as they gave. They all beat me but Jackey Jones, an old fellow that had but one eye; and if it had not been for him, I believe they would have killed, or starved, or drowned me among them. One night he was washed overboard: and after that I was beat worse than ever. It was a great storm, goody; I reckon you don't know what a storm is, ashore, even when the trees are snapping; I tell you what, the sea was boiling up, just like a big pot, and the ship danced about just like an apple-dumpling; all the difference was, the water was not hot. They were all big cowards, for all they had been so big with me; and down they went on their knees, crying and praying, like methodist preachers. The captain was white all over the mouth, the chief mate got drunk, and Big George, a sailor that used to be hard on me, came to ask my pardon for treating me so badly. I told him, we should have a reckoning about that some other time; and that night he was washed overboard, along with Jackey Jones, and we saw them no more. I tell you what, goody! it was the happiest time I had aboard that ship; for I supposed it would sink, and drown 'em all; which was a great satisfaction for me to think on. However, it cleared up again next day; and if we had not soon reached Philadelphy, I don't know what would have become of me; for they were all worse than ever, especially the captain.' 'And that wretch,' cried Elsie; 'did no one punish him for his cruel and barbarous oppression of a poor, friendless boy?' 'You shall hear,' replied the urchin, with a grin that might have adorned the visage of an Indian coming out of battle, with a sack full of scalps; 'he was for fastening me up when we came to the wharf at Philadelphy, to see his merchant, and learn what was to be done with me. But I sneaked away, when he was gone, and hid among some barrels, till he came back. Then I watched him come out of the ship again, and ran to a corner, where there was a bundle of green hoop-poles, at a cooper's shop. Well, goody, I took one of the hoop-poles; and when he passed by, down it went, and down went the captain, too, like a butchered ox, with a great yell like a school-boy, that brought the people up. However, I gave him two more, for as long as I had time; and then I had to scurry for it.' 'Good heavens!' cried Elsie, 'perhaps you killed him!' 'Well, if I didn't, I'm sure it was all the fault of the people that ran up so fast, so that I had not time. As for the rest of them, if I ever catch any of them up here among the hills, you may reckon what will come of it.' And as he spoke, he raised his eyes to an old musket, hanging on the wall, and nodded his head significantly.

"This," said the merry narrator, "is the very story I had from Elsie's lips, only that she spoiled it in telling; and I leave you to judge whether there was ever a more exquisite young savage in the whole world, than that same Oran Gilbert."

"Never, truly," said Miss Falconer, upon whom perhaps the unusual, yet natural, vivacity of her friend, had produced a still more pleasant impression than the story itself. "This Oran must have been the Paladin, the Orlando, the very Tom Thumb, of Hawk-Hollow;

'Though small his body,
Yet was his soul like any mountain big;'

and verily, if the other Hawks, callow or full fledged, were of the same colour and quality, you have begun the most diverting story in all your budget. Pr'ythee go on; there is a magic in the whole affair; for, while you speak it, it makes the teller herself again. Methinks you are now the same merry Kate I knew a year ago,—the bright Kate, no longer 'kerchieft in a cloud,' as Milton says,—the gay Kate, the madcap Kate, the Brandywine Kate"——

"Not a word about Brandywine, if you will have me play the fool longer," said Miss Loring, hurriedly. "And after all, there is nothing more to tell—that is, nothing more funny; and, after all, too, there *was* nothing funny in the sufferings of that poor, headstrong, vindictive boy; absurdity enough, I grant you, there was; but it was my wicked and hard heart that made me travesty an anecdote that poor Elsie considered serious enough."

She then went on to speak of the return of the boy's father, the building of the manor-house, the second marriage of Mr. Gilbert, and the exploits of his children. The peculiar temper of Oran soon determined the course of his life. While yet a boy of sixteen, he had extended his rambles over the mountains into the Wyoming valley, then occupied by two clans of Shawnee and Delaware Indians, who were often at feud together. "Among these barbarians," said the lady, "the young white Indian, for such he must be esteemed, fought his first battle, and took his first scalp. It was in the Grasshopper War"——

"The what?" cried Miss Falconer.

"Why, Hal, the Grasshopper War *I* call it," said Catherine, "out of tenderness to our sex; but all others call it the Squaw War. It was waged between those rival tribes I spoke of. The women of the two clans met together in a strawberry field, where they gathered fruit in company, very pacifically I doubt not, except a little scolding at one another. The children employed themselves, in the meanwhile, chasing grasshoppers; when, unfortunately, two boys belonging to different tribes pounced together upon a magnificent insect, that was perhaps the emperor of the field, and contended for the possession of the prize. Up ran the mother of the Delaware, and boxed the young Shawnee's ears; the Shawnee parent ran to avenge her child; and others immediately taking part, in a few moments the whole field was in an uproar: such scratching, scolding, and pulling of caps, were perhaps never heard of before. Out ran the men from their villages to help their wives, and to it they went pell-mell; and the war, thus begun, did not end until hundreds had been slain on both sides, and the Shawnees entirely driven from the valley. The less we say of this war, the better; for I heard it instanced as one small proof out of a thousand better, that men never fall by the ears, without the women being at the bottom of the contention. The Delawares, with whom Oran fought, made much of him, gave him a name which signifies the Boy Warrior, and formally adopted him into their tribe. As his brothers grew up around him, he enticed them one by one into the woods, and made them as wild as himself; and by and by, when those dreadful Indian wars, that followed after the defeat of General Braddock, extended over the whole western country, and even east of the Susquehanna, he acquired a singular reputation as a bold and successful scalp-hunter. I don't know what else to call him; he was not a soldier, for he never could be prevailed upon to go out with any body of soldiers, under the command of regular governmental officers. He went with his brothers, and seldom allowed even a neighbour to join his little party, though this was an object with all who knew him; for none of the Gilberts having ever been seriously wounded in any of their mad enterprises, the people had a superstitious belief that good luck and safety went with them.

"In the meanwhile, Mr. Gilbert had taken a second wife; and being wealthy, he was able to choose one of gentler manners and character than her predecessor, who, they say, was a fierce, masculine woman, though devotedly attached to her children. It is said, he married her in the hope that her kindness and gentleness might wean his boys from their barbarous career; but the expedient only served to confirm them in their habits. They conceived a violent dislike to their step-mother; and the only bond of union between them—I should say, perhaps, the only moderator and protector of the poor woman, was the girl, Jessie, whom they all adored, rough as they were, and who—while she lived, at least—caused them to treat the unfortunate lady with some show of respect. I may say, since you are in the poetical mood, and have already quoted one of Milton's clouds to me, that Jessie was, betwixt the timidity of the step-mother and the rudeness of her brothers,

>'A shelter, and a kind of shading, cool,
>Interposition, as a summer's cloud;'—

(I found that out myself!)—and, according to Elsie, she was one of the sweetest and warmest-hearted creatures in the world. They had a rich relation, an aunt, in the West Indies, who desired to adopt the maiden; but Mr. Gilbert refused to part with her. In her place he sent his youngest boy, an infant,—the child, and only one, of his second wife; I think Elsie told me, she died in giving it birth; but I am not certain as to that. This part of the story I never could understand perfectly; for whenever the poor widow speaks of it, she becomes dreadfully agitated. But certainly, it was most unhappy for all, that he did not send the girl."

"And why,—why unhappy, Catherine?" demanded Miss Falconer, losing somewhat of her serene self-possession, as she heard her friend's voice falter over the words.

"According to Elsie," muttered Miss Loring, with downcast eyes, "the misfortunes which crushed and ruined the whole family, might have been thus averted.—But, Harriet," she continued, "let us speak of these things to-morrow. What follows is dark, gloomy, dreadful; and I cannot speak it without giving you offence."

"I pledge you pardon and immunity beforehand," said Miss Falconer. "The ice is broken, and now I must dare the flood, though it be of gall and poison. Dreadful, indeed? What can be more dreadful than the state of a daughter, blindfold at the side of a parent whom all men are shooting at with the arrows of malice, which she hears hissing around her, yet knows not how to arrest? Speak then, Catherine, for you have placed me on a rack: nothing can be more painful than suspicion."

"Promise not to be offended with me then, dear Harriet," said Miss Loring, taking her hand, and looking deprecatingly into her face; "and do not think"— —here her voice quivered a little, and her eyes again fell to the ground,— —"do not think, because I tell you these things as I have heard them, that I necessarily believe them—or, at least, *all* of them."

"Certainly, my love," said the other, with a slight tinge of asperity. "As you will, one day, have a duty, like myself, imposed upon you, to repel all calumnies against my father, the sooner you become incredulous, the better."

Catherine smiled faintly, then blushed, and, as had happened before, at a similar allusion, the glow of embarrassment was again followed by paleness.

"I presume," she said, after a moment's pause, "that the Colonel has often spoken to you of the dreadful peril at the Moravian settlements, from which he was rescued by Oran Gilbert and his two brothers?"

"Never," replied Harriet, in a sort of dismay. "My father rescued from peril! and by the Hawks of Hawk-Hollow? Why, here is a drama opening upon us indeed! But it is not true, Kate!"

"This, Harriet," replied the other, "is a circumstance well known in the neighbourhood; and I wonder you have never heard it before."

"On all subjects connected with the family of the Gilberts," said Miss Falconer, "my father is reserved and silent—at least to me; and, Catherine, I confess with shame, this very circumstance has often filled my mind with the most painful misgivings. I know nothing about the Moravian settlements, either. You must therefore tell your story to ignorance itself. I know that my father was, in his youth, an officer in the colonial war establishment, and that he did duty somewhere on the frontiers, and came off with scars; but that is all. Speak, therefore, without reserve."

"The country west of yonder blue cliffs, (how sweetly they peep through the hollow of that hill, and over the yellow tree-tops!) has always been the theatre of the most bloody contentions," said Catherine. "That same Wyoming, of which I have said so much, has never been entirely at peace since that redoubtable war of the grasshopper set its inhabitants by the ears. It was settled by certain Yankees from Connecticut, who claimed, and claim yet, to erect a jurisdiction independent of Pennsylvania, and to this day the partisans of the two powers are quarrelling rancorously with one another, often shedding blood. When the inhabitants are driven away by enemies, they are obliged to cross a great swamp, to reach the Delaware. This has been crossed so often, and so many miserable wounded, and starving, and fainting wretches, have fallen down in the retreat and perished among its bogs, that it is yet called the Shades of Death. The wars that produced such suffering have commonly been waged in another county; but they have sometimes reached our own—(*Our own!* You see, I am making myself at home here!) The fall and winter of the year when Braddock was defeated in the extreme south-western frontier, were marked by many bloody incursions of the Indians, even in this county; and you may judge how terrible was their ferocity, when you hear that their enmity fell as heavily upon their friends as their foes. The poor Moravians, who, with a holy and unworldly zeal, had devoted their lives to the purpose of instructing and reclaiming them from barbarism, were among the first of their victims. The outer settlement of these poor missionaries was beyond the mountain, on one of the springs of the Lechaw, or Lehigh, as we now call it. It was beset, late in November, by the savages, and destroyed, together with many of the brothers. The next settlement was that called Gnadenhutten, where was much valuable property, and great stores of grain; and when the Moravians fled even from this in affright, the colonial government thought it of so much importance, that they directed it to be immediately garrisoned by a company of rangers. This was done; a fort was constructed in the neighbourhood, across the river, which was made the head-quarters of the company; while a detachment occupied the Moravian village. This detachment was commanded by your father, then holding the rank of lieutenant. And now, Harriet, I must tell you, that your father had enemies in these wild lands, even at that early day. I will not repeat what I have heard said, as the causes of enmity; for I doubt not they are mere scandals. I mention them only because some, I am told, yet declare that the barbarous attempt on his life was made by disguised white men, and not by Indians.

"Although from the time of the massacre of the over-hill Moravians, in November, until the end of the year, Indians were ever prowling in the woods, and occasionally carrying the tomahawk and flames to some lonely settlement, yet it was supposed that the presence of the soldiers at Gnadenhutten and the fort, would prevent their making any serious attempts this side the mountain. This induced a false and fatal security; and when the Indians did appear, the detachment and village of Gnadenhutten were completely surprised. It was upon New-year's day, and all the white men were amusing themselves on the frozen river, without arms, and of course they fell an easy prey to the savage assailants. Many were butchered, the village was fired, your father captured in the vain attempt to escape, and carried off to the woods.

"During all this scene of terror," continued the Captain's daughter, "there were no scalp-hunters among the white men so busy, bold, and famous, as the three Gilberts. Elsie Bell says, that Oran was then only nineteen, and the youngest two years short of that; but, it seems, men grow old fast in the woods, when Indians are nigh—(it is well the *women* don't.) They were upon an excursion, fighting for themselves, at the very time of this calamity; and it was their fate to encounter the party that bore your father away a captive. It seems that the savages, after completing the destruction of the village, retreated in small bands to distract and avoid pursuit, for there were many companies of armed men in the county, ready to march at a moment's warning. Some took charge of the prisoners, and others were to strike at small and retired settlements. Your father, who had been severely, but not desperately wounded, was left in charge of one little division, six in number, and was carried off by a path so remote from those followed by others, that, I suppose, it was this circumstance which caused evil-minded persons to affirm he was captured by private enemies and white men. Their course was at least very singular, for it carried them rather to the north-east, along the foot of the mountain, than to the north and west. They dragged their prisoner on till after midnight, which has been mentioned as an unusual circumstance, at least with Indians; and, at dawn, they tied him to a tree, and piled around him dead boughs and pine-knots, intending, as he now saw, to torture him alive."

The narrator here paused, and looked upon her friend, who, after a slight shudder, very composedly said,

"Poor pa! he must have been horribly frightened! I should like to know how he looked, the moment he made the discovery!"

Catherine heard her with unconcealed amazement, but appreciated her philosophy, when she added, with an affected laugh,

"Why, my dear Kate, as, after all, he was *not* tortured, it would be but folly to fall into hysterics. I never grieve over misfortunes that were never happening. But come; how got he out of this doleful dilemma? You said something about the three Hawks—Ah! you spoiled the dramatic point of the story, by enabling me to forestall a discovery. And so the three Hawks discovered the six buzzards, and fell upon them, and took their lambkin from them? They are no true fishing-hawks, after all; for it is the part of these ravagers, not so much to rob, as to be robbed. They should have been called Eagles, for it is these birds that take such little liberties with the feathered Isaac Waltons, as I have once or twice seen with my own eyes. But these were heroical kites, I must acknowledge."

"They were, certainly," said Miss Loring, not well pleased with the levity of her kinswoman; "and, methinks, you should do them the justice to consider that it was no child's play for three men—three boys we may call them, to assail six stout Indians, vanquish them, and rescue a poor doomed prisoner out of their hands. If you will not do justice to their courage, acknowledge at least, the dreadful cost at which they exercised their humanity. Hyland Gilbert, the second son, the best beloved of all, as Elsie assured me, was shot dead, while he was cutting your father loose from the tree."——

"Good heavens!" cried Miss Falconer, with an emotion, that seemed, however, to be rather horror than grief, "was this so indeed? Did one of them fall?"

"He did," replied Catherine, "and his poor brothers buried him where he fell. According to Elsie's superstitious belief, they were punished by the genius of their fate, for exercising their humanity on an undeserving object. You know *she*, at least, holds on to her angry prejudices. She said, that from that moment, which was the first unlucky one to them, the Gilberts never more prospered in their undertakings; every thing that came after was mischance and disaster; death followed death, sorrow succeeded sorrow, and now not one remains alive of the whole family, unless it may be the youngest son, who was sent to the Islands in his infancy, and of whom Elsie knows nothing whatever, although they have a report in the village that he also is dead."

"I am much obliged to Elsie," said Miss Falconer, sullenly; "after eating my father's bread, she might have the grace to abate her malevolence a little."

"Alas, Harriet," said Miss Loring, "do not call it malevolence; but the prejudice, the absurd and unjust prejudice of weak, dreamy old age, if you will. And you know, that she is ignorant from whom I derived the power to relieve her wants. I did but hint once that your father would befriend her, when she exclaimed, not in the heat of frenzy, but with a cold, iron-like determination, that she would gnaw the flints on the way-side for food, rather than receive a morsel of bread from the hands of Colonel Falconer. Indeed, your father himself directed me to conceal his agency in the benefaction."

"Peace to the silly old woman!" said Harriet, "and let us speak of her no more. Resume your story: I see, by your looks, that the worst is yet to come. But fear not: I am not so much shocked as I was, since the thing comes from that bitter old bundle of—oh, prejudice, my dear. Well, the two survivors saved my father's life—what then?"

"Then," said Catherine, "they bore him on a litter of boughs to their father's house; for, before they fled, the murderers had assailed him with their axes, and left him almost dying. The journey was very laborious; for to avoid the war-parties, now swarming through the country, they were obliged to steal along by circuitous paths,—and it was several days before they could procure assistance. They got him safe, however, to their father's house, and then played the good Samaritan with him. If you would like, I will show you the room where he lay, while recovering,—it is the chamber over the armoury, as you call it,—that is, my father's study, where he takes his afternoon's nap. Elsie told me there was a pane of glass on which he had cut his name with a diamond ring; but the sashes were changed, before she told me this, and I know not what has become of them. But, if you like, we will inquire about them.—He did not recover entirely before the autumn, and then he left the valley. I am told that there is an oak-tree on the lawn, at which he used to shoot pistols."——

"Catherine!" said Miss Falconer, with a piercing look, "you flutter about the subject, like a bird over the jaws of a serpent, unable to retreat and yet afraid to descend. Is there any thing so horrible to come?"

"There is indeed!" said Catherine, trembling; "but it is not true, cousin,—you must not believe it is true! It is about Jessie—they say she was very good and handsome—a kind nurse, simple-hearted, of an affectionate disposition, and"——

"Hold! hold!" cried Miss Falconer, vehemently, starting to her feet, with a pale face, and lips ashy and trembling, "this would be to make out my father a fiend! Saints of heaven! this is too much! Come,—let us proceed."

And thus muttering out her oppressive emotion, she darted down the stream, followed hastily by her friend.

Tall trees still overarched the rivulet; but its bank became smoother as they advanced. A few rods below, the channel was again contracted, but not by impending crags. A huge sycamore, ancient and thunder-scarred, but still flourishing, had been tumbled over the stream by some forgotten tempest; but so tightly were its roots twisted in the rocky soil of the one bank, and so tenacious was the hold of its gnarled and elbowed boughs upon the sward of the other, that it maintained its place despite the floods, which, it was evident, often washed over it, and thus afforded a bridge, rustic enough, but secure, though by no means easy of passage.

Upon this Harriet, still perturbed and driven onward by painful emotion, was about to place her foot, when she was restrained by the trembling grasp of her companion.

"What means the child?" she exclaimed, with a feverish accent: "there are no savages here."

"But," said Catherine, with a faint voice, "it was over there, by the rock, they dug the poor girl's grave!"

Miss Falconer recoiled for a moment, and then saying, with a firm voice, "It matters not—let us visit it," she sprang upon the bridge, followed by Catherine, and made her way across. About thirty paces below, the stream darted over a rock, making a cascade ten or twelve feet high; and it was the roar of this fall, borne downwards by the breeze, which had attracted the painter's curiosity, as he paused for a moment on the road side. It possessed no very striking beauty, nor was the body of water that leaped over the rock of any extraordinary magnitude; yet it had a violent and even impressive look, and the waters hurrying impetuously towards it from above, shot under the sycamore with an appearance of fury that might have tried the nerves of any over-timid person, crossing by so precarious a bridge.

CHAPTER VII

> Dull grave—thou spoil'st the dance of youthful blood,
> Strik'st out the dimple from the cheek of mirth,
> And every smirking feature from the face,
> Branding our laughter with the name of madness.
> Where are the jesters now?— —
> — — — —Ah! sullen now,
> And dumb as the green turf that covers them.
> BLAIR—The Grave.

  The spot which the maidens now reached, after crossing the rivulet, was wild and gloomy, yet exceedingly romantic. A little ascent led them up to a sort of platform, or shelf, of earth, the highest portion of the table-land, from which the torrent leaped downwards, making its way, in a series of foaming rapids, to the parent river. It therefore overlooked the sweeping hillocks and rustling forests below, and commanded a prospect of the river and the southern portion of the valley, both extensive and beautiful; and, indeed, a more charming nook could not have been imagined for one, who, though preferring personally to be surrounded by solitude, yet loved to send back his spirit to the world, and survey it from that distance which lends it the sweetest enchantment. On the summit of the platform lay two huge masses of rock, that approached each other in one place so nigh as scarce to permit a passage between them; towards the rivulet, however, the intervening space was wider, and covered with a grassy turf; and a sort of wall, composed of smaller fragments, ran from the one crag to the other, yet so rudely, that it was difficult to say whether the irregular barrier had been piled up by the hands of nature or man. Besides a majestic growth of trees behind and around the rocks, there was one tall beech flourishing within the enclosure; and from its roots there gushed a cool fountain, that went dripping and leaking through green mosses, until it yielded its meager tribute to the streamlet. Both the crags were overgrown with lichens and ferns; and under the larger one, which, in the afternoon, cast its shadow over the whole nook, there flourished a luxuriant array of arums, mandrakes, violets, and other plants that delight in cool and moist situations. On the face, and at the foot, of the eastern rock, where the sunshine lingered longer, were dusky columbines, rock-daisies, and other plants, now in bloom, and, in the summer, their places would have been supplied by the aster and the golden-rod; and at the foot of the rock, among a heap of brambles, that seemed to have almost choked it, there grew a rose-bush, the only remarkable thing present, being obviously of an exotic species. It bore a single flower, visible among the green leaves and white blossoms of the blackberry, and it immediately attracted the notice of the maidens.

"Elsie told me," whispered Catherine, with a voice of fear, "that the poor old father planted a rose-bush on the grave,—it is strange it should live so long.—She said there was a grave-stone too—ah! there it is!—Let us go away."

As Harriet, bolder than her friend, or affecting to be so, reached forward, to remove the brier from the more lovely plant, in hopes that the rude and thorny veil might conceal other flowers, it yielded to her grasp, and revealed a hollow or sunken place in the ground, at one extremity of which was a rude stone, entirely shapeless and undressed, yet so placed as to mark undeniably the couch of some human clod of the valley. No name, letter, or device of any kind,—no inscription to record the virtues of the dead, no legend to perpetuate the grief of the living,—appeared on the rude monument; and, indeed, however expressive the shape and appearance of the hollow place to those already aware that a grave had been dug in this unsanctified nook, it is scarce probable that a stranger, stumbling upon it by chance, could have believed that in that coarse and dishonoured fragment, his foot pressed upon a funeral stone. It was a singular grave—it was a singular cemetery; and the maidens regarded the brambled pit and the solitary flower with awe, the one because her spirit was especially susceptible of impressions from melancholy objects, and the other because the legend of her companion had invested the place with an interest personal, it might be said, to herself.

How little reflection is expended upon,—yet how much is called for, by the grave,—by the lowliest hillock that is piled over the icy bosom, by the grassiest hollow that has sunk with the mouldering bones of a fellow creature! And in this narrow haven rots the bark that has ploughed the surges of the great vital ocean! in this little den, that the thistle can overshadow in a day's growth, and the molewarp undermine in an hour of labour, is crushed the spirit that could enthrall a world, and dare even a contest with destiny! How little it speaks for the value of the existence, which man endures so many evils to prolong; how much it reduces the significance of both the pomp and wretchedness of being, reducing all its vicissitudes into the indistinguishable identity which infinite distance gives to the stars,—a point without parallax, a speck, an atom! Such is life,—the gasp of a child that inspires the air of existence but once,—a single breath breathed from eternity. But the destiny that comes behind us,—oblivion!

It is not enough that we moralize upon the equality of the sepulchre; that the rich man, whose soul is in the ostentation of a marble palace, and his heart in the splendour of the feast, should consider how small a pit must content him, or that the proud, who boast their 'pre-eminence above the beasts,' should know that the shaggy carcass and the lawn-shrouded corse must fatten the earth together. We should teach our vanity the lesson of humiliation that is afforded by the grave; neglecting the mighty mausoleums of those marvellous spirits which fame has rendered immortal, we should turn to the nameless tombs of the million, and in their deserted obscurity, discover the feeble hold which we ourselves must have upon earth and the memory of men. Friendship forgets what the devouring earth has claimed; and even enmity ceases at last to remember the resting place of a foe. Love ourselves as we may, devote our affections to others as we can, yet must our memory perish with us in the grave; and all the immortality we leave to be cherished among friends, is expressed in the distich of a poet, whom the anticipation of enduring renown could not blind to the transitoriness of real remembrance:

> Poor Pope will grieve a month, and Gay
> A week, and Arbuthnot a day.[1]

[1] SWIFT—*On the Death of Dr. Swift.*

But there were other thoughts necessarily associated, and other feelings excited by this lonely sepulchre; and while Miss Falconer preserved a moody and painful silence upon its brink, Catherine bent over it, scarce conscious that she bedewed the rose-bush with a tear, or that her own shadow had descended, as it were, into the pit, with an ominous readiness.

It was a delightful evening; the air was full of balmy freshness, the landscape resplendently verdant, and the sky cloudless, save in the west, where the sun was sinking among curtains of gold and pillars of flame; and the solitude and quiet of the whole scene, broken by no sounds, except the ceaseless turmoil of the water-fall, and the plaintive scream of the fishing-eagles, which had deserted their gray perch, to bathe in the pure floods of sunset, that beautified the upper air,—the solitude, quiet, and beauty of every thing around and nigh, were additional arguments for silence.

But silence, long continued, was not consonant to the restless and impatient temper of Miss Falconer; and notwithstanding the indignant incredulity with which she had interrupted her friend's narrative, the same curiosity which compelled the commencement of it, still thirsted for the conclusion. The presence of the dead, however, in so wild, so forlorn, so unblest a spot, where, as it would seem, the shame of proud but humbled hearts had dug the neglected grave, worked powerfully on her feelings; and it was with a hesitating and quivering, though an abrupt voice, that she demanded, after gazing for a long time on the grave,

"Did others,—did any beside this bitter-tongued woman, accuse my father of this thing?"

"I know not," replied Catherine, with accents still more unsteady; "all that I have gathered was from Elsie; and when she speaks of these things, as I mentioned before, she becomes fearfully agitated, so that I have sometimes thought her wits quite unsettled. She never pretended to tell me the whole story; nor indeed would I have been disposed to ask or listen, knowing it would be improper to do so. All these things have come in broken hints and exclamations. What others in the neighbourhood may say or think, I know not, never encouraging any to speak to me on the subject. The step-mother soon followed the daughter,—Elsie says, heart-broken; you may see her tomb in the village church-yard. The old father, too, became another man, gloomy, solitary, and indifferent to his friends, so that the neighbours ceased to visit him. His sons no longer hunted with the young men of the country, but went, as in their war-expeditions, alone; and when others thrust themselves into their company, they quarrelled with them, so that they began to be universally feared and detested. To crown all, as soon as the Revolution burst out, they went over to the enemy; and being distributed among the wild and murderous bands of savages forming on the north-western frontiers, they soon obtained a dreadful notoriety for their deeds of daring and cruelty. Of course, this remarkable defection of the sons caused the unlucky father to be suspected and watched. He was accused, at last, of aiding and abetting them in their treasonable practices; and soon, either from timidity or a consciousness of guilt, he fled, seeking refuge within the royal lines. This was sufficient for his ruin; for after the usual legal preliminaries, he was formally outlawed, as his sons had been before, and his property confiscated. He died soon afterward, either at New York, or in Jamaica, where he had gone to seek his youngest son—the lad he had sent away as a substitute for the daughter."

"And this son?" demanded Miss Falconer; "did you not say that he was dead?"

"Of him," said Catherine, "Elsie knows nothing; but if we can receive a belief that prevails in the village on the subject, it would seem as if the vials of wrath had been poured to the uttermost on the poor devoted family. They say, that the young man, just raised to wealth and distinction by the death of his munificent kinswoman, was one of the many victims to that dreadful tornado which ravaged the island of Jamaica two years ago. But I never heard how this intelligence was obtained."

"And the other sons? the rest of this brood of traitors!" demanded Miss Falconer, who strove to merge the unpleasant feelings that had possession of her bosom, in patriotic detestation of the unfortunate family.

"They met the fate they must have anticipated," said the Captain's daughter. "They perished, one by one, in different bloody conflicts; one fell at Wyoming, another at Tioga Point, where the combined forces of savages and refugees were routed by General Sullivan; Oran himself, with a fourth brother, was killed at the battle of Johnstown, near the Mohawk river, where another refugee leader, Walter Butler, not less blood-thirsty and famous, met a similar fate. Their death was terrible; they cried for quarter, being wounded and helpless; but the victors bade them 'Remember Wyoming, and Cherry-Valley,' two prominent objects of their cruelty, and killed them without mercy. Another, I have heard, was somewhere hanged as a spy; and these, with Hyland, killed as I mentioned before, and the youngest, deceased, if indeed he be deceased, in Jamaica, made up the whole seven sons, all of whom therefore died violent deaths. The eighth child,—the poor daughter,—undoubtedly sleeps under this rock; and there are none left to mourn her. The destruction of the family was dreadful and complete."

CHAPTER VIII

> Run! run! run!
>   Quickly for a surgeon!
> Call watch, constable! raise the hue and cry!
>   What's to be done?
>   Why the devil don't you stir, John?
> This way, that way, every body fly!
> > DON GIOVANNI.

Thus ended the sketch of a story, imperfect, perhaps tedious and unsatisfactory, but still a necessary preliminary to the series of events that completes the tradition. A mere womanly curiosity was perhaps at the bottom of the nobler feeling with which Miss Falconer sought to excuse to herself the impropriety of urging the relation. From the first to the last, it was meted out to her reluctantly; and nothing but the command she had long since obtained over a character less firm and decided than her own, could have persuaded the Captain's daughter to breathe a syllable of it into ears, which, she could not but feel, ought not to be opened to it. Miss Falconer had, moreover, overrated her powers of scepticism; she had provoked the story, as men commonly provoke an argument,—that is, with a resolution not to be convinced; but like the logician, in many instances, when the discussion is over, her incredulity was sorely, though secretly, shaken, and nothing but her pride and strength of character checked the humiliating avowal. Some circumstances a delicate consideration for the feelings of her friend, and an unconquerable repugnance to speak more on the subject than could not be avoided, had prevented the Captain's daughter from relating. These would have thrown a still darker stain upon the character of Colonel Falconer. There was enough, however, said, to force one disagreeable conviction upon Harriet's mind; and this was, that, if her parent were even as guiltless of ingratitude and wrong as her fondest wishes would have him, calumny had, at least in one secluded corner of the world, sealed him with the opprobrium of a villain. It was a sore addition also to her discomfort, that her penetrating mind discovered how deeply her kinswoman was affected by the hateful history: if she doubted, she did not doubt strongly. Vexed, humbled, displeased with herself and with Catherine, she rose from the rocky shelf, on which both had seated themselves when Catherine resumed the story, and prepared to leave the scene, equally mournful and unpleasant, when an incident occurred, which at once gave a new turn to her feelings.

The Captain's daughter had observed the look of dissatisfaction, and anticipated the movement, by rising herself, to lead the way to the bridge. As she started up hastily, her hat, which she had loosened from her forehead, to enjoy the evening breeze, now puffing among the flowers, fell from her head, and her beautiful countenance and golden ringlets were fully exposed. She raised her hands, naturally enough, to catch the falling hat, and thus assumed an attitude, of which she was herself unconscious, but which, to one spectator at least, had a character apparently menacing and forbidding. This spectator was no less a person than the young painter, who had rambled up the stream, and was now making his way across the sycamore, to obtain a view of the cascade, entirely ignorant of the presence of such visitors; for while they maintained their seats, their persons were concealed behind the low wall, and their voices drowned by the murmur of the water-fall.

A sudden exclamation, loud enough to be heard over this lulling din, drew Catherine's attention to the bridge; and there, to her extreme surprise, she beheld the young stranger struggling among the branches, as if he had lost his footing, while all the time, his eyes, instead of being employed in the more needful duty of looking to himself, were fixed upon her with an air of the most unaccountable wonder and alarm. The next instant, she beheld him, to her own infinite horror, fall from the tree, just as Harriet, starting up after her friend, had also caught sight of the strange spectacle. Both beheld the unlucky youth drop through the boughs, and both at once anticipated the most dreadful termination to such a misadventure; for a pitch over the cascade among the savage rocks below, could scarcely be less than fatal. The very instant she saw that the young man had lost his footing, Catherine uttered a loud scream, and then, driven onwards by an irresistible impulse, darted towards the river, to render him what aid she could. As for Miss Falconer, the shock had deprived her of her self-possession, and her tongue clove to her mouth with terror. She neither screamed nor rushed forwards to give aid, until her lethargy was dispelled by a distant voice, that suddenly echoed the scream of Catherine:

"Hark ye, Kate, you jade! hark ye, Kate, my dear Kate! my beloved Kate! what's the matter? I'm coming! I'll murder the villain! I'm coming, Kate!"

There was no mistaking the tones of Captain Loring, even altered as they were by anxiety and vociferation; and Miss Falconer recognising them, screamed out, "Quick, uncle, quick! for heaven's sake, quick!" and ran to the side of her friend.

The torrent, leaping along like a mill-race for the little distance that intervened betwixt the treacherous bridge and the fall, had immediately swept the young man from his feet; and as Catherine bounded to the verge, flinging out, with as much daring as presence of mind, the scarf of Harriet, which she had instinctively snatched up, in hope that he might seize it, she saw him swept by her like a feather in a whirlwind, and instantly hurried over the falls. The spectacle was really terrific; and as Miss Falconer caught sight of the dreary figure—the outstretched arm and the despairing countenance, revealed for one moment, as some rocky obstruction on the very brink of the cascade lifted the body half from the flood, and then instantly plunged it out of view—she lost what little courage remained, and was no longer capable of yielding the slightest assistance. If such was her overpowering terror, it might have been supposed that the Captain's daughter, who, whatever the vivacity and quickness of her mind, possessed little of the boldness of spirit that characterized her friend, would have been reduced to a state of imbecility still more benumbing and helpless. But this youthful girl concealed within the cells of a heart all of feeble flesh, a principle of feeling that could upon occasions, though she knew it not herself, nerve the throbbing organ into steel; and, at such times, if her brain was confounded, impulse governed her actions with an influence more useful, because more instant of operation.

Dreadful, therefore, as was the spectacle of the youth dashed down the abyss under her eyes, and almost in reach of her arm, she did not pause, like Harriet, to scream after the Captain, who was undoubtedly drawing nigh, and at an unusual pace; but leaving this to be done by her companion, she ran down the rocks that led to the base of the fall, and the next moment Harriet beheld her rush boldly into the water. The instant she reached the basin at the foot of the cascade, which was broken by rocks, black and slippery from the eternal spray, she caught sight of the body—for such it seemed—rolling in the flood where it boiled over a ridgy mole in a sheet of foam. It was scarce two paces from the bank, and though the torrent gushed over the rock with great impetuosity, it was shallow, at least in the nearer portion; and, unless too rash and daring, there was little danger she could be herself swept over the ledge among the deep and dangerous eddies below. She stepped therefore upon the rock as far as she durst, and stretching out her hand, succeeded in grasping the insensible figure, as it was whirling over at a deeper place and in a fiercer current. All her strength, however, availed nothing further than to arrest the body where it was; and she must have speedily released her hold, or been swept with it herself from the ledge, when a new auxiliary, attracted by the same cries that had alarmed Captain Loring, came unexpectedly to her assistance, crackling through the bushes, and bounding over the rocks on the opposite side of the pool, which was a wilderness of rock and swamp. No sooner had this personage beheld her situation, than he ran a little lower down, where the stream was again contracted, sprang across from rock to rock, and immediately darted to her side. With one hand he dragged—or, to speak more strictly, he flung her, (for his actions were none of the gentlest,)—out of the water; and with the other, he lifted the unlucky painter from the torrent, and bore him to the bank, saying, as he laid him at the maiden's feet, in a voice none of the mildest in the world,

"Why, here's fine sport for a May-day, and a rough end to a fool's frolic! How many more of you must I fish up?"

By this time the gallant Captain Loring, urged by anxiety for his daughter, (not knowing that the danger concerned another,) into a speed that he had not attempted for twenty-five years, made his appearance at the top of the fall, and seeing her stand shivering with fright over what she esteemed a dead body,—for the painter showed not a single sign of life,—with a stranger of questionable appearance at her side, he burst into a roar of passion, crying, "Hark ye, you vagabond villain! if you touch my girl"—when his rage was put to flight by Miss Falconer suddenly finding tongue, and exclaiming, "He has saved the poor youth's life;—that is, Kate saved him, and this man helped her. I never was more frightened in my life! Let us go down, uncle—I fear the young man is hurt."

Meanwhile, Catherine, whose courage and presence of mind had almost deserted her, so soon as she beheld the young man safe ashore, being roused by the rough accents of the stranger, and the death-like appearance of the youth, exclaimed, in tones of entreaty, for the man had turned away, as if to depart,

"Do not go.—Alas! you came too late! Help us yet a little, or the poor youth will die where he is. Pray, hold up his head—indeed, he is very much hurt!"

"Hurt! To be sure he is," cried the stranger, with infinite coolness, bordering upon a sort of savage contempt, or at least disregard, of the miserable spectacle, "knocked as clean on the head as if a refugee had been at him. So, d'ye hear, my young madam, there's no great need of troubling yourself more about him; and here come enough of your good folk to groan over him. As for me, I have no time for moaning. If you want help, just scream over again; and, I reckon, you'll have the whole road at your elbow."

Catherine had herself performed the office of humanity she had so vainly asked of the stranger; she stooped down, and beckoning to her father and Harriet, who were descending the rocks, to hasten their steps, she raised up the painter's head, and endeavoured, with a faltering hand, to loosen the neckcloth from his throat. Struck by expressions so rude and unfeeling, she looked up for a moment, and for the first time took hasty note of the person and lineaments of her preserver. He was a man of middle age,—perhaps forty or more, with a long shirt or frock of coarse linen thrown over his other garments, and a broad-brimmed, round-crowned, slouching hat, like the favourite *sombrero* of the Spanish islands, which was, however, painted of a fiery red, and varnished, so as to resist the rain. His stature was not considerable, nor was his appearance very muscular, yet he had given proof of no mean strength in the ease with which he dragged the painter and herself from the water. His countenance, without being coarse or ugly, had yet a repulsive character, derived in part from several scars, the marks of violent blows from sabres or other weapons, one of which seemed to have destroyed his right eye, for it was bound round with a handkerchief; but perhaps the forbidden air was rather given by the savage fire that glimmered in the other, and the perpetual frown that contracted his brows. His hair was grizzled, and fell in a long lock over either dark and bony cheek. His mouth was particularly stern, grim, menacing, and even malevolent of character,— or so the Captain's daughter thought. All these things Catherine observed in a moment; yet, however unfavourably impressed by them, she could not refrain from again imploring his assistance, saying, with the most earnest accents,

"If you be a Christian man, do not leave us. We are none here but two feeble women, and an infirm old man; and before we can procure assistance, the young gentleman may perish. We will thank you,—we will reward"——

"Good heavens!" cried Miss Falconer, who had now reached the foot of the rocks, and beheld the pale and bleeding visage that Catherine so falteringly supported, "he is dying!"

"Dying! Who's dying?" echoed the Captain, limping up to the group; "Adzooks; what! my painter? my handsome young dog, that was to paint me my son Tom Loring? my Harman What-d'ye-call-it from Elsie Bell's? Hark ye, Mr. Red-hat, or whatever your name is, I intended to arrest you on suspicion——Adzooks, I believe the young dog's dead! He looks amazingly like my son Tom. Hark ye, Mr. Harmer What-d'ye-call-it, how do you feel?

Why, adzooks, he's clean gone!—Hark ye, Mister Red-head, fetch him up the rocks——We'll carry him to the Folly."

While the Captain thus poured forth his mingled wonder and lamentation, a surprising change came over the visage of the stranger. He no sooner understood from the mention of the lodging-place and profession of the young man, that he did not belong to the party before him, and had therefore no greater claim upon their humanity than on his, than he at once dropped his rude and disregardful air, saying, as he released the others from the care of supporting the wounded unfortunate,

"I am neither stock nor stone; but I thought you had idlers enough to bury your own dead. And so the younker is a stranger to you? a bird of old Elsie's, and none of your own roost? And this young lady was trying to save his life? I beg your pardon, if I have been rough with you, young madam."—He pronounced these words with a tone mild, and almost regretful; then turning to the Captain, he resumed, "Well, Captain Loring, for I believe that's your name,—what shall we do with this broken-headed fool? You see, here's an arm broke, and a gash on the head that might do credit to a tomahawk! How shall we get him to Elsie Bell's? I can carry him, sure enough—but 'tis a long mile off.——And then for a doctor? Here's a shoulder slipped, Captain. The fool! that must tumble down this dog-hole water-fall! Captain, you have servants and horses—you must send for a doctor.—Poor boy, how he groans!"

"Hark ye, Mr. Red-head," said Captain Loring, "we will carry him to the Folly, and cure him like a Christian. Just get him up these rocks here, and I'll give a lift myself; and hark ye, Mr. Read-head"——

"But the doctor, Captain? the doctor?" cried the stranger.

"He is at the house!" cried Catherine, eagerly. "We saw him ride there ourselves!"

"Adzooks! to be sure he is! so Sam told me! What a fool I was to forget it!" exclaimed the Captain. "Come along, up the rocks, double-quick step—march!"

The eyes of the stranger sparkled at the announcement of surgical assistance being so unexpectedly close at hand; for he seemed to have conceived as sudden a liking to the luckless painter as had the Captain himself. He raised him tenderly, and with singular ease, from the ground, and without a moment's delay, clambered up the rocky path that led to the platform. Then striding rapidly to the treacherous bridge, though encumbered by a burthen at once so inconvenient and piteous, he crossed it with a better fate than had distinguished the attempt of the painter, and, almost before the others had reached the deserted grave, was making his way over the shaded path at a pace that soon promised to carry him out of sight.

"Haste, father, dear father!" cried Catherine, to whom the terrible scene of peril and suffering she had witnessed and almost shared, had given a new energy, and, indeed, a new nature; "haste, or the man will miss the path, and the young gentleman die. Or stay—I will climb the hill here, and run to the house for assistance, and Harriet will walk faster, and point out the way."

"The path is broad, the wild fellow pursues it," cried Miss Falconer, giving the veteran the impulse of her own activity. "What could have brought the young man to the brook? What could have brought this wild barbarian? Nay, uncle, what could have brought yourself?"

"Sam told me," muttered Captain Loring; and of a thousand broken and confused expressions that now fell from his lips, all that the maidens could understand, as they hurried him along, was that he had met one of his labourers at the park-gate, who had seen them take refuge in the wood, and was then engaged catching their ponies, which were running wildly about,—that he had instantly left his carriage, and was seeking them along the stream, when he heard the shriek of his daughter. Something else of much more importance, he seemed labouring to give utterance to; and this being nothing less than the fearful intelligence in relation to Colonel Falconer, which he knew not how to impart, his mind became so confounded betwixt fear of its effect upon the lady, indignation at the outrage, and the thousand other emotions which were distracting his breast, that the more he essayed to speak, the more mysterious became his expressions; so that the whole group had reached the door of the mansion, before a single suspicion of his object had entered the mind of either Miss Falconer or her friend. He mingled the oft-repeated name of her father with that of the dreaded Gilberts, and this again with Tom Loring's, and the painter's; now he burst into a frenzy of apprehension lest Catherine, whose garments were dripping with wet, and, in one or two places, spotted with blood from the wounds of Herman, should have suffered as many hurts as the youth himself, and now he fell into lamentations over the loss of 'that grand picture of Tom Loring dying!' which, it seemed not altogether improbable, death might prevent the poor painter ever attempting.

But if the Captain brought confusion with him to the mansion, it was evident, at the first glance Miss Falconer had of it, that the deranging fiend had been there before him, and still kept possession. The sun was then setting—a multitude of persons, old and young, sallow and sable, were bustling about in the shadows of the porch, some running to and fro with burthens in their hands, others shouting and screaming, or staring about them in speechless wonder; the carriage stood at the door, the ancient charioteer sitting whip in hand, as if expecting orders to start at a moment's warning, while a smart mulatto in livery was engaged strapping a portmanteau behind it. Horses, saddled and bridled, were hitched to trees, or held by servants; dogs were barking; pigeons flying about; and in a word, it seemed as if the inhabitants of the Folly, male and female, human and animal, were one and all preparing, in some ecstasy of confusion, to desert its troubled walls.

"In the name of heaven, uncle! what means all this?" cried Miss Falconer, recognising in the livery-servant a personal attendant of her own father, and in the portmanteau which he was fastening to the carriage, one of the repositories of her own womanly vanities.

Before the Captain could answer a word, the confusion was doubly confounded by the clatter of hoofs, and in an instant two horsemen in military apparel, came thundering up the avenue, as if the lives of a community depended upon their speed.

"My brother Henry, as I live!" cried the lady, starting forward. "Captain, what *is* the matter? Brother! heavens, brother! what can all this mean?"

At this, one half of the human elements of the chaos lifted up their voices, and groaned aloud, "Oh, the Gilberts! the bloody Gilberts!"

"Sister!" cried the foremost of the young soldiers, flinging himself from his steed, catching Miss Falconer in his arms, and speaking with a manner strangely compounded of horror and merriment,—"they have been at dad again! but don't fall into a fit—there's no murder this time! no, egad, only a few scratches. Don't be alarmed.—Ah, Miss Loring! my dear Miss Catherine!—you look dreadful pale—don't be frightened—beg pardon for coming in such a condition. Heard of it, Harry?—(my friend, Brooks,—Lieutenant Brooks, of the troop)—knew they'd send for you,—bent out of course—deflected, made a *detour*, as we say,—to fetch you. Not a moment to lose—must be in town by sunrise, if horse-flesh can carry us.—How d'ye do, Captain? All ready for marching?"

"Yes, all ready," said the Captain, recovering his tongue. "Don't be afraid, Harriet, my dear—Kate, bid your cousin good-bye. No great harm done,—only a little flesh wound that you can stitch up with your needle—by the lord, that's all! Must send you away—father sent a message after you— must have you to nurse him. Be a good girl, don't cry; 't an't all bad wounds do damage; saw many tomahawk-slashes at the fatal field of Braddock, and some got well. Tell the Colonel I'll be down to see him, and hope to fetch the assassin along."

"The assassin, Captain?" cried the young officer, as he leaped upon his horse, his sister having been already, almost without any exercise of her own will, thrust into the carriage, and the door secured. "Quick, Phil, you scoundrel, will you never have done strapping?—The assassin, Captain! oh yes, the assassin!—Remember the description—tall man, lantern-jawed, white horse, with a dappled near fore-leg, a black coat, and preaches!"

"Hah!" cried Captain Loring, with a shout of triumph, "saw the rascal, and meant to arrest him, but couldn't stand his sermons! I couldn't, by the lord!—Your horse, Phil! your horse! doctor, I'll take yours!—Whoop, Harry, you dog! down to the old witch's, and we'll nab him yet!"

While the Captain gave utterance to these expressions, he seized upon the nearest horse, and mounted him—a feat, that nothing but the frenzy of his enthusiasm could have urged him to attempt; for his infirmity had almost altogether incapacitated him from riding, save at the gentlest pace. But the recollection of the zealous Nehemiah, the assassin of his friend, now sheltered under a roof that he fancied, in the ardour of the moment, he could almost touch with his hand—and that holy impostor a villain so notorious and redoubted as the chief Hawk of the Hollow!—the fiery conception scattered his years and infirmities to the winds, and in an instant he was astride the beast of mettle, galloping over the park at full speed, followed by the two soldiers, as soon as they comprehended the meaning of his words— by the coach, which the venerable Richard set in motion upon an impulse of his own—and by some half a dozen of the male loungers, some on foot, some on horse, and all fired with the prospect of capturing a foe so famous and so deeply abhorred.

The pale gibbering ghosts, that start in affright at the magical alarum of the early chanticleer, could not have vanished from their doleful divan with a more impetuous haste, than did full two-thirds of those human beings from the mansion, who had given such life to it a moment before. In an instant, as it seemed, the hall was left to solitude; and the rough stranger, who still sustained the mangled frame of the painter, and had stood staring in astonishment at a scene so unexpected and confounding, had some reason to fear he was left to relieve the sufferings of his charge as he could, and to relieve them alone. A dark frown gathered over his visage, as he beheld the crowd rush away almost without bestowing a look upon his piteous burthen, or upon him; and he was about to mutter his indignation aloud, when it was pacified by a husky voice exclaiming in his ear,

"Hum, hah! bless my soul! what, drowned, eh? is the gentleman drowned? a case of suspended animation?—Hillo, Jingleum, stop! Come back, Pepperel! 'Pon my soul, 'tis the identical red-jacket we saw at the Rest! Why, what the devil's all this?—Beg pardon, Miss Loring!—Bless my soul, I hope you ain't hurt? Blood about your sleeve, and look very pale and nervous! A little wine, with"— —

"Think not of me, doctor," replied Catherine. "Attend to the young gentleman. This dreadful surprise and the hurry of my father—it will explain all, and excuse all. Aunt Rachel will show you a chamber: command every thing—every thing shall be done that you order. Hasten, doctor, pray hasten, and relieve the young gentleman's sufferings. Gentlemen, pray give your assistance to this good man, and heaven—yes, heaven will crown your exertions with success!"

With these hurried expressions, and still more earnest gestures, the young lady gave an impulse to the group now gathered about the wounded man, and he was immediately carried into the house and out of her sight.

"Oh, Miss Katy,—beg pardon—that's to say, Miss Catherine," cried a buxom, blubbering damsel, whose quavering treble had borne a distinguished part in the late din of voices, and who had no sooner laid eyes on the young lady, which she did as soon as the tumult was over, than she ran bustling hysterically to her side,—"never saw you in such a pucker! hope we shan't all be murdered. Such dreadful contractions were never heard of—great big hole in your sleeve—the Gilberts all come to life again, and will murder us as sure as we live!"

"Be quiet, Phoebe—come with me to my chamber—I don't think he will die!"

"Hope not, Miss Katy,—that's Miss Catherine; but they shot him right through the head with a blunderbush, and slashed him to pieces with a baggonet. Oh, the cruel murderers! And Philip, the yellow boy, says— — Lor' 'a' mercy! Miss Katy, what's the matter?"

"I am sick, Phoebe, very sick—it will be over directly. Don't call your mother—don't disturb any one; let them stay with the young gentleman."

With great difficulty, assisted by the girl, whose station in the house, without being altogether so exalted as that of an humble companion, was yet, at least in her own estimation, far removed from that of a menial— the young lady made her way to her apartment; when the impulse that had supported her energies through a scene of distress for so long a time, passed away, and was succeeded by prostration both of mind and body— by shuddering chills and assaults of partial insensibility, that terminated in fits of weeping, and these again in deep dejection of spirits, such as of late years had been a more prevailing characteristic than any other.

CHAPTER IX

Whither shall I go now? O Lucian!—to thy ridiculous purgatory,—to find Alexander the Great cobbling shoes, Pompey tagging points, and Julius Cæsar making hair-buttons, Hannibal selling blacking, Augustus crying garlic, Charlemagne selling lists by the dozen, and King Pepin crying apples in a cart drawn with one horse?— —

Then here's an end of me; farewell, daylight;
And, oh! contemptible physic!— —
                  WEBSTER—Vittoria Corombona.

Conducted by the old woman, an heir-loom dependant in the Captain's family, whom Miss Loring had designated by the familiar and somewhat endearing title of Aunt Rachel, the grim-faced stranger bore the young painter to a chamber, where he was laid upon a couch, breathing forth occasional groans, but still insensible. His bearer, having thus finished what might have been considered his peculiar charge, lifted up his eyes, and looked around him, not however with any intention of departing. On the contrary, his rude indifference seemed gradually to have melted away, and been succeeded by an anxious wish to render further services to the youth, or at least to be assured they should be rendered by others as capable as himself. He fixed his eyes upon the physician, as if to determine the amount of his professional ability by such outward manifestations of wisdom as might be traced in his visage and person; and the result was so little to his satisfaction that he resolved to remain in the apartment, to give the physician the benefit of his own counsels.

The man of science, who bore the undignified name of Merribody, was a youth of twenty-five or six, though the gravity of his countenance was worthy a practitioner of fifty. His frame was short, and roundest in the middle, and his limbs and neck of conformable brevity and dumpiness. His face corresponded with his body, being round as a melon, with features all highly insignificant, except his nose, which had a short and delicate pug that gave it some importance. His complexion had been originally fair, and his locks flaxen; but a few years' exposure to sun and sleet had communicated a certain foxy swarthiness to both, so that his eyes, which were of a light gray, were now entirely visible. His eye-brows had maintained their original creamy hue; and being the only part of the countenance possessing any great mobility, their motions up and down, and to and fro, were always distinguishable; and indeed they flitted about under the shadow of his hat, like two snowy moths entangled in a cobweb. Though no figure in the world could have been worse adapted to purposes of dignity, Dr. Merribody had thought proper to assume an important air, which he always preserved, except when irritated out of his decorum; a circumstance that not unfrequently happened, owing to a temper naturally testy and inflammable. His countenance he kept in a perpetual frown; and he cultivated an attitude he thought expressive of professional dignity, in which his feet were planted as far from one another as the length of his legs permitted, his head thrown back, or rather his chin turned up, for his neck was too short to allow much liberty to the temple of the soul, and his hands thrust into his breeches pockets; in which attitude he presented a miniature representation of the Rhodian Colossus. He had even bestowed much cultivation upon his voice, which being of a childish treble, and therefore highly incompatible with all pretensions to gravity, he forced it into artificial profundity, and spoke with a husky, catarrhal tone, a sort of falsetto bass, exceedingly pompous, and indeed sometimes majestic. However, the same testy temper which so often robbed him of his dignity of carriage, as frequently threw his voice into its hautboy alto; and on those occasions, he did not appear to advantage. At the present moment, the doctor certainly might be said to be in his glory; for the sight of a patient threw him into the best humour in the world;—and by the presence of his two friends, without counting the stranger and Aunt Rachel, he was assured of witnesses to his skill in a case, which he declared, while trudging up stairs, to be 'exceedingly critical and interesting.' Notwithstanding this favourable condition of things, however, the man of the red hat conceived but a mean opinion of Dr. Merribody's professional skill; and having eyed him a second time, without finding any reason to alter his opinion, he demanded, in no very respectful terms,

"Well now, doctor, here's the man lying half dead and groaning,—what's to be done with him?"

"What's to be done?" echoed the doctor, turning up the cuffs of his coat, throwing out his legs, and looking important and complaisant together; "Why, sir, we are to——but, hark'e, sir, who are you? Don't know you—thought you was Dan Potts, the raftsman, but see you a'n't. Who are you? and what are you doing here? Can't suffer a crowd in the room; it smothers the air. Must beg you to decamp, sir. Have plenty assistance, sir,"——

"Be content, doctor," said the man, drily, but not roughly. "My name is Green, John Green, the trader; every body knows Green, the York trader, as they call me. I fished up the young gentleman;—that is, I helped the lady; and I must see him through his troubles."

"Never heard of you, Mr. Green," said the doctor; "but you may stay. You have something the matter with your eye! Now I don't boast; but I believe I am good at the eyes—I will look at it directly."

"I don't doubt it, doctor," said Mr. Green; "but suppose, instead of talking of my eyes, you make the best use of your own. Here's the young man in great suffering."

"Oh, ay," said doctor Merribody. "The first thing to be done is to strip the patient, and see what's the matter with him. Method is the soul of business. Hurrah, Jingleum; come, off with his coat,—strip it off."

"*Rip* it off, you mean," said the trader, touching the fractured arm significantly, and indeed somewhat angrily. "Of all fools I ever heard of, those are the greatest who break their arms, when necks are so much less valuable. Here's his right arm smashed like a sassafras-bough; and, I reckon, slipped at the shoulder, too!"

"Ay! the deuce! you don't say so? a luxation!" cried the physician. "Set the old woman to work with her scissors. Aunt Rachel, my good woman, rip up this sleeve; and rip it as gingerly as if every stitch was the nerve of a man's elbow. A comminuted fracture, I can tell by the feel!—Here, Pepperel, pour some warm water into the basin, chill it a thought from the ewer, and soak this rag in it. A very genteel-looking dog, I protest!—Jingleum, lay out my pocket-case, tear an old shirt into bandages two and a half inches wide, and roll 'em up; and you, Mr. York,—that is, Mr. Green, hand me the crooked scissors there, till I shave some of the hair from the wound. A devil of a job, if it turns out a trephine case! We must send off to town for Dr. Muller and his case of round saws—I don't object to consult with Dr. Muller; and if it comes to trephining, why the sooner we are ready for it the better. Method is the soul of business!"

"The cut on the head is but a scratch," said the trader: "I v'e looked at it myself. Goody, rip up the shirt-sleeve here, or let me do it—there's blacker work to look at."

"Method is the soul of business," cried the doctor, whose spirits were beginning to rise to a rapture, as business thickened on his hand, and who now raised himself a tip-toe among his temporary assistants, like a generalissimo surveying the manoeuvres of his subordinates on a field of battle, which is perhaps to determine the destinies of a nation; "there's nothing like method!" he ejaculated. "Aunt Rachel, scrape me a little lint—there are more scratches to be filled.—Hah! what! what the devil's the matter?" he cried, as the trader, groaning with sympathy at the sight, tore away the damp shirt from the shoulder, and displayed it deformed and shapeless from luxation. "Bless my soul, what! a dislocation, really, under the *pectoralis major*, anteriorly luxed! Oh, here's the devil to pay! Method is the soul of business: but what method is there in having at once an arm broke, a shoulder disjointed, a head cracked, and to be half drowned into the bargain? Murdering work, sir! murdering work! Where the deuce can I clap my pulley? and where the deuce, now I think of it, am I to get one?"

"A pulley!" exclaimed the trader, with scorn and indignation; "a pulley to drag a man's arm off! Why, where's your fingers? Come, doctor, now's the time."

"Method is the soul of business!" exclaimed the physician, waxing wroth. "Are you a doctor, a surgeon, a gentleman of the profession, Mr. What-d'-ye-call-'em, that you take it upon you to instruct *me* what to do? I tell you, sir, a physician is not to be prescribed his duty, sir; and I allow no man to interfere with me in my practice, sir!"

The strength of this declaration was increased by its being delivered in the doctor's natural voice, high and shrill; but it produced little effect on the obdurate trader.

"Come, doctor," said he, "I know all about these matters of broken and disjointed bones, from the toe up to the top-knot, having had a hand in making many of them, as a man who has been an Indian trader, in wartimes, may well say. So take the benefit of my advice; for I intend to give it."

"Then, sir," said Dr. Merribody, with becoming indignation, "you may take the matter into your own hands; I wash mine clear of it. I'm not to be ruled by any ignoramus Indian trader, who, I believe, is no better than an Indian himself, and blind of an eye into the bargain; if you are to dictate, you Mr. What-d'-ye-call-'em, I'll have nothing to do with the case,—if I do I'll be hanged. No, sir! work away yourself, and kill the patient as soon as you like: he is at death's door already."

"Not at all," said Mr. Green, with a bitter sneer; "if he had been in any danger, I should have taken the matter up myself. Come, doctor," he added, more civilly; "don't be in a passion, and don't play the fool. I tell you, if it will be any satisfaction to you to know, that I, John Green, simple as I stand here, have seen more wounds and broken bones than you, and a dozen other such younkers, will ever have the mending of; and, for the matter of that, I have seen more mended than ever you will see hurt, ay, and helped in the mending, too,—as any man must, who has traded among Indians. So, come; look to your duty; the young gentleman will pay you for your services; and, as he seems to be forlorn-like, with no better friend at hand, I shall stand by him, to see he gets the worth of his money."

The amazement with which the insulted leech listened to these contumelious expressions, was prodigious, and would have been expressed otherwise than by a simple, common-place "whew!" had it not been for the dark scowl that clouded the trader's visage, at the first sign of explosion. It was a look of more than ordinary resentment or menace; and, indeed, expressed equal malignance with the grin of a wild-cat, preparing for the spring. The terror it struck to the bosom of the doctor, was communicated to his friends, who betrayed at first some inclination to enter into the controversy, but ended the heroic impulse in sundry grumbling murmurs.

"A devilish strange fellow as ever I saw!" growled the doctor in the ear of one. "A case of *monomania*, sir; he is mad, sir: yes! I see mania in his eye; he has been hurt on the head, you can tell by the knocks there, the scars on his phys'nomy; and his eye shows the infirmity. So we must humour him, sirs, we must humour him. — 'Tis the method; and method is the soul of business."

Thus apologizing for the surrender of his wrath and dignity, the surgeon betook himself again to his patient.

"Hum! hah!" he cried, laying his fingers on Herman's wrist, — "pulse irregular, intermittent. — The struggle between life and death — very low, sir, very low! — Aunt Rachel, make me half a dozen mustard-plasters, roast me a dozen bricks, and get me a coal of fire, to try if there's any feeling in him. One dare not bleed with such a pulse as this."

Green listened with visible impatience to the physician; and then, with as little consideration as before, exclaimed,

"What needs all these knick-knackeries? Clap this shoulder into place, and then think of them."

"My friend," said the doctor, his indignation supplying the place of courage, "I don't like to offend the feelings of any man; but you talk like an ass. Method is the soul of business; and there is no method in reducing a luxation for a man hovering upon the brink of the grave, unless you may consider the act a method of helping him into it. No, sir; the violence of the operation would do his business as expeditiously as a thump over the head with a tomahawk, which I think, as you are an Indian trader and fighter, you know something about. Yes, sir; I'll allow you to be a complete master of the science of tomahawking, skinning, and scalping; but when you come to talk of bones and dislocations, then, sir, I say, in the words of the Latin poet, *Ne sudor ultra crepidam* — I don't know whether it is *sudor* or *sutor;* but it means, 'Mind your own business.'"

"I speak of nothing but what I know," replied Green, impatiently; "and I say, now is the time to fix the bone with the least trouble. Feel the lad's muscles; they are as loose and limber as a girl's in a swoon; wait till he opens his eyes, and you will find them as tough as ash-boughs. So go to work, doctor; for if you don't, *I* will—I have clapped a bone in place before now. So, doctor, you or John Green, the York trader; and much good may it do you, when I tell the folks up the river how I out-doctored you!"

The argument was conclusive, and luckily it was given more in the spirit of persuasion than command; Dr. Merribody condescended to adopt the advice of the rude philosopher. As he had intimated, the muscles of the sufferer were in a condition so relaxed, that it required but little effort to restore the bone to its place.

"There! it is done!" cried the surgeon, triumphantly; "but it hurt him like the mischief! He groaned as if I had been cutting his throat. Now for the mustard-plasters"——

"Now, if you please," said the trader, "for your lancet; and leave such things for the old women."

The doctor was again offended; but the interference of his adviser had effected one desirable object, and he now thought him worthy of remonstrance:

"This, my friend," said he, striking his attitude, sinking his voice to its most majestic depth, and stretching forth his hand, to give emphasis to the oration,—"this is a case of concussion of the brain,—that is, while considered without reference to other minor injuries, such as the wound, the fracture, and the luxation. In concussion, sir, I would have you to understand, sir, the practitioner has to contend, or rather to provide beforehand, sir, against two insidious and dangerous consequences, *videlicet* depression and inflammation. Ehem, sir! do you understand that? If you don't, sir, you are no better than a—I won't say numskull, sir,—but something of that sort. Bleeding may undoubtedly prevent the latter, but it may as certainly aggravate the former,—it may sink the patient into the grave,—it may send him to the devil,—it may"—

"Open his eyes, and so rob the doctor of a patient," said the trader, gruffly. "Do you see how the blood begins to flush over his face? do you hear how hard he draws his breath? Bleed him, and he opens his eyes; warm him with bricks, and plasters, and such stuff, and he will have a brain-fever. Come, doctor, I'll take the blame. If it should hurt him, why a vein is easier stopped than a fool's mouth."

"*Probatum est,*" muttered the physician; "for nothing but a gag could do that for one that shall be nameless.—The fellow has some gumption, though," he muttered to himself. "Well, I'll bleed him but I *should* like to put Dan Potts, the raftsman, on him, or some such two-fisted fellow, and have him drubbed for his insolence! yes, I should like it!"

And grinning with the agreeableness of the fancy, the doctor phlebotomized the patient.

The wisdom of the trader's suggestion was again shown in the event. The blood, at first merely oozing in drops from the vein, at last gathered strength and volume, and the poor painter opened his eyes, and rolled them wildly from person to person. The trader surveyed him for a moment with a much gentler visage than he had hitherto displayed; then turning to the doctor, he said, softly, as if to avoid disturbing the patient,

"Now you can bind up the broken bone at leisure. Only keep him quiet, and the hurt is nothing. I did not mean to offend you, doctor—I have a rough way with me. Treat the young man well, and he will soon recover."

With these words, he took up his hat, left the apartment, and was soon heard stepping from the porch down to the avenue through the lawn.

"An impudent, ignoramus, unconscionable, rascal, with no manners, and half mad!" growled the doctor, giving his indignation full swing.

"A wasp-mouthed, sharp-tongued, malicious savage!" exclaimed his friends; and even the matron, who had all the time bustled about, seemingly regardless of all conversation that was not specially directed towards herself, concluded the chorus, by muttering,

"And a man that never goes to meeting, I warrant me!"

"Let's have candles here, Aunt Rachel!" cried the doctor, indulging his importance, in all the joy of liberation from restraint. "It is as dark as—oh! here they come, eh? Hark! there's horses' feet in the park! They're coming back from the Rest.—Bless my soul! I forgot all about the murder and the assassin! Hope they don't bring him here, slashed all to pieces by the soldiers; work enough on hand for one surgeon.—Only a simple fracture, after all! Hold the splints here, Jingleum. Don't be distressed, sir; won't hurt you more than I can possibly help."

With these words, the surgeon proceeded to tie up the fractured limb, the painter having recovered so far as to be able to wince and groan to the heart's content of the practitioner. Before the operation was concluded, Captain Loring came puffing and blowing into the room, and being instantly assailed by the doctor's friends with anxious questions concerning the result of the late assault upon the Traveller's Rest, answered in his usual hurried and broken manner,—

"Bird flown, adzooks—beat retreat in time,—struck colours, crossed the river; young Brooks and a posse after him; will have him before morning,—we will, by the lord! But, adzooks, here's my young painter that's to paint me that picture. Hark ye, Harman What-d'-ye-call-it, my boy," he exclaimed, taking a seat on the bed-side, and speaking with rough hospitality; "glad to see your eyes open. Mean to treat you as well as if you were my son Tom. How do you feel now, hark ye, my lad? What the plague sent you tumbling down the rocks, hah? A mighty stupid trick, that, adzooks! How d'e do?"

The young man's wits were not yet clear enough to comprehend the question, or to digest a reply. He merely turned his eyes, with a wild and ghastly stare, upon the interrogator, and then rolled them vacantly from one individual of the company to another. He sighed heavily, and mumbled a little, as the doctor proceeded to secure the splints, but made no resistance.

"I don't like that stare," cried the Captain; "he looks as wild out of the eyes as a squeezed frog; and that's no good sign. I remember me, Tom Loring stared the same way, when the doctor was fishing for the bullet among his ribs. He'll never live to paint me that picture! He'll die, doctor, won't he?"

"Can't venture to say, Captain," replied Merribody; "a very critical situation, sir, a very critical situation. But I never despair, sir; for while there's life there's hope. My preceptor, the late celebrated Dr. Bones, of Bucks county, used to tell his patients, 'he never despaired till he heard the joiners screwing up the coffin.' A very good rule, that, sir! We'll hope, sir, we'll hope. Pulse very full and vigorous—will take a little more blood, and remain a few hours to watch him."

"Stay all night," said the Captain; "won't let you go, sir."

"As to staying all night, Captain," said the physician, with an air, "I can't say. Must look to my patients in the village——but will stay to tea with great pleasure. Jingleum, hold the basin!"

The practitioner removed the bandage from the vein he had before opened, and (the Captain, in the meanwhile, hobbling out to inquire into the condition of Catherine,) had soon the pleasure of seeing his patient recover his wits so far as to be able to answer questions, though he displayed a much greater inclination to ask them.

His first demand was, "What's the matter? what ails my head, and my arm? and who are you all here about me?—Oh! ay!" he continued, "I remember—that confounded brook! I vow to Heaven, I thought I saw a ghost, though 'twas broad daylight! Heavens! how my shoulder aches, and my arm, how it twinges! Are you a doctor? Where's Elsie?"

"Well, now, I warrant me, doctor," whispered Aunt Rachel, "he begins to wander."

"My dear sir," said the physician, "I must beg you to hold your tongue. Take this cooling draught, and go to sleep; and, for your comfort, know that you are now in much better quarters than you could have had at old witch Elsie's. You are now in Captain Loring's house."

"In Captain Loring's! What, Avondale? Gilbert's Folly," cried the painter, starting up.

"Be quiet, sir," cried Merribody. "Lie down, and keep yourself quiet; or I won't insure your life two hours."

"Nonsense, sir," cried the patient, petulantly. "I will dress, and get me to the Rest forthwith; and I warn you to take your hand from my shoulder; for, besides that, you hurt me insufferably, I don't choose to be treated like a prisoner of war, nor to be quartered on strangers."

"I warn you," cried the physician.——"There! was there ever such a dolt?—Hartshorn, Jingleum!"

The painter's resolution was greater than his ability. His struggle to arise upset the little strength he had remaining, and he fell back almost immediately in a swoon. When recovered again from this, he seemed sufficiently sensible of his impotent and helpless condition; but was still reluctant to remain where he was. He conjured the doctor to have him carried in a coach, an arm-chair, a cart,—in any thing,—but certainly to have him carried to the widow's hovel. Then, discovering the physician to be inflexible, he lowered his tone, consented to remain in the Captain's house, but implored so earnestly that he should send immediately for old Elsie to nurse him, that the doctor's heart was moved, and he condescended to argue the matter:

"Sir," said he, "I never saw a man with such ridiculous notions. Mrs. Rachel Jones here is the best nurse in the world. Old Elsie Bell is a witch and an ignoramus, and knows no more about nursing than she does about Greek; and she would poison you with some quack weed or another. I never trust these old women, that ramble about among the woods. And then, sir, what makes you think she will come to you? Why, sir, it is notorious, she never comes nigh the Folly; they say she swore an oath, when the Hawks were driven out, never to cross the threshold again, until they returned to it. Sir, a lady in this house has as much as admitted, that the old hag refused to come to it point-blank, a dozen times over. She won't come."

"Try her," murmured the patient, eagerly. "Say, I conjure her to come to me; tell her I am sick, dying, and will trust nobody's nursing but her's. And, hark'e, doctor, where's my waistcoat? There's a key there—it opens my saddle-bags——that's it! Send it to her; bid her fetch me some linen, and such things as she thinks I may want. My life upon it, the good old soul will come. Send it, doctor, and I'll take all your vile stuff without grumbling,—yes, all you have the conscience to give me. It is an awful thing to take physic!"

Having prevailed thus upon the physician to send his message and summons to the Rest, though no one perhaps save himself, expected to see it followed by the widow in person, he swallowed, with divers wry faces, the draught repeatedly offered to him before, groaned heavily once or twice, and then turning his face towards the wall, endeavoured to compose himself to sleep, while the physician and all his attendants, save the matron, Mrs. Jones, stole from the chamber.

CHAPTER X

> The trout within yon wimplin burn
>   Glides swift, a silver dart,
> And safe beneath the shady thorn,
>   Defies the angler's art:
> My life was ance that careless stream,
>   That wanton trout was I.
>   BURNS.

To the surprise of every individual in the mansion, who had been made acquainted with the summons sent by the painter to his late hostess, it was answered in less than an hour by the appearance at the door of Elsie herself. She was followed by the little negro wench, bearing a bundle of linen and other apparel, and in a short time was inducted into the sick chamber, from which she contrived, before many hours, to expel dame Rachel, whom she had found listening very curiously to the sleeping murmurs of the sufferer, as well as all the officious auxiliaries. Indeed, she betrayed some inclination at first to be as free even with the physician, who had been easily prevailed upon to remain all night at the Folly, while his friends returned to the village; but the young man became so extremely ill in the course of the night, that she soon pretermitted her scruples, and was glad to receive the doctor's assistance in quelling the threatened brain-fever.

This remarkable repugnance of the old woman to divide with any one the labours of watching over the stranger's couch, excited no little surprise among the domestics, and seemed to them to attach a degree of mysterious importance to his character, which none had dreamed of attaching before. Long and anxiously, in consequence, did the good Aunt Rachel and her daughter Phoebe, in the dearth of all better occupation, apply their ears to the chamber door, and their eyes to the key-hole, in the hope that some murmur of the sick man, some whisper of his privileged attendants, or perhaps some movement in the room, might give a clew to the enigma, of the existence of which every circumstance now left them still more strongly convinced. Thus, they persuaded themselves that in the delirium, which all night long oppressed the painter's brain, he was betraying divers dreadful secrets, not at all to his interest to be generally known; and they demonstrated also to their entire satisfaction, that Elsie Bell, who had acquired by some witchcraft or other a complete knowledge of the young stranger's history, was imparting it to the physician, coupled with many injunctions on the one hand, and as many promises on the other, of honourable secrecy. Nay, they both affirmed, in after days, that they distinctly heard Dr. Merribody, in reply to some question or appeal of Elsie, say, with a manner highly characteristic of his dignified sense of honour, "The secrets of the sick room are as sacred as those of the confessional; and as for a doctor, Mrs. Bell, why you must know, we are all as mum as blacksnakes. A snake was the ancient symbol of physic, you know; because that's an animal which, if it don't *hold* its tongue, never makes any great noise with it!" They observed, too, as they surveyed her through the key-hole, that Elsie's countenance was darkened and troubled in an unusual degree; and once, they thought, they saw her shedding tears. However, they heard and saw little except what inflamed their curiosity to an intolerable extent; and, in consequence, they came within an ace of being caught in the act of eavesdropping by the physician himself, who came suddenly out of the room to demand ice to apply to the patient's head. Luckily, however, the degree of trust reposed in him by the widow, as they supposed, had filled him with uncommon importance, so that he made no remark on discovering them so near at hand, except to express his pleasure; "for," said he, "I supposed you were all sound in bed, and that there would be the devil to pay to get any out-of-the-way thing that might be wanted."

"Lord love you, doctor," said Aunt Rachel, "why we're all keeping awake, just a-purpose to be ready and handy; and besides, the young gentleman makes an awful groaning and taking on; and besides, there's my young madam, Miss Katy, who can't sleep a wink, out of concern for the young man; and she told me to ask you, doctor, what you thought of the young man's case, and whether he'll die or no?"

To this the doctor answered, with a look of great wisdom, 'that every thing depended upon circumstances.'

"And besides, doctor," said Phoebe, emboldened by the gracious reply vouchsafed to her mother, "she is mighty curious to know what all these things is, the young gentleman is talking about?"

"Sorry it is not consistent with the honour of the profession to gratify Miss Loring in that particular," replied the physician, with extreme gravity. "Must have ice, Mrs. Jones. Mighty fortunate I was able to remain all night! You must bring me ice, Mrs. Jones; and you must just scratch on the door, to give me warning; and then you must keep all quiet, and let none approach the room, unless summoned by myself. And if you can venture to disturb the Captain, and tell him to turn over on his side, (the *right* side, mind you,) he won't snore so hard. Very prejudicial, to sleep on the back, I assure you! It sets the liver tumbling over the lungs, and so half smothers one. But let me have the ice, d'ye hear; and keep all things quiet in the house."

Notwithstanding the skill, and (what was perhaps a less questionable virtue,) the zeal of Dr. Merribody, and the faithful vigilance of poor Elsie, the patient continued to grow worse, and was indeed, towards morning, in an alarming situation, and so remained during the greater part of the two following days, not a little to the surprise of the physician, who phlebotomized him with extreme liberality, expecting on each occasion to give the *coup-de-grâce* to the disease. The truth is, the doctor, from having witnessed its efficacy at first, had grown enamoured of the remedy, and now applied it, we will not say without judgment, but entirely without mercy; and had not Elsie at last rebelled against his blood-thirsty humour, and resolutely resisted all further encouragement of it, there is no saying where the matter might have ended, unless in the grave. However, as the patient possessed a youthful and vigorous constitution, capable of withstanding disease and his tyrant together, he was at no time in absolute peril of death; and being left a little to himself, he began at last to mend, and in the course of the fourth day was, to the infinite satisfaction of Captain Loring and his fair daughter, pronounced entirely out of danger. His convalescence was rapid, and would perhaps have been still more so, had it not been for the pains his hospitable host took to expedite it; for Captain Loring beset his bed-side from the first appearance of a favourable symptom, mingling many joyous congratulations with a thousand exhortations and instructions in relation to 'that grand picture of the battle of Brandywine, and Tom Loring dying!'

From Captain Loring he also learned some of the particulars of those bustling events, which had taken place during the evening of his insensibility. He was much struck with the strange transformation of the sanctimonious Nehemiah Poke into no less a personage than the refugee and assassin, Oran Gilbert, and was very curious to hear the particulars of his escape. They were told in a moment: the pursuers, headed by Lieutenant Brooks, (young Falconer having proceeded on his journey with his sister, and the Captain, much the worse for his gallop, having been forced to return to the Hall,) had followed across the river, and continued the search until nightfall rendered it useless to prolong it. They had, at one time, been close upon the fugitive's heels, having lighted upon a pedler, (not, however, Mr. John Green, the Indian trader, who was safely lodged at the time in the wounded man's chamber,) to whom the pretended preacher had sold his old gray horse, or exchanged it for a better; and from this man they obtained instructions, which put them in good hopes for awhile of coming up with him. Night, however, fell upon them, and the Lieutenant returned to the right bank of the river, to rejoin his friend and Miss Falconer, committing the whole charge of the pursuit to his volunteers, from whom the fugitive escaped, having baffled them completely. As for Mr. Green himself, he left the little inn betimes on the morning after the accident, and was seen no more.

In regard to the outrage upon Colonel Falconer, Herman was informed that it had been committed in a mode especially daring and audacious. He was entertaining certain gay and distinguished guests at his villa on the Schuylkill, and had stepped for a moment, in search of certain papers, to a little pavilion, which he had caused to be fitted up as a study, not sixty paces from the house, where he was presently found weltering in his blood by the guests, whom his sudden shrieks had drawn to the place. The assassin had already vanished, having added robbery, as Captain Loring averred, to murder. The sufferer had, however, recognised his well-known visage, and in the course of the following day some traces of him were discovered. It was found, at least, that a man answering the description had stolen a horse from a neighbouring farmer; and upon this horse, or one very like him, Mr. Nehemiah Poke, the parson, had been seen wending his way up the Delaware; and as no one knew or had ever before heard of this reverend gentleman, it was at once supposed that the assassin had assumed the character as a disguise. Before this second discovery had been made, a courier, whom the Captain stumbled upon in the village, was despatched to Hawk-Hollow, to recall Miss Falconer to the city. His intelligence therefore, though it caused the Captain to arrest the true offender, was not sufficient to legalize the capture, especially when this was opposed so strongly by the zealous exhortations of Nehemiah, and the discreet remonstrances of the painter. When Captain Loring remembered the agency of Hunter in robbing him of his prey, he burst into a towering passion, and reproached and railed at him with as little ceremony as he would have done with his own son, or near kinsman. It was in vain that Herman pointed out the improbability of a wild hunter of the hills, like Oran Gilbert, being able to assume the character of a ranting preacher, and preserve it so well, and endeavoured to convince him, that, if Nehemiah were really not the assassin, he must be some other and some secret enemy. The Captain swore that Colonel Falconer had no other enemy in the world, and therefore, of course, Nehemiah, the parson, must be the identical Oran of the Hollow. This opinion he maintained with such fury, that the painter, if indeed he had no stronger reason for holding his tongue, did not choose to meet it with an argument derived from his own previous acquaintance with Nehemiah. He suffered the Captain to have his own way, and believe what he liked; and, in consequence, the Captain soon dropped the subject altogether, to take up another that now occupied his brain, almost to the exclusion of every other. This was the picture of the battle of Brandywine, and Tom Loring dying, the consideration of which, and of the painter's ability to execute it to his liking, was the main cause of the extraordinary affection he conceived for the youth.

Another piece of information, which the young man obtained from the Captain, was an account of the agency of Miss Loring in his deliverance from the brook, and perhaps from death. He had turned upon her a despairing eye, at the moment when, as he was pitching over the fall, she had cast out the end of the shawl to him; but of this circumstance he had retained not the slightest recollection, and indeed, it is more than probable that his faculties were at that moment in a state of torpor. Not content with this deed of daring humanity (for if he had clutched upon the mantle, the chances were that she would have been jerked into the torrent after him,) she had plunged among the boiling eddies below, and thus preserved him from a second and perhaps greater peril, and all the time with imminent risk to herself. His emotions upon making this discovery, mingled surprise and admiration with the gentler sentiment of gratitude.

"Is it possible," he cried, "that a young lady should have such spirit, such presence of mind, such courage?"

"Adzooks!" said the Captain, setting the matter to rest at once, "isn't she *my* daughter? By the lord, sir, when my son Tom was but a boy of ten years, he could trounce all the boys of the Brandywine of his own age, and two years older."

"So heroic!" ejaculated the painter; "instead of committing me to my destiny, with a pathetic scream, to run at once to my assistance, like an angel, rather than a woman!"

"Adzooks," cried Captain Loring, "it was no such thing, when I carried Tom Loring home; for then she fell to weeping and bewailing; and hark ye, Herman, my boy, that's the way you must paint her."

"So noble! so benevolent! so humane!" continued Hunter. "Noble impulses are only produced in noble spirits.—And I really, then, owe my escape, perhaps my life, to the humanity of this young lady, to whom I was but a stranger!—Captain, it was the noblest act in the world!"

"Adzooks," cried the Captain, "do you think so? Why then, by the lord, we'll paint that too! And, now I think of it, 'twill make a most excellent picture! Why, yes,—what a fool I was, not to think of it before! 'Twas very brave of her, and it shall be painted: You shall stick yourself at the bottom of the brook, and my Kate Loring fishing you out, with Harriet and me on the top of the rock; and as for that rusty fellow, the pedler, why you may leave him out."

"I am very curious about that man," said Hunter; "but 'tis no matter."

Then he fell to musing, and in spite of the noisy rapture with which the Captain danced about his bed, filled with the new conception of immortalizing paint,—of a picture which was to perpetuate the heroism of his daughter as effectually as the other was to record the glorious death of his son,—the painter indulged his meditations for a considerable time. The result was, first, a perfect conviction that the sooner he made a due acknowledgment of his gratitude the better; and, secondly, that he felt himself strong and well enough to undertake a duty so pleasing, without further delay. In this opinion Captain Loring coincided with great satisfaction; and neither the physician nor his nurse being at hand to restrain him, (for so soon as he recovered his wits, and began to amend, they deserted his bed-side, returning only at stated periods,) he got up and dressed himself as well as he could, the Captain having in the meanwhile, descended, to apprize his daughter of the meditated visit. It was indeed lucky that the Captain did so; for after the young man had risen, and caught a view of himself in a mirror, his resolution melted away like wax in the fire.

"Heavens!" said he, "how villanous I look! Such lobster eyes, and such lantern-like jaws! That confounded doctor has bled me like a Turk: I wonder he did not make a Turk of me in earnest, and leave me with a poll as naked as a peeled yam. Truly I am now the *Caballero de la Triste Figura*, Don Quixotte in good earnest, as far as looks go; and truly I had better get me to bed again, and wait a month or two, before showing myself to any handsome young lady."

His objections, however, to descend were overruled by the Captain, and having been announced at his own instance, and the young lady having expressed great satisfaction at the happy change in his condition, as indicated by a renovation of strength so unexpected, he was even forced to do as he proposed, and suffer himself to be conducted into her presence.

Miss Loring was evidently surprised and shocked by the change in his appearance, which was still odiously visible, notwithstanding the great pains he had been at to arrange his battered person to advantage. The hair, massed over his forehead, to hide an envious patch, added but little ornament to his bloodless visage; nor did the splint on his right arm, the riband-ties of his sleeve which could not wholly conceal it, and the black silk sling that supported the arm on his breast, impart any peculiar elegance to a person of ghostly tenuity. However, the surprise of the young lady, though confirmatory of his own assurances in relation to his unprepossessing looks, served the good purpose of drawing what blood was left in his body into his cheeks, and thus, for an instant, removed one item of deformity.

The little confusion into which he was thrown by this inauspicious reception, was luckily driven to flight by the boisterous and triumphant introduction immediately commenced by Captain Loring.

"Look ye, Catherine, my girl," he cried; "here's my young Herman Hunter, the painter, that you fished so finely out of the water; and, adzooks, he says, he'll paint the action for you, as well as your brother Tom on the Brandywine, and General George Washington on the fatal field of Braddock! You see how quick we are curing him—begin to have quite an opinion of that fellow, Merribody!—As soon as we get his arm out of the stocks here, he's to begin. Don't intend to let him go back to Elsie's; but Elsie's a good nurse,—will say that for her. Have somebody to talk to, now! Will have cousin Harriet back as soon as possible. So be civil to my young Herman What-d'ye-call-it.—Think he looks very much like my poor Tom!"

With such characteristic expressions, the ancient soldier dispelled the young man's embarrassment; and Herman now turning his eyes upon the maiden with a disposition to be pleased, he found, in her countenance, so much to admire of beauty both physical and spiritual, that his approbation added a double emphasis to his expressions. Indeed he spoke of her act of heroism, and his own gratitude, with a warmth and energy of feeling that, to her own surprise, nearly startled the tears into her eyes, while they filled the Captain with a new sense of his daughter's merits.

"Adzooks!" he cried, in a rapture, "he tells the truth, and he speaks like an honest fellow! 'Twas the noblest deed in all the world, and 't shall be painted."

Anxious perhaps to escape the praises of her father, which, as he had a whimsical docility of temper, might be obtained at any moment,—rather than to avoid those of the guest, which struck her as being unusually agreeable, Miss Loring hastened to protest against all panegyrics, by referring to the more efficient aid rendered by the trader; and then, with an attempt at pleasantry, to lead the conversation still further from herself, she required to know 'to what mysterious cause of alarm on Mr. Hunter's part she owed the happy opportunity she had enjoyed of playing the heroine?'

"You will be astonished, Miss Loring," he replied: "but you were positively the cause yourself."

"I?" said she. "Ah! I understand," she continued, with a smile of infinite mirth—"you were thinking of the assault made by the two dragoons upon poor Elsie's habitation, which we were so near taking by storm; and you looked for nothing less than a repetition of the charge, while you were at a disadvantage on the narrow bridge!"

"By no means," said Herman, sharing somewhat of her animation, and smiling—"I really took you for a spectre; and being of a superstitious turn"——

"A spectre!" cried Captain Loring; "does my Catherine look like a ghost?"

And "A spectre!" re-echoed Miss Loring, though with a more serious emphasis.

"I had heard," said the young man, "that there was a grave beyond the falls"——

"Adzooks!" exclaimed Captain Loring, "I never heard of it.—Who's buried there? One of the Hawks, hah? By the lord, I'll root him up—have no such villain's bones lying about the place"——

"Father," said Catherine, "it is a woman's grave."—Which answer instantly checked the veteran's rising indignation, and some little disgust with which Hunter heard him threaten the lowly sepulchre with violation.

"In truth," resumed the painter, "my mind was affected by the solemn scenery that conducted me to the burial-place; and when I had reached the bridge, and, lifting up my eyes, beheld a figure rising, as it seemed out of the earth, and to all appearance commanding me, by menacing gestures (for such, Miss Loring, was your appearance,) to retire, you may judge how much my imagination was excited. I assure you, such was the hallucination of my mind, that I beheld, even in *your* countenance, the pallid hues of death, with tears, too, dropping from your eyes, and such an expression of mingled sorrow and displeasure, as I thought could exist only on the visage of a disembodied spirit. In the sudden alarm produced by such an impression, I forgot entirely where I was, and so stepped off the narrow bridge into that malicious torrent, and thereby, as I may also add, fell under the obligation of owing you a life—an obligation, which, I assure you, is of so agreeable a nature, that"——

"If you say so," cried Catherine, perceiving that her father was preparing for another burst, and interrupting the speaker with a smile, "I shall undoubtedly expect you to give occasion for some second display of my heroism, by leaping into the brook again, as soon as you have recovered your strength. You have indeed lowered my own vain estimate of the obligation conferred, by showing how much I was the cause of your misfortune; and I now perceive, that I shall not have entirely atoned for my fault, until you are wholly restored to health. Allow me therefore to work out my pardon, by assuming the character of a mentor and governess.—You are yet unfit for the toils of a courtier, and the exertions of the visit have already exhausted your strength. I must command you back to your chamber, to rest and recruit your spirits; and to-morrow, if Dr. Merribody consents to such unusual grace, I will perhaps permit you to enjoy another half-hour of liberty.—You must obey me, Mr. Hunter; my father is a soldier; and, in his house, you are under martial law."

The painter would willingly have disputed the orders of the 'Lieutenant-commandant,' (for such Captain Loring, transported with her military spirit, immediately pronounced his daughter to be,) but Miss Loring spoke as if she had assumed the command in earnest; and Hunter admired how so much firmness could be expressed with so much pleasantry, and how both these qualities could be mingled in the same spirit with the maidenly gentleness becoming her youthful age. But, indeed, the young lady had found it convenient to put on both the former appearances, to terminate an interview irksome to herself, and perhaps prejudicial to the convalescent; for no sooner had he taken his leave, and her father with him, than she immediately walked into the garden, the supervision of which was the chief delight, and indeed passion, of her existence, and, sitting down under an arbour of honey-suckle and trumpet-flowers, indulged herself in a long fit of weeping.

CHAPTER XI

> Ladies' honours
> Were ever, in my thoughts, unspotted ermines;
> Their good deeds holy temples, where the incense
> Burns not to common eyes. Your fears are virtuous,
> And so I shall preserve them.
> BEAUMONT AND FLETCHER.

The happy constitution which had empowered the young artist to contend successfully with fever and phlebotomy, soon enabled him to exchange his quarters under the Captain's roof for those he had occupied so short a time in the cottage of Elsie. This was a change he made with no little reluctance; for, independent of the superior comfort of Gilbert's Folly, there was a charm in the society of the Captain's daughter, which, with all the drawback resulting from the addition of the Captain's company, was not to be replaced by the attractions of the melancholy widow. Nevertheless, a consciousness that his presence at the mansion, however welcome to its inmates, was, at best, an intrusion, soon forced itself upon his mind; he felt that it was highly improper to take advantage of the affection of a whimsical old man, and the kindness of a solitary and almost unprotected girl; and accordingly he revealed the determination he had made to leave them, upon the third visit he made Miss Loring. His resolution was however combated with such violent hostility on the part of the veteran, who commonly devoted three-fourths of his time to expatiating upon the subjects of the three great pictures, and with such agreeable dissuasives on that of the lady, that his resolves easily melted away, and his sojourn was prolonged for a week or more beyond the period of his first visit. At last, however, he grew ashamed of his effeminate abandonment to an enjoyment which he had no right to consider his own; and one morning, having surveyed himself in the glass, and discovered with peculiar satisfaction, that his cheek-bones were burying themselves in their former insignificance, and that his eyes were twinkling again with their natural sunshine, he took the sudden resolution of retreating to the Traveller's Rest that day; and this design, maugre all the furious opposition of the Captain, he was strengthened to put into immediate execution, by the frankly-expressed consent of his fair governor.

"Yes, I will go," he soliloquized, in his chamber, to which he had ascended for the purpose of collecting his scattered moveables; "it is plain enough, the girl is vastly delighted to get rid of me. 'You are now well enough to be released from captivity.' These were her very words; and she smiled as she uttered them, as if my discharge were a deliverance to herself!—Well,—and why should it not be?" he muttered, after a pause; "Why should my presence be a pleasure to her? and why should my departure afflict her? and why should I care whether she be pleased or not? A girl engaged,—betrothed,—and betrothed to a Falconer! Tush, I am a fool. I was a fool to come hither, too. The devil take the wars, and the king's commission into the bargain. I will leave the place—I would my arm were but sound, and I would leave it to-morrow,—ay, I vow I would!

'Oh, the bonny bright island.'—

I wonder she don't sing: for a speaking voice, she has the richest *soprano*,—a *mezzo-soprano*, I think,—I ever heard; it is a positive music, mellow, rich, and wild, like the hum of a pebble in the air, darted out of a sling—a most delicious, wondrous, incomprehensible voice. And then her eyes——Death! what care I for her eyes?

'Oh, the bonny bright island'—

Pshaw! I would I were home again.—Home? *home!*" he muttered, with long pauses betwixt each interjection, and nodding his head the while, as if surprised at his own reflections. Then, as if these silent comets of the brain had returned to the orbit in which they had so lately vapoured, he resumed,—"At all events, old Elsie's is not far off; and in common civility I must call and see her two or three times.——And, besides, I don't see how I can get off without painting the Captain 'that grand picture of the battle of Brandywine, and Tom Loring dying.' What an absurd old fellow!—A precious picture I should make of it! Yet I must do something to requite their kindness.—Kindness! There's no doubt she saved my life. The Captain swears, nothing living that gets into the deep eddy under the fall, can get out living. His cow lay under there three days. To think I was so near my head-and-foot-stone! and to think this girl, this Catherine Loring, saved me from the destiny of a crumpled-horn! The most remarkable, fascinating.——Ah! the island's the place for me, after all.

'Oh, the island! the bonny bright island!'

Well, now she's in the garden among the flowers, and the Captain's taking his siesta. A little medicine, with some of its concomitant starvation, is quite a good thing for the voice."

During all the time of this soliloquy, the young man had ever and anon, sometimes insensibly to himself, been humming the *refrain* of a familiar air; until at last, being seduced by the sound of his own voice, and betrayed into a mood of melody by his reflections, he gradually fell to humming with more confidence; and, finally, supposing no one to be nigh, he even began to sing, though in a low voice, the following idle stanzas, that had been all the time jingling through his brain.

I.

Oh the island! the bonny bright island!
    Ah! would I were on it again,
Looking out from the wood-cover'd highland,
    To the blue surge that rolls from the main.
How sweet on the white beach to wander,
    When the moon shows her face on the sea,
And an eye that is brighter and fonder,
    Looks o'er her bright pathway with me!

II.

Oh the island! the bonny bright island!
    Never more shall I see it again,
Never look from the wood-covered highland,
    To the blue surge that rolls from the main.
Never more shall I walk with the maiden,
    On the beach I remember so well:
Farewell to my hope's vanished Eden—
    Oh my bonny bright island, farewell!

"Pshaw,—nonsense!" he went on, pursuing his reflections; "'the island, the bonny bright island,' is a very fine thing, but what do I care about it? I wonder if Elsie spoke the truth about the match? If I thought the girl's heart were not in it.—Pshaw again! She is the merriest-hearted creature I ever saw,—only of quick feelings, and strangely attached to the memory of her brother: her eyes always fill when the Captain talks of him—the very name makes the tears start; and good heaven! how superb her eyes look, with tears in them! But then the Captain is poor, and she knows it,—bent upon the match, and she knows that, too; and young Falconer is a soldier, and a handsome fellow, and she knows that, too. And he was here! I wish I had seen him. He has wealth, too—so have *I*; he is gay and handsome—I am neither sour nor ugly.—'Sdeath! where am I getting? I will find out, at least, what are her feelings towards him: if her heart be not in the match, why then.— —Could any man stand by and see such a saint of heaven bartered away, sacrificed—sold to tears and captivity?"

Here he fell to musing again, and again his spirits seeking that vent to melancholy, he began to hum an air, extremely mournful, the words of which were in unison with his reflections.

I.

    Darkly the wretch that in prison is pining,
        Turns to the dim, dismal grating his eye;
    Darkly he looks on the day-star that's shining,
        The far-soaring eagles that float in the sky.
        In the pale cheek, so furrow'd and wet,
            The story of anguish is spoken;
        The sun of his hope it is set,
            The wing of his spirit is broken.
    Darkly the wretch, &c.

II.

    Heart! in thy dreary captivity heaving,
        The fate of the poor, hopeless pris'ner is thine—
    To look through a grate at the world thou art leaving,
        And slowly the long silent sorrow resign.
        But the vial is emptied at last,
            The bolts have been shot from the quiver,
        And the future has buried the past,
            With the tears of the captive, for ever.
    Heart! in thy dreary, &c.

Having despatched this second madrigal and his preparations together, he descended into the little apartment in which Miss Loring was wont to while away the time in reading, or plying her needle,—which latter employment she often followed in company with the girl Phoebe and the matron. On these occasions there commonly prevailed a proper degree of female noise and chatter; for which reason such convocations were strictly forbidden during that portion of the afternoon which Captain Loring devoted to napping—not indeed because any sound short of the blast of a trumpet or the roar of a musket, could disturb his slumbers, but because his brain was of too excitable a nature to sink into repose, so long as a single vocal murmur came to his ear. Herman had chosen this period to take his departure, for the sake of avoiding any altercation with his violent host; and he now stepped into the parlour, which opened into the garden, where he expected to find the Captain's daughter. However, he had no sooner entered the apartment, than he saw her therein, sitting by herself, plying her needle with unwonted industry, and her eyes filled with tears.

"Good heavens! Miss Loring," said he, "I hope nothing has happened?"

"By no means," she replied, displaying her countenance frankly, with a smile, and then proceeding, without any embarrassment, to wipe her eyes. "You must know, in the first place, that I come of a tearful tribe, a very lachrymose stock, and shed tears very often for no comprehensible purpose, except to pass the time; and in the second place, I have been paying the auditor's tribute, and rewarding your music with the utmost stretch of sentimentality,—that is to say, by crying. I wonder where you could light upon such melancholy tunes? But I like the last song extremely: that release from captivity,—that ending of

'The tears of the captive for ever,'—

I should suppose you would have sung that line to the gay whistle of a blackbird!"

"I assure you, Miss Loring," said the painter, "my deliverance comes to me with no such spirit of rejoicing. I am ashamed you overheard me—I thought you were in the garden; I would not have otherwise presumed to hum so loud."

"Oh, I like your singing, I protest; and if you remain long enough in the valley, I shall claim a future exertion of the faculty, perhaps even a serenade. But beware of my father; if *he* discovers this new virtue in you, rest assured, you will have to sing him Yankee Doodle and God Save Great Washington, all day long; and this too," she added with a mirthful smile, "without any hope of escaping from 'that grand picture of the Battle of Brandywine and—and Tom Loring dying.'—Ah, Mr. Hunter," she said, apologetically, for her eyes again glistened, and her lip quivered, as she pronounced the familiar name, "you have perhaps laughed at my father, perhaps you will laugh at me, when you behold our usual insanity on the subject of my brother. But he was one whom it was not easy to forget,—one long to be remembered by both sire and sister.—But I see you are displaying your generalship; you intend to beat a retreat, while the enemy is sleeping. Perhaps you are wise. Richard will have the carriage ready in a few moments."

"Not so, Miss Loring: I will depart on foot, like a pilgrim, as will be best. An unlucky jolt in the carriage over a stone, might bring me under the tender mercies of the doctor again." And he touched his wounded arm significantly.

"You are right," said Catherine, after a pause. "The distance is short; Richard shall escort you, for fear of accident; and Phoebe and myself will add to your retinue as far as the park-gate. Do you really consider yourself equal to the walk?"

"I do," replied the young man; "but pray be not in such a hurry to discharge me. In a very few days,—perhaps as soon as I am able to resume the saddle, I must take up my line of march, (to borrow your military illustration;) from Hawk-Hollow, with but little expectation,—that is, I think so,—of ever seeing it again."

"Must you, indeed? I thought you were to explore every cliff and brook in the county. However, I cannot blame you. I am afraid my father's strange conversation about 'those grand pictures,' must annoy you; and you are right to escape."

"On the contrary, Miss Loring," said the painter, "I am sincerely desirous to gratify him in that fancy; and, though sorely convinced of my inability to paint him any picture worthy acceptance, yet, were my arm well, I should do my best to paint him something; and if I had but a portrait or miniature of your deceased brother for a few hours, to secure a likeness"——

"You must not think of it seriously, Mr. Hunter. It is but a whimsical fancy, which my father will soon forget. There is no portrait of my brother; he was but a boy of eighteen, and his likeness was never painted. Indeed, I wish it had been, for my father's sake."

"Perhaps I can yet gratify him," said the painter. "I owe you a deep debt of gratitude—I have some skill in taking likenesses, and sometimes obtain them, even with but little aid of the sitter. The Captain has averred that you yourself bear an extraordinary resemblance to your brother——Perhaps, perhaps, Miss Loring, if you were to honour me so far—that is to say"——

"Ah!" cried Catherine, with sparkling eyes, "I see! Do you think it possible? I am indeed like my poor brother, if I can trust my own recollections. Do you think it practicable, from *my* visage, to construct a likeness of my brother's? Then, indeed, I would sit to you, and gladly!"

"With such a resemblance to begin upon," said Herman, greatly pleased with the satisfaction of the young lady, "and the help of your recollections and criticisms, I do not doubt of success; and then the pleasure of presenting such a portrait!"——

"Of *presenting*, Mr. Hunter!" cried Catherine; "we cannot permit you to think of that. We will not convert your gratitude for a slight hospitality into an excuse for taxing your professional exertions."

"Professional, madam?" said the other, with some little petulance; "I hope you will not consider me a mercenary, hireling dauber?"

"A dauber, we hope not,—mercenary, assuredly not;—and hireling is a word not to be applied to one who receives payment for any generous labour," said Catherine. "If you insist upon painting 'the grand picture' for nothing, Mr. Hunter, you will certainly escape from all trouble in relation to it. Not even my father would think a moment of imposing such an unrecompensed task upon you, or such dishonour upon himself."

"You mortify me, Miss Loring," said Herman: "I can scarce call myself a painter by any thing more than inclination. If I have adopted the profession, it is not to make my bread by it; and indeed I can scarce say, I have adopted it at all.—That is," he added, in some confusion, for Catherine regarded him with a look of surprise—"In short, Miss Loring, it has been my good fortune to be put above the actual necessity of adopting this profession, or any other, for my support. I paint, because I love the art, and have nothing better to do; it suits my idle habits. I never have received a recompense for my labour, (you should have called it my amusement, for such it is,) and perhaps I never will;—not that I scorn recompense as being degrading, but because I need it not. The pleasure I feel in the labour is my reward; and I am doubly rewarded, when my poor sketches afford pleasure to those whose good opinion I covet. You have thrown me under obligation, Miss Loring; and I claim of your generosity, or if that word will not be permitted, of your justice, an opportunity to oblige in return."

"Your argument is singular, yet almost conclusive," said Catherine, with a pleasant accent, yet with a more distant air. "And so you are no poor painter—a wandering son of genius—after all; but a knight of romance, roaming the world over, with palette for buckler, and brush and maul-stick in lieu of lance and sword? Really, you have lost much by the transformation: it was a great pleasure to me, to think I could patronise you—encourage an unfriended genius. But now—ah! my folly offends you! I beg your pardon; I will trifle no more."

"I am not offended, Miss Loring," said the youth, who had coloured deeply while she spoke; "but I *did* think your tone satirical, and indicative of a suspicion that I was not what I profess myself to be. Suffer me then to be a poor painter, as I really am; though not a man in very restricted pecuniary circumstances. I confess, that I was presumptuous, to think you—that is, your father,—would accept any gift at my hands; yet the persuasion that

I had it in my power to give you—that is, *him*, a particular gratification, emboldened me to think I might presume to attempt what I thought a mere simple, allowable compliment."

"Pray, Mr. Hunter," said Catherine, "say nothing more about it. I believe you are right, and I wrong. We act here"—and here she smiled as merrily as before—"entirely upon impulses and instincts; and if impulses and instincts be conformable, as doubtless, some day, they will, we will accept the picture as freely as it is offered. But I see you are impatient to go;"—this was a discovery authorized by no particular symptom of dissatisfaction on the part of the painter, who, on the contrary, seemed well pleased to continue the tête-à-tête;—"you are impatient to go, and here comes Phoebe.—Phoebe, my dear, have the goodness to call Richard, to attend Mr. Hunter to Mrs. Bell's.—I am glad to see you walk so firmly, and look so well.—I will positively be your escort to the gate. It becomes me in my function of Lieutenant-commandant; and I will dismiss you with all the honours of war."

Thus speaking, and whiling away the walk with light and joyous conversation, Miss Loring conducted the guest to the park gate; where her eye suddenly caught sight of a little bush, of no great beauty of appearance, but exhaling an agreeable odour. This she instantly began to rob of its branches, expressing pleasure at the discovery.

"It is sweet-fern," she said, in answer to the painter's question, "not very rare, to be sure, but the first specimen that has come into the paddock of its own accord; all the rest I planted myself. Now, sir, this is neither myrtle nor sweet-grass; but it is good to smell at; and in token that my extreme hurry to drive you out of my father's house proceeded from no ill will, but from true benevolence, and as much friendship as one can feel at a week's notice, I present you this same odoriferous plant, and advise you to make a medicine of it. It is said to be a fine tonic and cordial; and, I warrant me, Elsie will know all about it."

"I shall apply it to a better use," said the painter, gaily. "You know, it is fern-seed which enables man to walk invisible.—Now, as a knight of romance, I may have need of such a magical auxiliary."

"Oh, if you laugh at me for that," said Catherine, "I see there is peace between us."

"You could have added but one more injunction," said Herman, "to make the gift agreeable. Had you told me to follow its example—you know it came into the paddock of its own accord!—I should have"——

"Thought me immensely witty," said Catherine. "Certainly, Mr. Hunter, I will expect you to call upon my father if you remain in the valley; and certainly, if he do not fetch you to the Folly to-morrow, I shall be vastly astonished. But pray, sir," she added, observing that the gentleman looked mortified, and abashed, "do not consider such an invitation necessary. A visiter at Gilbert's Folly is too much of a Phoenix—a *rara avis*, I think you scholars call it,—to be turned lightly away. I wish you, sincerely, a happy and speedy recovery.—Good day, sir—I commit you to Richard's keeping."

With these words she turned from the gate, plucked another branch from the fern-bush, and then, with Phoebe, pursued her way back to the house. The painter received her valediction with much less satisfaction than had been produced by the fragrant present. He saw her return to the bush, and then, looking once back, and waving her hand, resume her steps, walking on towards the mansion; and he was himself astonished at the feeling of melancholy that instantly came over his spirit. "What is there in her," he muttered within the recesses of his bosom, "that should interest me so strongly? Why should I be gladdened by the wave of her hand? why darkened at once by the turning away of her face?—She *is* unhappy after all, whatever skill she may have to conceal it; and, by heaven, it is a piteous thing to ponder on. Well, well.—Such an admirable creature! so gentle, and yet so firm! so frank, yet so modest! so merry, yet so dignified! so natural in manners, yet so refined! so sensitive, yet sensible! so kind,—nay,—openly affectionate of disposition, yet so womanly in all!—sure I shall never more see her equal!"

Thus the young man mused, remaining so long with his eyes following the retreating figure of the young lady, that Richard, the venerable coachman so often mentioned before, thought fit to presume upon the arguments of his age and standing, as a faithful and highly-prized servant, and interrupt the meditations of his charge. He first scraped his feet over the gravelly road, then coughed, then hemmed, and at last opened his lips, and spoke:

"A-well-a, massa Hunta," he said, "werry bad practice this here, 'sposing broken bones in the open air, 'specially when a gemman are sickish-like. No offence, massa,—but why we no go down to Missus Elsie's?"

"Right, Richard, let us go," said Hunter, walking down the hill, but ever and anon casting his eye over his shoulder, as long as Miss Loring was visible, or a single flutter of her garment could be detected among the green shades of the avenue. "How long have you lived with Captain Loring, Richard?"

"Ebber since he wa' born.—Wa' a mighty fine boy, Massa John Loring!"

"Oh, then you were in the family long before Miss Catherine was born?"

"Lorra-golly, yes!" said the negro, with a triumphant grin; "Massa no s'pose young missus born afo' her fader: Lorra-massy, yaugh!"

"An excellent, lovely young mistress!" said the painter.

"Lorra, massa, yes; a lubly young missus; and makes lubly fine hoe-cake, if massa Cap'n would let her.—Old Nance taught her, when she wa' no bigga naw my foot. Massa must know, old Nance wa' *my* wife Nancy. So't o' nuss'd young missus Katy, for all what missus Aunt Rachel say; always liked old Nance betta, 'case how? Why old Nance larned her all she knew, make hoe-cake, corn-cake, johnny-cake, short-cake, hominy, pie, pone, and cream-cheese."

"Well Richard, and so you are to marry her off, and see her no more?"

"Golly, massa, yes; what for she young lady, if no?"

"And when's the wedding to be, Richard? Merry times you'll have!"

"Lorra, massa, don't know. Some says one day, some anoder. Wa' to been married soon, but faw the white nIgga Gilbert, what cut the Colonel's throat!"

"What, so soon?" said Herman, feeling a sudden thrill run through his frame. "Why, Richard, they were in a hurry, for such young folks. Miss Catherine is only seventeen—a very great hurry!"

"No, massa; long standing 'fair that; and put off, put off, Lorra knows how long; 'case young missus says she too young. Lorra-golly! old Nance wa' but fo'teen o' so; and I reckon there's more naw all that. An old nigga man, what's brought up a gemman, knows what's what!"

"Eh, Richard! you don't say so? You have the secret then? Come now, my old boy, here's a dollar. Come, put it in your pocket."

"Saddy, massa; God blessa massa!"

"Well now, Richard, what's the reason the marriage has been put off?"

"Golly! massa gib me the dolla' to tell?" cried Richard, looking alarmed.

"Certainly, Richard.—It's not a long secret, I hope?"

"Lorra, massa, can't do dat. Gib back a dolla', if massa call him back; but no tell on young missus. Brought up a gemman, massa; and no tell secrets out of the house."

"Oh, well, never mind, Richard; keep the money; I did not want to bribe you to tell any thing improper on your mistress; and I am glad to see you are so honest. It makes no difference: but what's the reason your young mistress does not like the Colonel's son?"

"Not like Massa Harry?" cried the coachman, in great dismay. "Sure old fool Dick no tell massa dat?"

"Oh, no; you kept the secret very well. But it is quite odd the young lady should not like so fine a young man?"

"Yes, massa, wery strange; but women's women, massa. Massa Harry werry fine young man."

"Well!" muttered the painter to himself, "I am playing an honest gentleman's part with this old ass, truly! I'll befool him no more. It is true, then!—even this dolt can tell that his mistress is sacrificed. So young, so fair, so good!—I would I had never seen her."

With such reflections as these, and many others of a painful nature, the young man continued his path; and, finally, having come within a short distance of the hovel, he discharged his attendant, and bade him return to the mansion. He then pursued his way alone, and reaching the solitary cottage, took possession of his former quarters with a sigh, a saddened brow, and a spirit no longer composed and mirthful. The bunch of fern he placed betwixt two leaves of paper, with as much care as became the first tribute to an herbarium.

CHAPTER XII

> Oh, now I see where your ambition points.—
> Take heed you steer your vessel right, my son:
> This calm of heaven, this mermaid's melody,
> Into an unseen whirlpool draws you fast,
> And, in a moment, sinks you.
>
> DRYDEN—*The Spanish Fryar.*

The summer had just set in, when the painter returned to the Traveller's Rest, with the prospect, so rapid was his convalescence, of being able to leave the valley within the space of a fortnight. But week came after week, June exchanged her green cloak for the golden mantle of July, the laurels bloomed on the hills, and the fire-flies twinkled in the evening grass, and still he lingered among the pleasant solitudes of Hawk-Hollow, as if unable to tear himself away. This faintness of purpose, for weekly, at least, he vowed he would depart, he excused to himself, by pleading the strong necessity he was under of delighting Captain Loring's heart with a picture, which he could not begin until his arm was released, not only from the wooden bonds of splints, but from the weakness resulting from the fracture. Until that happy period arrived, he was a frequent and indeed a welcome visiter at the mansion, his society being not less agreeable to Catherine than it was absolutely indispensable to her father. Young as she was, and with a spirit so gay and frank, there was much good sense in all Miss Loring's actions; and this had been doubtless sharpened by the necessity, imposed upon her so early, of playing the matron in her father's household, and guarding against the consequences of his many eccentricities. It was this good sense which taught her the propriety of getting rid of the stranger guest, as soon as humanity would sanction his expulsion; and this she had, in part, indirectly confessed to the party herself, with her usual good-humoured openness. This being accomplished, and Herman now assuming his proper station at a distance, and visiting the house as an avowed favourite of her father, she felt herself delivered from restraint, and received him without reserve. His manners and conversation were at all times those of a gentleman; and this is always enough, in America, to entitle a stranger, of whom no evil is known or suspected, to hospitality and respectful consideration, especially at a distance from the larger cities. That curiosity, which travellers have chosen to saddle upon Americans as a national characteristic, along with the two or three forms of speech that have belonged to the mother-land since the days of Chaucer, is in no country less really intrusive than in America. If it be irksome, and, at times, ludicrously impertinent, it is easily satisfied. It springs, indeed, not from a suspicious, so much as an inquisitive, disposition; and is the result of a certain openness of character, such as arises under every democratic government, and is well known to have prevailed to an extraordinary extent among the old Greek republics, notwithstanding the proverbial craftiness of individual character. With this curiosity is associated an equal quantity of credulity; and Americans are very content to receive the stranger, whose deportment is at all prepossessing, entirely upon his own self-recommendations. No jealousy accompanies an introduction made only by accident; and the same generous confidence is reposed in the new acquaintance, which the bestower will expect, under similar circumstances, to have lavished upon himself.

It did not, therefore, enter into the thoughts of Miss Loring to question Hunter's claims to such friendly courtesies as were accorded to him; and if any doubts of the propriety of continuing his acquaintance had occurred, they must have been dispelled by a remembrance of the circumstances under which he was introduced. Her happy instrumentality in rescuing him from a dreadful peril, had given her a right to be interested in his behalf; and the great pleasure the young man's society afforded her father, was an additional argument to banish reserve. The visits of Herman were therefore received and encouraged; the young lady's spirits, animated by such companionship, became more elastic and joyous; and Captain Loring rejoiced in the painter's acquaintance as much on her account as his own. "Adzooks, Kate," he was used to exclaim, "the young dog is as good company for you as cousin Harry,"—so he often called Miss Falconer, as well as her brother,—"and the lord knows how much *better* for me! And then the picture, Kate, adzooks, is'n't it a charmer! that is to say, it *will be*; but the young dog won't show it to me."

The picture,—'the grand picture of the Battle of Brandywine, and Tom Loring dying,'—had been at last begun, or rather a drawing in water colours, meant to represent that double calamity; and from the few samples of proficiency in his art which Herman had already shown, the expectations of the daughter were almost as agreeably kindled as those of the parent. The painter had presented Catherine with a few little sketches from his portfolio,—landscapes, representing views of Southern scenery, which to her appeared highly spirited, while to the Captain they seemed sublime,—only that *he* had a perverse facility at seeing rocks and stumps of trees in groups of kine on the meadows; and in distant flocks of sheep, nothing better than so many rambling killdeers on the barren upland. Notwithstanding these unlucky mistakes, he conceived so high an opinion of the artist's ability, that he strenuously urged him to begin the Battle of Brandywine upon a scale of magnitude commensurate with the grandeur of the subject; 'He would have it,' he said, 'done magnificently. He would go down to the village, and buy Ephraim Gall, the tavern-keeper's, big sign, that had the great Black Bear on it; or he would have another made just like it; and, he had no doubt, his young dog Haman,'—for the Captain could never fall upon his protegé's true name,—'would beat John Smith, the sign-painter, hollow,'—a flight of panegyric that somewhat nettled the artist, but vastly diverted Miss Loring.

But the greatest accession to his reputation was obtained when Herman, as the only means of securing a likeness of the Captain's deceased son, prevailed upon Catherine to sit to him for hers, and the radiant features beamed at last from the ivory. The delight with which the Captain seized upon this happy effort of art, was not merely boisterous; it was obstreperous,—nay, uproarious; and Catherine, laughing and weeping together, acknowledged that, in thus enrapturing her father's heart, the painter had made her his friend for ever.

"Now, Captain," said Hunter, with a beaming eye, "now, all I have to do, is to take that sketch home"——

"Shan't let it go out of my hands!" cried Captain Loring. "Why, it's my Kate herself! Give up my heart's blood first." "You shall have it again, Captain; I promise you that. It is only to copy it, you know—that is, to paint the likeness of your son from it."

"Shall do no such thing—must do another," cried Captain Loring; and it required all the arguments of the painter, backed by those of Catherine, to prevail upon the obstinate old man to surrender the sketch, that it might be devoted to the purpose for which it was executed.

Thus passed the time of the painter in an employment, which, as much as his conversation, recommended him to the friendship of two isolated beings, simple-hearted, guileless, and unsuspicious of any coming ill. Thus he passed his time, confiding and confided in—the gayest, the merriest, and perhaps the happiest visitor who had ever been admitted to the privileges of Avondale; yet, all the time, whether rambling with the frank maiden in search of summer flowers to transfer to her garden, whether listening to the gay music of her conversation, or gazing, in the exercise of his art, upon her beautiful features, drinking in a poison which he felt and feared, yet without knowing the deep hold it was taking upon his spirit, until the sudden crash of coming events made him dreadfully aware of its influence. He was neither too young nor too short-sighted to be ignorant of the impression made on his feelings by each daily interview with a maiden so bewitching; nor did he attempt to repress the humiliating consciousness, that, in thus giving his heart to the affianced bride of another, he was preparing for himself a retribution of pain and penitence, and perhaps of shame. From the moment in which he discovered himself treasuring away with such jealous care, the gift of withering fern,—a bagatelle of compliment, which, he well knew, was only given by Catherine to remove a mortification she had inflicted,—he saw that he was sporting upon the brink of a precipice—trifling upon some such slippery bridge as that of fatal memory over the streamlet, from which his folly might at any moment hurl him. With this consciousness before him, he perceived the necessity of flight, yet fled not, deeming that the power of escape at the right moment could not be denied him—of taking some antidote with the poison, but took none, resolving it should be swallowed thereafter; and, in fine, while still thinking that he resisted, or was prepared to resist, when the peril should become urgent, he gave himself up to the intoxication of the new passion, and, in reality, sought every means to augment it.

> 'When the flame of love is kindled first,
> 'Tis the fire-fly's light at even,'—

the flash of an insect, which one can admire, without fearing its power to create a conflagration. A vague impression that Catherine's want of affection for the licensed lover would prevent the completion of the marriage contract, gave a sort of encouragement and hope to his selfishness, which he interpreted into the more generous sympathy of one who lamented her hard fate, and desired only to shield and protect her. In this delusive thought, in this romantic willingness to watch over the safety of another, he lingered around the vortex of fate, until the ripple became a current, and the current an impetuous tide, from which there was no escape, except by exerting his remaining strength to the utmost. At the very period when the exertion should have been made, he bore to his solitary chamber the idol lately completed by his own hands, and as he gazed upon it, felt that the moment of salvation had passed by.

"Yes, it is now too late," he muttered, apostrophising the miniature; "I have fooled myself a second time into the whirlpool; and who, Catherine, will play thy part with me again, and again save me? It *is* too late; it is too late to retreat, and now therefore I must go on—yet with what hope go on? With none. She heeds me not, she dreams not of my folly, she cares not. Friendship is the grave of love; and in her friendship my love is entombed, before it has breathed twice in existence. I will speak to her, and be derided!—I will confess myself, and be driven from her presence! And this is honourable of me too! to take advantage of her unsuspicious frankness, her anxious desire to gratify her father, and steal a portrait from her! I saw she doubted the propriety of sitting; and yet I, by base dissimulation and affected indifference, cajoled her to consent. Well, if I can copy, I can destroy; and if this fool—this slave—this Falconer wed her, why, then good-by to the knavery and the folly together! I will tarry, at least, until I see the privileged woer; and then, if she like him not, if she recoil—nay, if she shed but a tear of repugnance, may heaven forsake me if I do not——Well, what? Kill him!——There has been enough of that among us already."

Thus murmuring to himself, and expressing invectives against his folly, with the usual arguments for continuing to indulge it, he sat down before a table, and despite his convictions of the impropriety, if not the meanness of the act, began to copy the miniature. He laboured assiduously until he had completed the outline, and then exclaimed, with a species of reproachful triumph,

"Now, foolish father of the best and loveliest! though you rob me of my labour, yet have I secured its counterpart. Send me a thousand leagues away, and within this dim outline shall my hand reproduce the image of your sacrifice.—But here come the fools again! Now for a smooth face, a merry voice, and a frolic with my jolterhead admirers."

The vow which the painter had made, when the doctor and his two friends passed by the widow's cottage, and smiled at his choice of lodgings, that he would make them fonder of the Traveller's Rest than their own village quarters, he had in part fulfilled. Whatever was his secret and growing care, it was yet confined to his own bosom; and he was altogether of too joyous a temperament, had he even desired to nourish his melancholy, to bear a sad spirit in company. He was one of those who suffer most, and suffer longest, by grieving only at intervals, and enjoying themselves heartily among friends. The idea of a continuous grief, of any duration, at least, is preposterous. The body can live upon the rack only a few hours, or days; and the spirit's powers of endurance are not much greater.

His gay and agreeable manners had strongly recommended him to the trio; and the two lawyers, having nothing better to do, were wont to mount their horses, and accompany the doctor on his professional visitations, which he continued for some time after the patient had taken refuge within the Traveller's Rest; and even after he insisted upon being cured, they wasted their tediousness upon him at least twice or thrice a week, in the way of friendly calls; and he was wont to entertain them as well as he could. Of the doctor he had made a conquest by asking for his bill, and paying it in good English guineas, a handful of which coin gave doctor Merribody more sensible delight than could the bushel of paper with which he expected to fill his saddle-bags; the amount charged against the unlucky amateur being some few thousands of dollars,—Continental currency.

One of the doctor's friends, whom he usually addressed by the familiar title of Jingleum, but whose real name was Jackson, or Johnson, or some such unhappy dissyllable, was the poet of the village, and a bard of renown for at least ten miles round. Him the painter won by praising his verses, and what was still more captivating, by singing them, and what was yet more enslaving, by requesting permission to cull all the stanzas of a *cantabile* nature from the long blue-covered log-books, in which Mr. Jingleum had carefully recorded his labours. Seeing what a congenial soul he had found in the painter, Jingleum freely supplied his wants, and wrote divers madrigals at his suggestion, with which Herman charmed the ears of Miss Loring. The poet soon became his intense admirer and perpetual visiter; they grew fast friends, and soon came to regard each other, the one as the divinest poet, the other as the most finished singer, under the moon. It would have been an interesting sight, could one have invaded the sanctity of the painter's apartment, on such occasions, to see them together, industriously fixing a tune to each affecting ditty,—a labour that was sometimes none of the lightest; and sometimes, when the genius of the bard, as it often did, chose to disdain the base bonds of metre and rhythm, and none of the thousand melodies in their service could be forced or wheedled into nuptials with his independent verse, they were fain to betake themselves to their own resources, and finish the business with such a *quodlibet* as they could manufacture between them. It was a divine enjoyment to the poet, when they had at last succeeded with any refractory song, to hear his lines breathed out from the mellow lips of his friend; for then his poetry seemed as celestial as his pleasure. His bliss, however, was not complete, until he lighted by accident, one day, in the village, upon a battered guitar,—an instrument of such venerable antiquity, that there was not a soul therein who was able to pronounce for what unheard-of purpose such an extraordinary engine had been framed, until Herman Hunter, swearing it could discourse most eloquent music, and was *not* a banjo, managed, by dint of much exertion, to fit it up with fiddle-strings and the savings of some demolished harpsichord, and set its dumb tongues twangling: it was not until he heard his rhymes trolled forth to the clatter of this romantic instrument, that the joy of the poet mounted to the heaven of ecstasy. He would sit distilling with delight, while the lips of his friend warbled over the seraphic lines, and while his fingers hopped over the amaranthine strings; and then, sometimes, with a sudden feeling of inspiration, he would snatch the lyre, as he poetically called it, into his own hands, doubtless expecting an overflow of ineffable harmony from the mere fulness of his spirit, until warned by the dreadful dissonance of his touches, and the remonstrances of his admirer, he found, however extraordinary it seemed, that the drum and the jewsharp were the only instruments the playing of which came by nature.

This peculiar friendship betwixt the bard and the singer it is perhaps necessary here to mention, in order that it should be understood to whom should be given the credit of those canzonets sung by the painter, which seem to have any peculiar reference to his own condition. He did not carry his affection so far as to bestow any of his private confidence on the bard; nor did the latter ever suspect that any call, however urgent, for a ballad especially sad and amatory, was to be understood as indicating a passion deeper than that of the mere songster. There was little suspiciousness in the poet's frame, and no scandal-mongers in the neighbourhood. It was indeed the golden age of that part of the world; although the country was somewhat overflowed with paper-money.

It was one result of this generous spirit, doubtless, that caused the story of the resuscitation of a Hawk of Hawk-Hollow to be so soon forgotten. The account of the outrage upon Colonel Falconer, as having been perpetrated by Oran Gilbert, did indeed at first create a considerable sensation; and many excitable individuals, hearing of the chase after the fugitive Nehemiah, mounted their horses, and resumed the trail, the next day, with the resolution of sifting the mystery to the bottom. But the trail ended where Lieutenant Brooks had left it; the raw-boned white horse had passed through divers hands, and was, in course of time, supposed to have been recovered by the rightful owner; but the rider had vanished as if swallowed up by the earth, or melted into the air, and was never more heard of. The story died away, or was remembered only as a jest, which finally expired in the vapour of its own silliness. The reasonable men laughed at their late fears, and forgot them.

About the present time, however, there arose a rumour, no one knew how or why, which created a new sensation among the credulous and foreboding. It was whispered that a band of tories was secretly forming among the hills; but where, or for what purpose, no one pretended to say. It was a vague and mysterious apprehension, that spread from person to person, by virtue, perhaps, of its enigmatic character; for no inquiry could detect a better reason for its prevalence. As it carried its contagion further and further, men began again to talk of the Hawks of Hawk-Hollow; the refugees, in imagination, rose again from their tombs, and the scalp-hunter stole anew through the forests. The rumour had reached the Traveller's Rest; but it made little impression on the spirit of the painter.

He laid aside his drawing in haste, so soon as he heard that clatter of hoofs in the oaken yard, which, he thought, betokened the coming of his friends; and having secured it beyond the reach of any prying eye, he descended to meet them.

CHAPTER XIII

> "Unto you," quod I, "with all my whole assent,
> I will tell trouthe, and you will not bewraye
> Unto none other my matter and entent."
> "Nay, nay," quod he, "you shall not see that daye:
> Your whole affiaunce and trust well ye may
> Into me put; for I shall not vary,
> But kepe your councill as a secretary."
>
> HAWES—Pastime of Plesure.

Instead of the bard or the physician, Hunter discovered that the clatter which had interrupted his secret labours, was caused by the arrival of a personage entirely unknown, and, as he soon began to believe, unworthy his notice. He was a stout but ill-looking man, with a soldier's coat and hat, both worn and shabby, and Herman inferred at once, that he was some private from a disbanded regiment, returning to the life of industry and obscurity he had left for the wars. As he reached the porch, Herman saw that Dancy, the farmer, who happened to be about the house, was showing the new guest the way to the stable; and, however unprepossessing his appearance, he soon perceived that he had already struck up a friendship with Dancy, who talked and laughed, as they jogged together round the crag, as if with an old acquaintance. This set the painter's heart at rest; and he soon afterwards discovered that the man, being as humble in his desires as prospects, had visited the Traveller's Rest less in search of entertainment than employment, and had agreed with the widow, or rather with Dancy, who assumed the privilege of striking the bargain, to remain and assist the hireling in the labours of the approaching harvest, in consideration of receiving free quarters and forage during that period.

In the conversation of such a man it is not to be supposed the painter could have looked for any source of interest; and, accordingly, he merely gave him a glance as he strode away with Dancy, leading a sorry gelding in his hand, and then took a seat on the porch by Elsie, whose wheel, as usual, was droning out its monotonous hum near the door. Though hand and foot plied their accustomed task with accuracy and effect, it was evident that the poor widow's thoughts were not with her employment; on the contrary, she was engaged in profound and sorrowful contemplation; and, indeed, for a sennight past, Herman had observed that her fits of abstraction were unusually deep and frequent.

He sat down at her side, and addressed some few questions to her in relation to the stranger, but received such vague and irrelevant answers as convinced him her meditations were too engrossing to be easily broken. He proceeded therefore without delay to seek some other means of amusing his mind; and casting his eyes towards the distant hall, he was, in a few moments, plunged in reflections as absorbing, or even more so than her own. Indeed, his interrogatories, though they did not immediately rouse the old woman from her lethargy, served the purpose of interrupting and distracting her thoughts a little; so that she, by and by, woke up, and recovered herself so far as to look round her, and perceive she was not alone on the porch. She surveyed the young man very earnestly, until, at last, tears gathered in her eyes, and her wheel stood still. The sudden ceasing of the sound at once broke the spell that enchained the painter's spirit; and looking up to Elsie, he displayed a countenance on which the turn of some darker thought had imprinted a character of sternness, and even fierceness.

Elsie rose up, and stepping towards him, laid her palsied hand upon his shoulder, saying, in tones both solemn and impressively appealing,

"Drive these thoughts from your bosom, and now depart. Why should you rest longer in this place? Your limb is sound, your strength is restored; and now begone, ere the calls of others, and the anger of your own heart, shall drive you into acts of blood, which, if you die not among them, you will live only to repent."

"Fear me not, mother," said the youth, with a faint smile. "On this subject, I have told you my resolution before. I am, at the least, as good an American as yourself; and whatever may have been my original loyal and subjugating propensities, I have now not a wish, nay, not a thought, of playing the enslaver. Nothing on earth shall draw me into the matter you think of."

"Ay, but revenge though!" said the widow, warningly. "You are dreaming of him whom you think you should hate, and thirsting perhaps for an opportunity to shed his blood?"

"You are deceived, Elsie. I will never lift my hand against him, unless in self-defence. God is the avenger, and, one day, he *will* avenge. I hate, Elsie, but I will not shed blood."

"And why then do you remain? If *he*, whom neither knife nor bullet can destroy, looks upon you again, as surely he will, and that perhaps sooner than you dream of, he will entice you into his bloody schemes; and though he escape, yet will you perish."

"Into his schemes I will not be enticed," said Herman; "and I rather hope, by argument and persuasion, to draw him from them."

"Argument and persuasion! and these to be tried on *him?*" muttered Elsie, looking around her as if in dread. "When you can argue the wolf from the neck of the dying deer,—when you can persuade the rattle-snake not to strike the naked foot that is trampling his back, then may you think of turning him from his purpose, or changing his wild and dreadful nature. He will have revenge, and I know that he will obtain it. Years have passed by,— (how many and how bitter!)—the gray hair has joined with the black, the smooth brow has turned to the furrowed, but the purpose of his heart has not grown old and fainted; all is now as it was, and so will be till the end. Think not of drawing him to your opinions; but be certain he will draw you to his. Go not near him, avoid him, let him not see you, or speak with you."

"Fear me not, Elsie"———

"I *do* fear you. Alas, young man, trust not yourself in his power; if he touches you with his hand, you will fall. God forbid you should be joined with him in the matter that is coming! I had rather you were struck down by lightning where you stand;—better were it for you, had you slept under the Fall of the Grave."

"Sure, Elsie," said the young man, "there is nothing so criminal and horrid in the enterprise, after all. The rescue of a poor captive,—a boy, too, of nineteen years, and the only son of a doting and noble mother, condemned to death unjustly and perfidiously, (that is a harsh word, Elsie!) to expiate a crime committed by another,—sure, this is an enterprise of humanity rather than iniquity."

"And do you think this is all?" cried Elsie. "A darker project is in his mind, and a darker deed will be soon accomplished. Why then do you stay? Have you not seen enough, and mourned enough? I tell you, when the marriage-day comes, the wronger will come, and after him the avenger; and who knows what dreadful deeds will be done, before all is over?"

"If it be a marriage of blood," said the youth, "why so let it be. They are, I firmly believe, leading Catherine Loring like a sheep to the shambles. If they mean to wed her to young Falconer against her will, why then, though there should be no other man in the world to befriend her, I will stand by her myself;——I will, Elsie," he exclaimed, impetuously; "and, if Falconer do not at once surrender his claims, I will compel him!"

"What!" cried the widow, starting from him in dismay: "What is this I hear? What! you,—have *you* looked at Catherine Loring, then, as a creature to be loved! Have *you* dared"— —

"Nonsense!" cried the young man, with a visage of flame; "I am enslaved to her by gratitude, and I wish to do her a service. I owe her a life, Elsie; and I will yield it up ten times over, before she shall be driven into a marriage she abhors, and which, I believe, is breaking her heart."

"Miserable, insane, cruel young man!" cried the widow, with unexpected energy,—"and it has come to this, then? You have repaid her humanity and kindness, by stealing away her affections from her betrothed husband, and so making a lot, sorrowful enough before, still more wretched! You have"— —

"Hold, Elsie," exclaimed Herman; "it is you who are insane. You told me yourself, she was averse to the match.— —And, as to stealing her affections, I have done no such thing—they are not so lightly come by. If they were, Elsie,—nay, if they were really mine, Elsie, why should I not make my claim to them, as well as another? I am neither poor nor humble, neither degraded nor corrupted; in all things of worldly good, I am young Falconer's equal, and perhaps, in some, his superior."

"Ay!" cried the widow, with increasing vehemence, "and if she smiled, and if that would win her, you would shoot Harry Falconer through the brain! Is it not so? This is dreadful! Oh, young man, begone; remain not a moment longer in the valley. You will commit a crime worse than self-destruction, and one more hard to pardon!"

"I will commit no crime, Elsie; and none have I yet committed. Your anxiety is absurd; and so is your suspicion. That I have the most friendly regard for Miss Loring, the most ardent friendship, is true; but as to loving her, Elsie, that—why that is all nonsense."

"Perhaps it is," cried the widow, "and Heaven grant it may prove so. But go not near her again, do not expose yourself to the intoxication of her society. If not a wrong to yourself, it is an unkindness to her. If you talk to her of escaping from the marriage she hates, and she finds she has a friend left in the world to aid her—ah, that would ruin her! The desire of escape may madden the wisest."

"Fiddlesticks!" cried the youth; "I have no such coarse and meddling ways of testifying my regard; and a presumption of that kind would banish me from her presence for ever. But, Elsie, I tell you, I cannot bear the thought of her being married against her will."

"And how can you prevent it? By wedding her yourself? That cannot be. By breaking her heart? Yes, there you may succeed——it is breaking already; and when you have added one more pang to it, it will soon cease to suffer. Hearken, young man; if you persist in this thing, you will be a villain. Go up to the grove—get you to Jessie's sleeping place; and consider how fast you are treading in the steps of him who slew her."

"I, Elsie! This is extraordinary!"

"It is true. Both of you were carried, sick and dying, into the house of a stranger; both of you were received by guileless and open hearts; and, when you have gone a little farther in your folly, it can be perhaps said, that both left sorrow and death behind them."

"Elsie, this is shocking? Do you think me such a villain as that man?"

"I do not," said Elsie; "if I did,—if I thought you were now, like him before you, plotting, even in conceit, a wrong to that noble girl,—if I thought this," she added, with singular asperity, "I would put hemlock into your food, though you were the child of my own sister, and you should die before morning!"

"I commend your zeal in the lady's cause, and will myself endeavour to imitate it. But there, an end, Elsie; we will talk of this no more. Your fears are even more groundless than injurious. I will leave the valley soon—perhaps very soon; and I will murder no one, while I remain in it."

So saying, to end a discussion which was becoming disagreeable, he left the house, resolved to make his way to the scene of his late disaster. In this resolution he continued, until he reached the park-gate; when, suddenly observing the flutter of a white garment under the trees near to the mansion, he turned from his path, and again found himself in the presence of the Captain's daughter.

And thus it happened with him on the next day, the next, and again the next; until the little thread that tangled his spirit had become a web from which there was no escape, unless by rending away some of the vital limbs it encircled. He sang and painted as before; nay, he assailed the Battle of Brandywine with zeal and industry, and had advanced so far with the work, before the occurrence of unlooked-for events chilled his enthusiasm and palsied his hand, that he was able to carry it to the mansion, and exhibit it to the father and daughter, that he might derive all the advantage of their remarks on the most difficult feature of his subject,—that is to say, the figure of the Captain's deceased son.

In the meanwhile, he confirmed the good impression he had long since made on his two friends, and was indeed admitted to such intimacy with both, as marked, not only their sense of his merits, but their own simplicity of character. In the case of the Captain, he certainly began to fill up the gap made in his affections by the death of his son; and as for Catherine, she soon appreciated the value of a friendship based upon grateful recollections, and, what seemed to her, a delicate and purely disinterested regard for her weal and happiness.

The situation of this unhappy girl,—for such, in truth, she was,—was of a nature to engage her feelings warmly in favour of any one approaching her with real friendship, as it was also to touch the sympathies of the discerning and compassionate.

> "Naught is there under heaven's wide hollownesse,
> That moves more dear compassion of mind,
> Than beautie brought t' unworthie wretchednesse,
> Through envie's snares, or fortune's freaks unkind."

She was still very young, yet old enough to feel the desolation of her father's house and fortunes, and to be willing to sacrifice her own happiness to secure that of her parent. At the very moment when her father became a beggar,—an outcast from the home of her nativity,—her charms had won the heart of the young Falconer,——'A lad,' as Captain Loring was wont to say, 'after a man's heart, and a woman's too;' and the enamoured youth, with his father's fullest approbation, and indeed warm encouragement, claimed permission to throw himself at her feet, and received it. Perhaps the consideration of her father's misfortunes had greater weight with Catherine than the temptation of wealth and splendour; and perhaps the indifference of a young and wholly unoccupied heart had also its share of influence in determining her decision. It is certain, if she did not consent with alacrity, she did not refuse so earnestly as to make the Captain believe the proposal was otherwise than vastly agreeable to her; and, in truth, it was some considerable time before she began to lament her easy consent, and to feel that there was merit, because pain, in the sacrifice. The great youth of the pair (for at the time of betrothal, the lover was yet in his minority,) had caused the nuptials to be deferred until the close of the spring of the present year, but a short time previous to which the attempt was made on the life of Colonel Falconer; and that occurrence had necessarily produced another postponement. In the meanwhile, the maiden had grown older and reflected more deeply; and the regrets that began to wake in her spirit, though, at first, she scarce knew why, became more frequent and painful, as fame, or scandal, brought to her ears stories of wild frolic and dissipation on the part of her absent lover. These reports, to be sure, were combated by Miss Falconer, and the excesses they proclaimed made to appear, as they always are in the case of the rich and happy, only the natural outbreakings of a joyous and generous spirit. But Harriet's skill could not prevent her friend discovering that the young soldier had little beside a comely face and a merry temper to recommend him to her favour; and perhaps no circumstance will sooner prejudice a woman against a lover, not previously adored, than the discovery that his mind is inferior to her own. The *passion* of love is a material instinct; the *sentiment* is a particle of the divinity, and can only exist when called into action by the breath of spirit. Woman's love is only deserving the name when it is purely a sentiment, and based upon reverence for the idol of her affections. In a word, Catherine found she was to be wedded to a man she could never hope to love; and it required her constantly to keep before her eyes the situation of her father, himself wholly incapable of retrieving, as he had been of preserving, his fortunes, to prevent her openly repining. To him, therefore, she could not look as a friend, in her difficulty; his affection could be indeed counted upon, but it could be exercised in her favour only at the price of his ruin. As for Miss Falconer, though she loved her well, she knew that *her* spirit was entirely with her brother, and that she encouraged, and did all she could to promote, the match, for his especial benefit, as a means of weaning him from a gay and dissolute career, which threatened, if not speedily checked, to terminate in confirmed profligacy.

With feelings of this kind constantly weighing upon her breast—a consciousness ever present, that in the death of an only and beloved brother, she had lost a friend to whom she might have unbosomed herself in grief, and from whom she might have expected sympathy and relief,—it is not extraordinary that the kindness even of a stranger, expressed ever with delicacy and gentleness, and uttered not so much in words as actions, should make a strong and enduring impression upon her feelings, and that she should bestow upon him the frankest evidences of regard.

"Ne evil thing she fear'd, ne evil thing she meant."

A circumstance—and it was the only one—which seemed at first to threaten a speedy interruption of their good understanding, served in the end even to strengthen her confidence and friendship. In an unguarded moment, and while under a strong impulse, the young man alluded to the approaching nuptials, and that in a manner so plainly indicative of his knowledge of Catherine's feelings, and of the sacrifice she was to be compelled to make, that she was justly alarmed and offended. She felt as a woman, that this was an indecorum and presumption of the most unpardonable nature; and the reproof it brought upon the offender's head, was the stronger for being mingled with the tears of humiliation. But even this was forgiven, when several days elapsed without bringing the youth back to the mansion, and she reflected how much his offensive intermeddling must have been caused by the sympathy she was ever so glad to possess. She was really rejoiced, when her father, astounded and concerned, and finally enraged, at the unaccountable absence of his favourite, sought him out, and dragged him, almost by force of arms, to the mansion, and she heard his footsteps once more sounding on the porch; and Herman soon perceived that she had discharged from her mind all anger, if not all remembrance of his ungoverned zeal, and was disposed to treat him with as much confidence as before. In truth, she was one of the few we meet in the world, and perhaps as seldom even in woman as man, of that angelic quality of spirit, which mingles inaptness to take offence with the greatest readiness to forgive it; and as all he had said was made offensive not so much by its nature as by the position of the offender himself, and would have been proper in the case of a near kinsman or old and familiar friend, she easily persuaded herself that the very rudeness was an evidence of regard, which she did wrong to punish with severity. She never perhaps afterwards smiled with the same gayety, or conversed with the same unreserved freedom; but she treated him with much confidence; one proof of which, from its singular nature, and the important, though secret, influence it had upon the young man's conduct, it is necessary to mention. She took occasion one afternoon, when her father was sleeping, and her female companions were occupied afar-off in various domestic duties, to call his attention to the subject of the outrage on Colonel Falconer, with which, as an intimate at Gilbert's Folly, he was, of course familiar. 'She had,' she said 'a letter from Miss Falconer in relation to the unhappy and mysterious affair, and to certain steps that lady was taking in consequence of it. These,' she added, 'though of a singular nature and questionable propriety, she would not perhaps have presumed to communicate to another, as they were in a degree confidential, were they not accompanied by a call upon herself for co-operation, under circumstances so perplexing and embarrassing, that she felt herself at liberty to ask Mr. Hunter's assistance and advice,—the former for her friend, the latter for herself. She judged, from many expressions he had let fall, that Mrs. Bell had made him acquainted, in part at least, with the history of the Hawks of Hawk-Hollow; for which reason, he would be able to understand the letter without comments from her. He had seen one individual who figured prominently in the letter; and his opinion and recollections of *him* would undoubtedly be acceptable to Miss Falconer. On the whole, she was persuaded he could assist her in what she felt to be a difficulty; and perhaps he might be able to suggest something for the benefit of her friend.'

With this preliminary explanation, she proceeded to read Miss Falconer's letter, not stopping at those parts which alluded to the painter himself, and of which she made diverting use, though here and there for obvious reasons, altering some of the expressions, and apologizing for others in a humorous way. It may be supposed, and with justice, that she carefully abstained from reading all those passages in which she was herself spoken of, in connexion with her affianced lord; and, indeed, the occurrence of these always caused her lip to quiver, and her finger, tracing the lines as they occurred, to hasten onward to the next fitting paragraph.

The letter was to the following effect:

> "And so Monsieur Red-Jacket is alive and well, and handsome, and paints, and has a good singing voice, and is altogether a genteel young personage! Well now, though I detest his very memory, and never see a scarlet waistcoat, without thinking of two galloping fools, and another standing on a porch grinning, I am quite glad you fished him out of the river, since you have thereby got such a conformable well-behaved young man to keep you company, for lack of a better,—the doctor and the rest of those village noddies being all insufferable, as I always agreed. If he can really succeed in obtaining your likeness, retain him in the Hollow by all means, even if you have to break an arm for him over again. We must have at least two copies, one of which will set our beloved Harry frantic, and the other I will keep myself. The man may fix his own price; and, besides, I'll patronise him, though I *do* detest him. Harry shall sit to him, I assure you; and perhaps I also—just as I happen to like him—that is his painting, not himself. Do you remember, as we sat at the sycamore tree, I wished him 'a harder sleep that night than he ever had before?' There's something odd in the coincidence; a hard night he had of it, from your own account, poor rogue. I only thought of an old bed and damp sheets, such as I supposed it likely enough he would find at that old witch's. I will wish bad luck no more, believing I have some magical power that way, which might, sooner or later, lead me to commit murder. However, I have more important matter for discoursing on.
>
> "Papa is recovering fast; indeed, he was pronounced out of danger before I reached him; and he already talks of banishing me again to the green fields. To tell the truth, I have grown more inquisitive than ever; and it is plain, he is tired of me. That story, Kate, has set my brain spinning; but

blessed be thou for telling it! There will such good come of my knowledge as will perhaps astound you, and him too.—But you shall hear.

"The assassin is wrapped round about with mystery,—a most singular doubt. My father is, or rather *was*, (for he never pronounced the wretch's name, except in the first moment of confusion and terror,) positive that the blow was struck by the Hawk of the Hollow; and who should know better? Yet, I can tell you, there are circumstances pointing so strongly at another man, that every body pronounces him guilty, except myself and, I suppose, papa; and these they are. There was (I speak of the man as if he were dead, for he seems to have killed and buried himself,) a certain vagabond in our town, called Sterling, or Starling,—a man of much shrewdness, some talent, and possessing a degree of rough humour and wit which made him a favourite with many of our citizens, some of them quite respectable, and delegates in Congress. Nobody exactly knew how the man lived; though it was generally supposed by gambling. An accident of no great importance in itself, revealed the fellow's true character and occupation to my father, who forthwith acted as honour and patriotism commanded him to do. This Sterling was a spy,—a pensioned spy, whose duty was to reside at our Congressional head-quarters, and by cultivating acquaintances among the honourables, pick up as much intelligence in relation to secret legislation as he could; and there is no doubt, the villain has laboured so well in his vocation, that the British commander-in-chief has been often apprised of our intentions as early as our own leader. It is said that Sterling was once an actor; they say, he has strong comic talents, but has a mad conceit he was made to shine in tragedy. He once got up a sort of company in our town, with the expectation of establishing a theatre. However, his friends all turned upon him the first night, the piece being tragedy, and laughed and ridiculed, and finally carried the matter so far as to hiss the poor wretch off the stage. They say, my brother Harry (I believe it was before he entered the army,) was a ringleader among the hardhearted censors.—An exemplary youth, he! He was ever a most incorrigible mischief and plague, notwithstanding his excellent heart; and the duel he fought with his captain last winter, (a warm friend of his now,) was caused by one of his freaks of humour.—But marriage cures all that, you know.—However, I must speak of Mr. Sterling.

"My father obtained such proofs of the treason of the lord of the buskin as might have brought him to the gallows, and he was thrown into prison; from which, however, he escaped as soon as was convenient. I think, it happened eleven days before the outrage was attempted; and long before that, he was supposed to have succeeded, by verifying Shakspeare's words, (that is, by esteeming the world at large the boards of a theatre, and playing many parts thereon,) in passing the lines of the army, and reaching New York in safety. Indeed, he was, in a week's time, almost forgotten. But now comes the marvel.

"My father had entered the pavilion, (as I wrote you before,) to get certain papers. They were the very documents in relation to this man's case,—the proofs of his treasonable practices, &c., which were put into papa's hands, when he volunteered to conduct the prosecution. The man was really such a favourite, that all others were quite cool in the matter, and rather disposed to let him off, than push matters to extremity, especially as hostilities were almost over: even Harry interceded for him. Papa, however, was determined to bring him to justice; and therefore volunteered in the case. He had these very documents in his hands, when the assassin, (whoever he was,) who had previously concealed himself in the pavilion, or stole into it after him, suddenly assailed him; and, what is curious, it was found, when they came to examine afterwards, that these papers had all vanished, together with my father's purse, and a small-sword which he always kept hanging up in the study.

"The next thing discovered was, that a certain horse, the property of this Sterling at the time of his arrest, but which some one had seized upon and sold, to satisfy some claim or other, had disappeared from a neighbouring farm, where it was at pasture. The animal being traced, it was found that he had ambled up the river, supporting the weight of an individual, who, although assuming to be a fanatical parson, had so many points of resemblance to the original owner of the horse, that it was immediately affirmed, he could be no other than Sterling himself, playing off a character of which he was notoriously fond;—a ranting, canting parson, as Harry says, being one of the impersonations with which he was wont to set the table in a roar. You know the rest of this man's story; his sudden appearance at Elsie Bell's, at the very moment when we were discoursing of the Hawks under the sycamore;—his flight over the river, and his sudden disappearance. I suppose, he assumed some new disguise that deceived the pursuers.

"These things favour the opinion of the mass, who will believe nothing less than that the murder was attempted by Sterling, in revenge of my father's zeal in bringing his villany to light. But now remember, that papa was the only one who *saw* the assassin; that he knew the faces of both parties; and that he affirmed the villain to be Oran Gilbert, without so much as mentioning Sterling's name. Can there be any striking resemblance between the two traitors? Might not a course of extraordinary coincidences have assisted the Hawk in adopting (even without knowing it himself) the appearance and manner of Sterling in disguise? Nothing should be thought too incredible in such a case, for the whole matter is a wonder.

"I have not space to mention all I wish, or all I have learned, that confirms my father's words. This, however, is certain: Oran Gilbert *is not dead*, but alive, and is engaged *somewhere* upon *some* villany; but where and what—ay, there's the rub. I have received intelligence not to be doubted a moment, that he was in New York, and that he left that city, about two months since, on some secret enterprise.

"Now, Kate, I have little more to tell you, except that I have turned thief-taker; that I am convinced Oran Gilbert was the midnight assassin, and is, at this moment, lying in wait in a certain place, with the expectation of renewing the attack on my father's life; and that I, weak woman as I am, have laid a trap for the cruel and remorseless villain, which may bring the doom he is projecting for another upon his own head. Don't stare; and don't say any thing of the matter. You cannot comprehend the spirit that now inspires me; I am playing the part of a man, but in a very ladylike way, and all to guard my father from the knife that is still outstretched against him. You shall know all in good time—sooner perhaps than you imagine. It is necessary to my purpose that I should have a minute description of Gilbert, his height, figure, eyes, hair, nose, mouth, his age, &c.: get it of Elsie Bell, and don't let her suspect you have any object beyond mere simple curiosity. If we could make the old creature speak, I warrant me she could tell us enough of the villain. I entrust this matter to you. Don't scruple: you *can* deceive as well as any body, when the spirit of woman seizes you; and the end we have now in view will excuse a mountain of duplicity. You can also make inquiries (but, mark you, *not of her*—don't let her suspect suspicion,) in relation to the appearance of the preacher Poke. Your bonny Red-Jacket, the dauber, can doubtless answer satisfactorily on this point, painters being commonly good observers. As for your father, I interdict all counselling with him; for, first, his memory is not to be relied upon, being somewhat dependent upon his imagination, you know; and secondly, because we must take no more confidants into the confederacy than we can help. Every thing depends upon secrecy. I long to tell you the whole matter, but dare not *yet*—no, not even so much as the names of my counsellors, auxiliaries, agents, &c. By the way, did you observe Lieutenant Brooks? He is very genteel and agreeable, I assure you—and the shrewdest, boldest-witted brain for his youth I have ever seen. He will attend upon Harry, and you will adore him.—But my third sheet is out, and so I must conclude.

"As for your fourth of July jollification that you talk of so sentimentally, I hate all such merry-makings. What do I care about Jingleum, and his orations? Could they find no more reasonable Demosthenes? And then the folly of dragging up drums, and cannons, and militia companies, dogs, horses, and women in their Sunday clothes, to the sacred solitudes of Hawk-Hollow! Sure, you are all gone crazy: it is profanation. I should not wonder if the martial din of the jubilee should bring a regiment or two from the lines upon you. We shall see what will come of it.

"*Addio*——Do my bidding, and keep my counsel.

"*Mem.* It is very odd, I forgot the postscript."

The contents of this epistle, as Catherine saw, greatly surprised, and indeed confounded the painter; and it was some moments before he could shake off his embarrassment so far as to comment upon it. 'He esteemed it very singular,' he said, 'and very improper, that Miss Falconer should engage in an enterprise such as she so significantly hinted at; and he thought she was impelled by a species of frenzy. Her suspicions, that the assault upon her father had been committed by a Gilbert, were ludicrously absurd. How was it possible her father should, in a single glance, and almost in darkness, recognise a countenance he had not seen for more than twenty years? How could it be believed that such a man, a refugee captain, long since formally outlawed, should force his way into the very strong-holds of his enemy, commit a crime of unexampled daring, and then, with audacity still more astonishing, direct his steps towards the district where he was so well known? How incredible, that a man of his wild and stubborn habits could adopt a disguise so outré as that of Nehemiah! How much more incredible, having taken such pains to shed a foeman's blood, that he should have done his work so bunglingly! The idea was preposterous. Every thing went to show that Sterling was the assassin; and it was quite probable, nay, it was almost certain, that Nehemiah and Sterling were one and the same person. He could not pretend to say, or to know, or to be very certain, of course; but he was sure Nehemiah was an impostor, much more familiar with tags from play-books than scraps from the Bible, and so he had told the man himself, though not in direct words; the consequence of which was, that he instantly took the alarm, crossed the river, and escaped. As to the request made of Miss Loring in relation to the information she was expected to obtain of Mrs. Bell, that was as unworthy of Miss Falconer as compliance would be on the part of Miss Loring. It was quite proper, indeed, she should ask Elsie for information, but not without apprizing her of the object in view. But even this was needless; *he* had heard Elsie speak of Oran Gilbert's appearance, and he could assure Miss Loring that no two persons could be more unlike than he and the ranting Nehemiah, the one being a man of middle size, the other a giant. He would advise Miss Falconer to adopt two measures, which would go farther to effect her objects, (which, he supposed, were, to protect her father from future danger, and to punish his enemy,) than all the witty and masculine stratagems in the world. If Oran Gilbert were really alive, and within the American lines, then let her persuade her father to remain in the city, afar from his dreaded vengeance; *there* he most certainly was safe. To punish the assassin, application should be made to the British commander-in-chief at New York; and as the atrocity was purely of a civil nature—a case of malicious, inexcusable violence—it was highly probable he would be at once brought to justice.'

With remarks of this kind, which appeared to her to be founded in good sense, he satisfied Catherine that her confidence had not been misplaced or unprofitable; and the time waxed on, without causing any abatement of her good opinion, or any interruption of an intercourse highly agreeable to her own feelings.

CHAPTER XIV

I called on Vengeance; at the word
She came.
>   SIR EUSTACE GREY.

The letter of Miss Falconer contained an allusion to an approaching festival, which she characterized as a '4th of July jollification.' This day was already rendered sacred in the affections of Americans; and the prospect of a speedy and successful close to the battle of independence had disposed them, throughout the whole confederacy, to signalize its recurrence with all the pomp and glory of observance. The spirit had awakened even in the precincts of Hawk-Hollow; and the villagers, taking advantage of the patriotic offers of Captain Loring, had made extensive preparations to celebrate it among the solitudes of that lovely valley. They assembled in public meeting, appointed committees of arrangement, purveyors, marshals, and masters of ceremonies; and that the occasion might not pass without a due share of national glorification, they selected an orator, who, it was universally supposed by all his friends, would electrify the souls of his auditory by a display of impassioned and heaven-inspired eloquence. It happened, however, that the appointment of Mr. Jingleum to this honour had disgusted the adherents of another candidate; and the consequence was, that, in the end, there were two different celebrations, held at different places, one in the village itself, which being more convenient to the mass of citizens, was much more numerously attended than the rival jubilee in the Hollow. Indeed, the spirit of faction running very high, there were found so many arguments against holding the convocation at the latter place, that the current of public opinion soon set decidedly against it, and it promised to be quite a failure. It was indeed but thinly attended; although circumstances arose to give it an *éclat* entirely wanting at the other.

The gentlemen of the committee, finding how matters were going, redoubled their exertions, and by adding preparations for a *fête champêtre* to those for the more public object, succeeded in awakening an interest on the side of the female portion of the community; so that, as the day drew nigh, they began to hold up their heads and boast aloud, that, go the day as it might, the beauty of the country would be found displayed only in the valley. The scene of festivity determined upon was the little promontory at the mouth of Hawk-Hollow Run, and the river-bank at its base, where were such green plots as might have enticed fairies, as well as mortal women, into the joys of the dance. A small piece of ordnance was dragged upon the promontory; the venerable habitation of the fishing-hawks was tumbled about their ears, and the tall and naked trunk that supported it, converted into a gigantic flag-staff, from which the striped banner was seen waving as early as the afternoon of the 3d. A scaffold some five or six feet in height was also erected around the trunk, and a tribune, or orator's desk, with seats behind it, constructed thereon; the whole forming a rostrum suitable to the occasion, which the good taste of the supervisors caused to be canopied and adorned with branches of laurel, that were also wreathed around the tree almost to its top. The whole of the day preceding the celebration was occupied with these and other preparations, in most of which the painter contributed his personal assistance with great zeal. He had consented, after first flatly refusing the honour, tendered him at the instance of his friend the poet, to accept the appointment of reader of the Declaration, with the pronouncing of which sacred instrument the exercises of such a celebration are always begun; and although, on many occasions, when his auxiliaries were all as busily occupied as himself, he betrayed a strong disposition to desert, and betake himself to the distant mansion, there was no one, when all were assembled together under its roof, sharing the hospitality of the Captain and the smiles of his daughter, who exhibited a more disinterested anxiety to hurry all back again to their duties.

The evening came, and the preparations having been completed, the bustling Committee-men mounted their horses, and retreated to the village, leaving Gilbert's Folly to solitude; for not even Herman returned to it that evening. But an unexpected guest made her appearance, an hour after night-fall. As Catherine sat musing on the porch, perhaps moralizing, as she watched the spark of the fire-fly, now struggling in the moist grass, now flitting among the oak-boughs, and traced the resemblance it seemed to figure forth to the life of man,—a tissue of linked light and darkness,—a bolder beam flashed along the park, the roll of wheels was heard on the gravelled avenue, and before she had time to wonder or surmise, a carriage stopped at the door, and in a moment she was clasped in the arms of Miss Falconer.

"Brava for my dear self!" cried the lady; "my generalship is complete—I take even my friend by surprise! Wo therefore to my enemies! for this is a part of my practice. *Eureka! Eureka*, Kate! as the old philosopher said, when he discovered what the little fishes knew before him: I have discovered the enemy, and to-morrow I will take him! Never trust me if Congress do not order me a vote of thanks for my doughty services.—Where's your father?"

"Sleeping in his arm-chair," replied Catherine, confounded by the vivacity of her friend's expressions; "tired with entertaining so many people, and being so much on foot; and I believe he would have gone to bed, except for Mr.—that is to say, Monsieur Red-Jacket."

"Hang Monsieur Red-Jacket!" cried Harriet, quickly: "If he is here, get rid of him,—I've a thousand things to tell you.—Not here, then? but coming? Shut up the house, and fasten the doors—no admission to any superfluities to-night. And pa's sleepy, too? Pack him off to bed, dear Kate; tell him 'tis ten o'clock; or wait till we get the carriage away, and all quiet, and don't let him know of my arrival; we'll surprise him in the morning. I tell you, you unconscionable girl, I have such a secret to relate!—a secret so big and mighty, that I have been more than half dead with keeping it already!"

Ardent as were the lady's desires to escape the welcome of the return for that night, she was doomed to a disappointment. The bustle of arrival broke the Captain's slumbers, and he rushed into the porch, after a host of domestics bearing lights, expressing his rapture that 'his dear Harry' had arrived at such a lucky time; "For," said he, "we've laid in two hundred and fifty charges for the six-pounder, and we'll have such a roaring racket as has never been heard this ten years; and there's Tom Terry, the trumpeter,—was regularly brought up in the troop school, and blasts a charge to make your blood boil! and there's the drums and fifes! and there's my boy Haman to read the Declaration! and, by the lord, now I think of it, there's the Battle of Brandywine and Tom Loring dying! There never was such likenesses painted by mortal man."

The Captain yawned fearfully while he spoke; but his enthusiasm was fast dispelling his drowsiness. Miss Falconer groaned in spirit; but woman's wit came to her assistance. She imitated his example, opened her lovely mouth, with an expressiveness his own could not resist, exclaimed, "Oh, how tired I am!" and concluded by vowing she could not keep her eyes open, but must retire to rest forthwith. In this manner, she succeeded in escaping to Catherine's chamber, whence she immediately expelled both Phoebe and her mother, charging the latter, as the Captain had also signified his disposition to retire, to lock up the house, and admit no visitors to disturb her or her companion.

As soon as these instructions were given, she turned to Catherine, and cried, with extraordinary eagerness,

"The man with the red hat! that fellow that helped the painter out of the brook,—what has become of him?"

"I know not," replied Catherine, surprised at the question.

"What! has he never been seen in Hawk-Hollow again?"

"Really, I know not—I have never heard: I suppose not."

"Oh, you poor owls! blind birds that you are!" exclaimed Harriet, laughing, yet preserving an earnest air: "I believe, if Beelzebub himself came riding into the valley, nobody would suspect him to be a bad Christian, provided he kept his tail in his coat-pocket. As for the cloven hoof, he might wear that naked; no one would think of looking at it. And Gilbert, the Hawk of the Hollow? have you heard of him no more?"

"Oh, there is some idle rumour among the people, but I think it foolish. But, Harriet, you got my letter, with the advice I gave you? You must know, I had that from a sensible person I was obliged to take into the secret"— —

"Good Heaven!" cried Harriet, in alarm, "you have not told any one? Catherine, how could you? This may ruin all."

"I do not know what it is to ruin, Hal; but it will not ruin by betrayal of the secret. Mr. Hunter is"— —

"Mr. Hunter!" exclaimed Harriet, in as much wonder as dismay. "What! Red-Jacket? a stranger, a vagabond dauber, to be made the repository of such confidence! Really, Kate, you will drive me mad. How could you be so insane?"

"These are severe rebukes, Harriet," said Miss Loring, "and perhaps, in my case, they are just and well deserved; but you will not be so harsh with Mr. Hunter, when you know him better. He is a gentleman, Harriet,—in every particular, a high-minded, honourable man. On his good will and friendly co-operation, I knew I could rely; he was shrewd, sensible, and had seen one individual you inquired after; I had no other person to look to for advice. I acted with my best discretion, Harriet, and for your sake."

"Well, don't pout now," cried Miss Falconer, throwing her arms round her neck. "Soldiers—that is, generals,—as Harry vows, are ever pestilent scolds; and you must lay my shrewishness to the door of military impulses. The thing can't be helped; I don t blame you; if Red-Jacket be really a sensible fellow, why there is no harm done; and, as I said before, I'll patronise him; and if the matter be not blown already, in good truth, he will not have time left him to do mischief. But now for my story—and know, Catherine, in the first place, you are surrounded by cut-throat tories,—by skulking refugees,—by the Hawks of Hawk-Hollow!"

"Sure, Harriet, you are raving!" cried the Captain's daughter, in affright.

"It is as true as that the stars are shining above us," said Miss Falconer, her eyes flashing with a soldier-like fire; "and to-morrow, when you look only for mirth and merry-making, you will perhaps see—ay, Kate, *see* them fight their last battle. It is well you had me to watch over you, you poor cowardly mouse; or you might have been scalped and murdered, a week before your wedding-day. But all's safe, Kate; so leave trembling, and put yourself under my protection. To think we had that blood-stained demon so near to us, when we were talking about him! Nay, to think we had him in the house here, and my brother and myself standing hard by! Truly, Kate, had I known him, and could have laid my hand on a pistol, I should have fired it at the audacious monster—though I have no doubt, I should have hit some one else. That vagabond, malignant-mouthed villain with the red hat—who would have dreamed that blood-coloured covering was on the head of Oran Gilbert?"

"Impossible, Harriet! Remember, that he was in the house here nearly an hour,—that Green, the Indian trader; and at that very moment, the party was chasing the true murderer beyond the river."

"Nonsense!" cried Miss Falconer,—"nonsense and ignorance together. Listen to my story, and talk no more of impossibilities."

She then proceeded to relate, that, having recovered from the shock and confusion of mind produced by the sudden intelligence of her father's mishap, she began at once to gather all the information she could in relation to the outrage, and rack her ingenuity to penetrate the mysteries that attended and followed it. The information communicated by Lieutenant Brooks in relation to the fugitive of the white horse, though it added to the perplexities of others, threw a gleam of light upon her active imagination. It has been mentioned that this young officer, while in full pursuit of Nehemiah, had lighted upon a certain pedler who had, but a few hours or moments before, exchanged horses with the parson,—a piece of traffic which the trader was then bitterly lamenting; for though he confessed he had received a reasonable 'boot,' or consideration, he declared he was never more cheated in his life, the horse being knocked up and almost wholly worthless, as any one, he said, might see; he had been thrown off his guard by the holy character of Nehemiah; "for who," said he, "would think of being cheated by a parson?" He was very desirous, so great was his rage at the imposition, to guide the party himself after the cheat; but his horse being incapable of keeping up with the others, they were fain to receive his instructions, and leave him behind.

Two suspicions instantly entered Miss Falconer's brain; first, that in the indignant pedler, the pursuers had found and suffered to escape, the very rogue they were seeking; or, (and the second conjecture seemed to her the more rational,) that they had lighted on some agent he had despatched across the river for the purpose of misleading the avengers, he himself assuming a new disguise, and boldly remaining in the Hollow, until the hue and cry were over. She could give no particular reasons for turning her suspicions upon the Indian trader, save that his fierce countenance and savage bearing had made a strong impression on her imagination; and as she did not for a moment dream that the assassin could be any other than Oran Gilbert, she was as ready to discover his identity in the person of Green as in that of Nehemiah. In all this there was evidently, as Catherine in fact perceived, a degree of confusion and hallucination in Miss Falconer's mind. The idea had seized upon her, and it was impossible to shake her faith in the conception. It was in vain that Catherine urged the impossibility of merging the gigantic bulk of Nehemiah in the more moderate proportions of the trader. Her mind was made up; on that persuasion she had governed all her actions; and the result satisfied her that she was right, as the events of the morrow would show to the whole world.

She went on to relate, that, having communicated her suspicions to Lieutenant Brooks, as well as her belief that the bold outlaw would soon gather about him all the disaffected of the country, and strike some unexpected blow, that he instantly declared his readiness to sift the matter to the bottom, and at once devised a scheme that had already satisfied himself and his superiors of the justice of her monitions. A certain private of his own company, a man of bad character, but of the most crafty and daring spirit, had been selected as a fitting instrument; and, after a singular course of duplicity, which she related at length, had not only discovered that a band of refugees was already formed in those deserted solitudes, but had intruded himself among them. He had managed to communicate with his officers through *her*; he had discovered that the band, which was scattered in squads through the country, was actually commanded by Oran Gilbert; and though he had never yet set eyes on this redoubtable chief, he had heard and communicated enough to prove that he and John Green the trader were one and the same person. He had discovered, also, that one object of the rising was to be the rescue of young Asgill, the British guardsman, then under peril of suffering, by the mere law of retaliation, for the execution of Captain Huddy, mentioned in a previous chapter; after which was accomplished, (and until then no danger was to be apprehended,) he did not doubt they would begin to burn and murder, according to the usual system of tory tactics. One effort had been already made by the desperate partisan, single-handed, to rescue the young prisoner, while riding out on parole; and this was only defeated by Asgill's firm refusal to dishonour the pledge he had given his enemies. It was designed therefore to carry him away by force, which might easily have been done, so much license being allowed him in riding out for exercise, had not the communications of Parker (for such was the bold agent's name,) put the keepers on their guard. By the same hands, she had been informed of one haunt of the outlaws, at which Parker was himself posted, and where he pledged his soul to yield up the tory captain on the day of the approaching festival, provided the instructions he gave should be implicitly followed by his officers.

She then drew, from among divers other mystic-looking documents, a scrap of dirty and crumpled paper, which she declared, with a laugh, was the last epistle she had received from her new and highly esteemed correspondent, which was as extraordinary in style of writing as in appearance, being obviously the production of a rude and illiterate soldier, making unusual efforts at composition on account of the dignity of the correspondence and the character of the correspondent. It began by styling Miss Falconer 'Honourable madam to command,' and ended, after a postscript, in which he showed a discreet regard for his own safety, by cautioning the lady to 'let all the boys on duty remember the two rabbit-tails he was to wear in his hat,'—'as a sign for to be known by, and not shot at by accident; for, these vagabond refugees being uncommon crusty cut-throats, there was no use in being banged at on both sides,'—and by 'hoping, as before, that her honourable madam was well, and begging her pardon for singing a soldier's song,—

'God bless George Washington, God d——n the King!'

and was dated on the '29th June, if I reckon right, in the year of our Lord, Anno Domini, 1782.'

It was stated in this precious epistle, that the different squads were to meet on the 4th July, at a general rendezvous within seven miles of Elsie Bell's tavern; but for what purpose he could not divine; they were, however, to meet their captain there. The place he could not describe; but as he was ordered, with six others, to take post in it two or three days before the 4th, he promised, on the night of the 3d, to deposit a letter containing a full description of the place, together with his final instructions, at a certain spot near the park-gate, which he described with a soldier's precision. There was much other matter in the scrawl, which Catherine only read so far as to satisfy herself that this bold traitor had laid a scheme for surrounding the whole lurking party; and Harriet assured her, that his advice had been followed to a letter, that, at that very hour, a strong force was marching thitherward from the army, and would be, by sunrise, perhaps earlier, in command of all the escapes from Hawk-Hollow.

"Besides this," she cried with triumph, "you will see some visitors among the feasters you have not dreamed of,—Harry himself, Mr. Brooks, and Captain Caliver, at least,—to receive the instructions of the last letter.

That, Kate, we will seek at the dawn of day: see how methodically my martial swain discourses of the place of deposit:<'p>

> "'It's a spot you can't miss,—but to be certain, you should start from the middle of the gate, facing right towards the house,—march nineteen steps, then halt, face to the left, dress, and fetch five steps and a half more, which fetches you to a bush that has a sweet smell, with long leaves, notched like a saw,'"— —

"My bush of sweet fern, as I live!" cried Catherine, in whom the revealments of her friend had produced an agitation bordering on terror.

"Do you know it, then? Good luck to my trusty Parker, knave though he be. I have promised him a hundred guineas for his services; and, o' my word, I'll make papa double them. Can't you lead me to the bush to-night? But no—he may not yet have sought it out, and the sight of persons stirring in the park might frighten him away. Come, Kate, out with the light; we must sleep fast, and be up early: I will rouse you at the first gray streak of the dawning, I warrant me; for I shall be dreaming of the matter all night. Oh, that letter! that letter! if a maiden adoring looks for the billets of her swain with more anxious impatience than I do for honest Parker's greasy hieroglyphics, sure am I, I should myself soon die of expectation, so soon as I got me a wooer. Oh, lack-a-day, Kate, kiss me, and good night; for I think we have talked evening into midnight."

Anxious as was the lady's desire to fall instantly asleep, she was doomed to a disappointment. Scarce had she murmured out the last good night in the arms of her friend, when a sudden strain of music woke in the outer air, mingling the jangling of strings with the hum of a thousand nocturnal insects, flitting among the trees. Surprised, nay, almost startled at the sound of a guitar (for such her practised ear instantly knew the instrument to be,) in a region so remote and unsentimental, she raised her head from the pillow, and had soon the satisfaction of hearing an agreeable voice, manly yet capable of much tenderness of expression, added to the instrument.

"Oho, Kate," said she, "do you hear that? Now suppose my mad confederates should have stolen a march upon me, and, in their zeal, made the dawn of the 4th out of the midnight of the 3d? They say, Mr. Brooks sings well and plays—but, foh! I never heard that voice before—I was dreaming. Listen!"

She held her peace, and hearkening with no little curiosity, was able to distinguish (a window of the chamber having been left open to admit the balmy night-air,) the words of the following little serenade.

THE WHIPPOORWILL.

I.

Sleep, sleep! be thine the sleep that throws
Elysium o'er the soul's repose,
Without a dream, save such as wind,
Like midnight angels, through the mind;
While I am watching on the hill,
I, and the wailing whippoorwill.
      Oh whippoorwill, oh whippoorwill.

II.

Sleep, sleep! and once again I'll tell
The oft-pronounced, yet vain, farewell:
Such should his word, oh maiden, be,
Who lifts the fated eye to thee;
Such should it be, before the chain
That wraps his spirit, binds his brain
      Oh whippoorwill, oh whippoorwill.

III.

Sleep, sleep! the ship has left the shore,
The steed awaits his lord no more;
His lord still madly lingers by
The fatal maid he cannot fly,
And thrids the wood, and climbs the hill,
He and the wailing whippoorwill.
      Oh whippoorwill, oh whippoorwill.

IV.

Sleep, sleep! the morrow hastens on;
Then shall the wailing slave be gone,
Flitting the hill-top far, for fear
The sounds of joy may reach his ear;
The sounds of joy!—the hollow knell
Pealed from the mocking chapel-bell.
      Oh whippoorwill, oh whippoorwill.

"Mighty well!" exclaimed Miss Falconer, so soon as the roundelay was finished. "That is one of Jingleum's madrigals, I dare be sworn; for there's the 'ship' and the 'steed' in it; and I never yet saw or heard of one of his compositions that had not a touch of salt water and the saddle. And so the dear ape has got to singing, has he? and he mourns the merry marriage-bell, the goose-cap! Really, I had no idea the youth had so good a voice."

"You are mistaken," said Catherine, who, Miss Falconer almost suspected, was asleep, for she did not lift her head from the pillow, and rather muttered out the words than spoke,—"it is the young gentleman,—Mr. Hunter."

"Hah, indeed!" cried Harriet, quickly: "And *he* has got to chains and chapel-bells, too? But, pho, I forgot you told me about his singing. This serenading, though, is somewhat presumptuous. Well now, good youth, get you gone, and let us to our slumbers. I'll rouse you, Kate, I warrant me.—Why, good heaven, what is the matter? Crying again, Catherine! Sure, if I spoke roughly to you, Kate, I did not mean to offend you; and you must remember, it was on my father's account I became so suspicious, and averse to strange advisers and confidants."

She did not doubt that Catherine was brooding over her former hasty and reproachful expressions; and she knew her too well to be surprised, when the maiden replied to her apology only by flinging her arms round her neck, and sobbing on her bosom. Before she could attempt to soothe her, the serenader again struck his instrument, and began chanting a melody of extreme sadness, but to words of such mystical purport, that they instantly engaged her whole attention, in an eager desire to penetrate their meaning.

> Shall I speak it to the night-wind?
>   Shall I breathe it to the sky?
> It is spoken in a whisper,
>   It is uttered in a sigh:
> And the sigh shall be the saddest,
>   And the whisper shall be low,
> Like the sound of hidden runlets,
>   In their melancholy flow.
> There's a sigh comes on the west wind—
>   Hark! it rustles through the leaves,
> Like the moan——

But here the artist abruptly ceased singing; his voice and the sound of the instrument were as suddenly hushed as if annihilation had on the instant rapt him into the world of spirits. Miss Falconer sprang from bed, and ran to the window, hoping to discover the cause of so extraordinary an interruption, but without any success. A sable cloud, gradually stealing up from the west, and at intervals glimmering with faint flashes of lightning, had invested the heavens, and all was darkness, especially under the lime-trees near the window, from which the music proceeded. She thought, at first, that she heard the murmuring of voices, as if the singer had been arrested in his task by the coming of a second individual; but they were low, and so mingled with the rustling of leaves, that she doubted if her ears had not deceived her. She peered through the curtains and the vines that encircled the window, into the darkness, without being able to detect any thing like a moving figure; and she listened with as little effect for the sound of voices or footsteps. Whatever had brought the serenade to so abrupt a close, it was certain that it was over, and that the singer had departed.

"Perhaps," she said, as she again threw herself into the couch, "the tender youth is afraid of the rain; and in truth, there was a drop fell upon my hand. So much for spoiling a lady's rest, good Red Jacket! I hope he may get a ducking before he reaches the hovel. This is rather an odd sort of a man for a painter. Good night, Kate—now we will sleep in comfort and quiet."

CHAPTER XV

"I do not like thee, Doctor Fell;
The reason why I cannot tell,
But I don't like thee, Doctor Fell."

Anxiety, expectation, and perhaps an unusual degree of restlessness on the part of her friend, who soon fell asleep, kept Miss Falconer awake until a very late hour; and when she opened her eyes, after a short and uneasy slumber, she found a streak of sunshine playing on the window curtains. She started up hastily, yet so softly as not to discompose the Captain's daughter, with regard to whom she seemed to have altered all her resolutions. She arrayed herself with such celerity and silence as indicated a desire to escape while Catherine yet slumbered; and indeed it appeared, that, so far as the sleeping maiden was concerned, Miss Falconer had changed her feelings, as well as designs. She eyed Catherine occasionally with a countenance on which suspicion seemed struggling with anger; and when she had completed her toilet, she stole up to the bedside, and surveyed her with a look of anger, which was the more extraordinary as Catherine, at that moment, presented an appearance of the most attractive and, in fact, seraphic beauty. Her hands were clasped together under her chin, as if some thought of rapture were shining through her spirit; a smile of such delight as can only come from a heart both guileless and happy, beamed from her visage; her lips moved, as if breathing the accents of joy, though no sound came from them; and the tears that stole from beneath the closed eyelids, were evidently shed in pleasure, not sorrow. Miss Falconer's countenance darkened, as she gazed; but she gazed only for a moment; and soon stealing from the bedside, she crept out of the chamber.

The rattling of the latch, as the door closed, dispelled the dream of delight, and Catherine instantly arose, and prepared to follow her friend, whom she had in vain called after to return. Miss Falconer had already left the house, and long before Catherine reached her, she saw that she had found her way to the memorable bush of fern. She saw also, without explanation from her friend, that some singular accident had defeated, at the very moment of its accomplishment, the plan so subtly laid and so zealously pursued. No letter or scrap of any kind was found in the appointed place; yet it was evident the bush had been visited by at least one, perhaps by two persons, in the course of the night. It was deranged and torn; two flat stones were found lying at its roots, which Miss Falconer did not doubt had been designed to protect the paper from the dews of the night, as well as the eyes of passers-by; and there were foot-prints in the grass, some of which were very distinct, having been left since a light rain, that had fallen during the night.

The chagrin and dismay of Miss Falconer at this unlooked for termination of her hopes, entirely drove from her mind the recollection of her late displeasure, together with its secret cause. She wondered and lamented, and devised a thousand suppositions for explaining the phenomenon, but without satisfying herself. Was it possible the treachery of her agent could have been discovered by his comrades, at the very moment of its consummation? Could such a discovery have been made by accident, and in the dead of the night? What now was she to do? how supply the information of which she had been robbed? how act upon that already received? how avert the ridicule of the coadjutors she had drawn into her schemes? how propitiate her brother?—For sure he had not ceased laughing at her, from the hour he was let into the secret, and would make it the theme of raillery to his dying day.

To the latter questions Miss Loring could frame no answers; but in regard to the former and more important, she expressed her doubts whether the agent had really visited the appointed place at all. It was *not* probable he could himself have found his way to the bush at night, or that another should have followed him to it. The marks of footsteps were, in all likelihood, left by some of the patrons of the jubilee, collecting shrubs and flowers to adorn the rostrum—her garden had been thrown open to them for the purpose, and, she doubted not, they had already despoiled it. What was more probable than that some of those persons, returning from the house to the promontory, should have nosed the sweet-smelling shrub, as they passed by, and appropriated its leafy honours, along with those of other plants discovered on the way? Parker might yet come, and deliver his communication in person; or perhaps he found it impossible to escape the vigilance of his wild comrades, now rendered doubly watchful by the gathering of so many people in their neighbourhood. It was plain that Harriet must now give up the prosecution of the scrutiny into the hands of more fitting agents. If there were refugees in the land, a single word could convert the assembled revellers into soldiers, who would instantly scour the hills in every direction, and rid their peaceful solitude of such dangerous intruders; and if the companies and officers Miss Falconer had spoken of, had taken position in the woods, a general rising of the people must result in the capture of perhaps the whole gang. It was plain, at least, that the wisest plan to be followed was, to remain in tranquillity, until her military friends arrived; when it would remain for them to determine what further steps were to be taken.

The frustration of her sanguine hopes threw a shadow over Miss Falconer's spirits, and plunged her besides into a fit of peevishness, which she, before long, indulged to an extent that both surprised and pained her friend. Thus, her father making his appearance the moment they returned to the house, and, so soon as he had expressed his joy at seeing her, declaring she should see 'his excellent young dog, Hunter, the painter, the greatest genius and most capital fine scoundrel in the whole world,' she let fall certain expressions of scorn that might have stirred the Captain's choler, had his mind not been wholly occupied with 'the grand picture,' which it was now in his power to exhibit. The painter had laboured with much zeal, and, three or four days before, had brought his sketch to the mansion, to receive the father's and daughter's criticism on what had been done, as well as to introduce the Captain's figure; and he was easily prevailed upon to accept his patron's invitation, and continue his labours, until the sketch should be completed, on the spot.

Notwithstanding her dissatisfaction of mind, Miss Falconer could not deny, that, so far as he had gone, the artist had exhibited no little skill in the design and execution of his piece. It represented the young hero lying across the knees of his father, while Catherine knelt at his side, her hands clasped between those of her dying brother. A dead horse, a young oak-tree, shivered by a cannon-ball, a broken gun-carriage, and two or three other characteristic objects, made up, with this group, the fore-ground of the picture; while the back-ground, to which little had been yet done, was sketched over with hills and trees, and a confused medley of contention— broken columns of men, flying horses, and wreaths of smoke. With the three portraits Miss Falconer was very much struck; she had the vehement testimony of Captain Loring, and the melancholy assent of his daughter, in regard to the likeness of the expiring youth; and she could see with her own eyes, how well the painter had succeeded with both the others; though, as Captain Loring averred, 'he did not like so much red on his nose;' "and as for the tears that the young fellow has put into my eyes," he exclaimed, blubbering as he spoke, "why that's all nonsense, for I never shed a tear in my life—adzooks, I didn't!"

As there was a violation of the unity of place in the introduction of Catherine upon the battleground, so also there was an evident anachronism, which the painter had been guilty of, in depicting her, not as a little girl, as she was at the period of her brother's death, but a woman, such as she now appeared. The fault, such as it was, was easily pardoned, since it perhaps allowed a wider scope for expression; and on this visage, it was obvious, the artist had exhausted his skill. Independent of its beauty, it had such an air of deep grief as almost conveyed the history of the after life and feelings of the subject—secret sorrow, and a sense of lone, unfriended destitution, never to be banished a moment from her bosom.

While the three were engaged surveying the sketch, the painter himself entered the apartment. Piercing, almost fierce and menacing, was the look with which Miss Falconer regarded him; and her recognition of his salutation was haughty in the extreme. She observed, too, with high displeasure, with what frank and almost eager haste Catherine extended him her hand, and how her voice trembled in the uttered welcome, as if it were bestowed upon one endeared by long years of friendship; and she turned upon Catherine a look that almost frightened her from her propriety, when the latter, leading Hunter up, to present him with a more ceremonious form than her father had thought fit to use, said, as if to bespeak her good will at once,

"This, Miss Falconer, is my good and valued friend and *confidant*," (she strove to pronounce the word archly,) "Mr. Hunter."

"It is very well," said Harriet, turning coldly away, and fixing her eye upon the picture. "I am admiring his work, and striving to understand it."

"I do not pretend to be very perspicuous," said the painter, disregarding the mortifying reception and the perhaps equally ungrateful sarcasm. "Mystery is said to be an ingredient in the sublime; and as that is my aim, *of course*, (it belongs to the aspirations of all youthful candidates for immortality,) I always contrive to be as full of mystery as possible."

To this speech, which was uttered with an air of pleasantry, Miss Falconer only replied by a second penetrating stare; and then fixed her eye again upon the sketch. The painter, determined not to find offence where it was palpably meant, resumed his discourse, saying,

"I am afraid that my foolish music, last night, may have disturbed Miss Falconer. I forgot she had a right to be fatigued after her journey, until the plash of a rain-drop in my eye, as I lifted it romantically to heaven, brought me to my senses, and, ludicrously enough, in the very middle of one of Mr. Jingleum's best pieces."

"You knew, then, that I——Oh, certainly! the carriage rattled by Elsie's door. I am sensible of the compliment, sir, and return you my thanks."

These expressions Miss Falconer uttered with much vivacity, and began the question which she ceased so abruptly, in a voice of eagerness. Indeed, she felt that she had been almost thrown off her guard; and she therefore, without any purpose, except to divert the attention of those present to another subject, and certainly with no definite object in view, said, laying her finger at the same time on the sketch,

"I do not well understand this tree, sir. What kind do you call it?"

"Oh," said Hunter, with a smile, "that is a palm."

"A *palm!*" cried Miss Falconer, eyeing him with surprise; "and pray, sir, how came a palm on the hills of the Brandywine?"

The question threw the painter into confusion, which was increased by the keen and searching glances of the critic, over whom this third violation of propriety seemed to produce as strong an effect as the detection of it did on the unlucky artist.

"A palm! good heavens," he stammered, with a laugh; "and I did not myself discover the incongruity before? Ah, Miss Falconer, you are the very princess of censors; and I am glad you saw the fault, before it might have been too late to remedy it. But 'use doth breed a habit in a man,' as the great poet says; and painters are only flesh and blood, after all. This comes of taking my first lessons in painting, among the lagoons of Carolina. I must look close: I warrant me, I have stuck a live-oak into the picture also."

"Really, sir," said Miss Falconer, whom the opportunity of playing the critic seemed to have put into a better humour, "I must beg pardon for my ignorance. I thought that in Carolina we had no palms, except cabbage-trees; and this has a marvellous soaring, long-leaved, cocoa-nut appearance, judging from the prints I have seen of that tree, for of the tree itself I am quite ignorant."

"You are right, madam," said the painter; "the cocoa-nut is, in every way, a much finer palm than the cabbage-tree; and for that reason, I have always been accustomed to take a painter's license with the latter, to make it as graceful and stately as possible. Painting, you know, is a sort of palpable poetry; and one must not be tied down too closely to nature."

"The cocoa-nut has an immensely long leaf, has it not?" demanded Miss Falconer.

"Full fifteen feet," said the painter, warming into enthusiasm; "and each one so much shaped like a great waving feather, that you might deem it a plume plucked from the wing of Lucifer, or some other colossus of demons. One can never forget its majestic appearance, who has once looked upon the tree."

"You have been, then, in the Islands?"

"Certainly, madam, yes;—that is to say, in my early youth, when the tree made a great impression on my mind. You may judge, therefore, how natural it is that I should amend our inferior palms by adding somewhat of the beauty of those that belong to the tropics."

"Oh, very natural," said Harriet; "but it is quite droll you should put one upon the Brandywine."

And with this indifferent remark she closed a conversation that seemed, even to the unsuspicious Catherine, to be somewhat embarrassing to the painter, though she was glad to find how quickly it dispelled her friend's peevish humour.

They were soon summoned to the breakfast table, to partake a hasty repast, previous to visiting the scene of celebration, towards which several merry-makers were seen directing their way, even at this early hour. Miss Falconer appeared surprised that the young man did not instantly take his leave; but she soon discovered he was there for the purpose of attending her kinswoman to the promontory, that duty having been expressly delegated to him by the Captain, who had accepted the honourable and highly responsible command of the six-pounder, and the three or four vagabonds who were to serve it, and had therefore duties of his own to look after. He soon deserted the table, saying he left his young painter 'to look after her and his Kate; his rogues were coming after the powder, and he knew they would shoot off some of their legs or arms, adzooks, unless he accompanied them back to the hill.'

In the meanwhile, Miss Falconer, discharging her hauteur and petulance altogether, talked freely with the Captain's guest, and appeared much interested in his conversation, and many obvious good qualities. But it was observable, that as her ease and frankness increased, those of Hunter proportionately fell, until he became visibly reserved, and almost silent. This mood, however, did not last long; and by the time the little party was on its way to the scene of festivity, he was as gay and spirited as ever.

CHAPTER XVI

> Then came the felon on his sable steed.
> THEODORE AND HONORIA.

The festival, so far as events allowed it to proceed, was rather a picnic, of a somewhat patriotic character, than a true national celebration; and such indeed it might have been esteemed, had it not been for the occasional roar of the six-pounder, and the ambitious din kept up by the muskets, and the drum and fife of a small company of volunteers, the only portion of the county military who could be induced to honour Hawk-Hollow with their attendance. Few, however, as were the persons present, they claimed to form in themselves the flower of the district; and rather rejoicing in than regretting the absence of the great multitude, they proceeded with zeal to despatch what was esteemed the business of the day, in order that they might the sooner advance to its pleasures. In fact, all interest in the proper business of celebration was soon found to be confined to Captain Loring, the officers of the day, and their immediate adherents and partisans; the greater number of revellers, both male and female, preferring to ramble about in groups along the river shore, rather than to sit in solemn expectation on the promontory, awaiting the beginning of the proceedings. There were more attractive charms to the mass in the grassy glades below, where attendants were busily occupied in preparing for the feast and the dance, some arraying stores of napkins and platters along the course of the brook, and others matting together bushes and branches of trees, so as to form temporary canopies. In some places might be seen a knot of Sabbath-clad bumpkins, moving among the horses that were tied under the trees, and discoursing learnedly upon their good and bad points; in others, were collected divers rural beauties, admiring one another's bonnets, or exchanging, like merchants at a fair, their little stock of innocent scandals— the peculiar products of their respective neighbourhoods; and in one place, an amalgamation of the two interests was already effected, and a romping country-dance begun upon the green sward. Some idlers, incapable of any other exercise of their faculties, had begged pins of their cousins and sweethearts, converted them into minnow-hooks, and were already angling from the rocks; some, more gallant, were paddling their favourites about in canoes; some were singing; some rejoicing in the felicity of a jest; and in two different places afar off, was heard the screaming plaint of flutes, sounded by as many youthful followers of the Musagetes, who had stolen to their solitudes alone.

In the meanwhile, those who were most zealous in the cause which had brought them together, remained on the top of the promontory, whiling the time in conversation, until the moment should arrive fixed on for opening the rites of the day. The prospect from this elevation was extensive, and, at one spot, it comprehended a view of a horse-path sloping down the hills on the further bank of the river, which, in seasons of drought, like the present, was there fordable. It looked besides over a part of the valley, and afforded a clear glimpse of the public highway at a place near to the park-gate, where it ran over a hill. Both these roads possessed, on the present occasion, a peculiar interest in the mind of Miss Falconer, and she had chosen her resting place, with the view of keeping them always in her eye. She was followed to it by a select group, consisting, besides the Captain's daughter, of the painter, the orator of the day, Dr. Merribody, and a few of that immediate coterie. Her vivacity on this occasion was remarkable; but it was observed by many that there was a degree of restlessness and even uneasiness in her deportment, which were displayed in her frequent changes of conversation, and the piercing looks she occasionally bent on all present, as if in some sudden and short-lived fit of abstraction, that rendered her unconscious of them herself. These glances she bestowed more frequently upon her friend Catherine than any other person present; though some supposed they proceeded from solicitude; for it was now remarked that the Captain's daughter was thinner and paler than of old, as if suffering from some hidden or not yet fully developed, indisposition. There was an air of lassitude in her countenance and movements; and the bursts of merry humour that once marked her conversation, were now few and far between.

The individual who shared her piercing looks in the second degree, was undoubtedly the painter, with whom she carried on a conversation frequently very animated, and distinguished by a kind of malicious ambition, no one knew why, unless it proceeded from sheer good will, to betray him into inconsistencies and contradictions. She took occasion to recur to the subject of the serenade, and requested him, with many compliments, to resume 'the pretty little ditty of the Sigh and the Whisper,' as she called it, which had been so abruptly terminated on the preceding night by the rain-cloud, and the request being backed by that of others, he very good-naturedly consented to sing, objecting however to the lay in question, that being entirely of a serenading character, and therefore unfit for chanting by day-light. "Instead of that," said he, "I will sing you the song of *River, O River*, which always brings back the dear Pedee to my recollections." And so saying, with but little of that hemming and coughing, which we have good authority for esteeming the 'prelude to a bad voice,' he immediately sang the following little roundelay, turning his eyes the while, with a mournful earnestness, upon the Delaware, as if *that*, by a turn of prosopopoeia, was made to supply the place of the Southern river.

I.

River, O River of light! whereon
    The eyes of my youth were cast,
And many an idle hour and day
    In mirth and joy were past;
Still bright and quiet thou flowest on,
    As flow'd my earlier years,
Without a ripple, save those that rise
    Beneath my dropping tears.

II.

River, O River! the trees still shake
    Their leaves in thy passing tide;
And the nodding flowers the glass'd flowers see,
    That mock them as they glide.
'Twas thus, even thus, in ages gone;
    But others,—alas, all flown!—
Were wont to sit on thy gray old rocks,
    Where now I rest alone.

III.

River, O River! thy charm is gone,
    For those that gave it are fled;
And the thoughts thou wakest are dark and sad,—
    The thoughts of the distant dead.
None of them rest where they should rest,
    By the waters they loved to see;
And thy green banks a grave shall yield
    To none, unless to me.

IV.

River, O River! my lady yet
    Walks on thy verdant shore;
But though she smiles on thy bright blue waves,
    She smiles on me no more.
I will not look on thy happy tide,
    Nor list to thy breeze's stir,
When knowing, however she sighs by thee,
    Another sighs with her.

A deep sigh came from the breast of Jingleum; but before it had reached any ear but his own, Miss Falconer fixed her eyes on the singer, and asked him, with much inquisitorial emphasis,

"Pray, sir, how came those 'gray old rocks' into the Pedee?"

"*How!*" echoed Herman; "Truly, I know not; that is a question for a geologist."

"Really, sir," said the lady, maliciously, "I am surprised they should be found in the Pedee, which, I have heard, rolls through a quagmire."

"You are right, Miss Falconer. The Pedee *proper* is without rocks; but the Yadkin, which is the upper portion of it, and mountainous, has as rugged a bed as any other river. But allow me to say,"—this he uttered with a smile of triumph, as if aware of her desire to catch him tripping,—"you appear to suppose the song commemorative of my native river; whereas, if I can believe the poet, my friend Mr. Jingleum, it relates entirely to the Delaware before us."

"Ah! I forgot—I thought you were speaking of the Pedee; and I longed to show my knowledge of geography," said the lady. "But, hark, sir; there is the roll of the drum; the volunteers are cocking their pieces, the Captain is just priming the artillery, and now we shall have the signal for beginning the ceremonies.—I hope, sir, you have well studied the Declaration?"

"I have, madam," said the youth, who seemed to discover something offensive in the bantering question; "and, however incompetent to the task of pronouncing it with eloquence, or even effect, I believe there is no one present who has given it more thought than my own unworthy self."

At the signal thus indicated, the various truants on the river-bank were seen thronging hastily up the hill, and the orator, reader, and officers of the day, immediately ascended the rostrum. Before the preliminaries were all completed, an exclamation from Captain Loring, who had mounted with them, drew the eyes of all across the river.

"Soldiers, by the lord! adzooks, soldiers!" he cried, and the patriots beheld three horsemen, in military attire, riding down the horse-path on the opposite bank of the river. "Look, Harry, my dear, look!" continued the Captain, eagerly; "'tis our brother Harry, I'll be sworn! Could tell him among ten thousand. Sits his horse like a general; and a wonderful handsome dog—and, see, he is waving his handkerchief!"

But Miss Falconer was at this moment staring at another object in a contrary direction, of more attraction even than her brother. She beheld a single horseman, riding slowly along the road by the park-gate, wending his way towards the cottage of Elsie Bell, and apparently too much wrapped up in his own reflections to bestow a glance, or even a thought, upon the scene of commotion presented by the promontory. The distance of the road was at least a mile; but it was easy to perceive, first, that the man was mounted upon a white horse, and, secondly, that his head-gear was of a flaming red colour,—two circumstances that filled both the eyes and the heart of the gazer with fire. She turned her face to the rostrum, on which Hunter was already displaying the record of a nation's enfranchisement; but interrupted his proceedings without ceremony, crying eagerly,

"You have a painter's eyes, Mr. Hunter—do you know that man on the road yonder? A red hat, I think?—a rawboned horse?—An acquaintance of yours, Mr. Hunter?"

"An acquaintance?" echoed the painter, with a look of surprise. "At this distance, it is impossible"——

"Mr. Jingleum, what say you?" cried Harriet, hastily; "or you, Mr. Pepperel?"

"The midnight oil, Miss Falconer," murmured the modest bard; but was interrupted by the lawyer, saying,

"It is necessary, before arriving at a conclusion, to examine into the premises; and before deciding upon this matter, I should like to have, not only the evidence of my own eyes, but the evidence of the eyes of other persons," — —when he was, in turn, silenced by the sudden exclamation of Dr. Merribody.

"I know the fellow, as well as I know my own patients," he cried, pursing his eye-brows together; "'tis that scoundrelly quack fellow, John Green, the Indian trader; and I hope he may come here before night, that somebody may get drunk and trounce him."

"Bravo!" cried Miss Falconer; and turning towards the river, she waved her handkerchief, as if to hasten the advance of her martial friends.

"Nonsense!" cried Hunter, eagerly, but manifesting some little agitation. "What! Green, the good fellow that pulled me from the brook? Nonsense, doctor; that man is twice as tall; and besides, he rides quite a different horse."

"I'll stand up to it," said the doctor, with dignity. "As for his horse, why these traders are always buying and stealing; and there's his red hat, as clear as a bunch of sumach, the red-headed villain! But never mind any such vagabonds: read away, Hunter, my boy, and let Jingleum begin; for I am as hungry as a horse-leech, and I long to be at something more substantial than all your confounded orations."

"Hang the reading," cried the painter, petulantly; "let us see what's in the wind first.—We should at least be civil to the army officers: you see, they are regulars; and, there, they have given up their horses to old Richard, the coachman, and are running up the hill, like three hounds after breakfast.—Rogues, you will be sorted! and fair Britomart, you shall this time wave the lance of cunning in vain!" The last expressions were muttered within the recesses of his own heart.

In the meanwhile, the three officers, ascending the hill quickly, were met by Miss Falconer, who flew to meet them, crying, "To horse, gentlemen, to horse! the game is riding into your very arms."

These words were heard even at the rostrum, and filled all present with surprise; which was not much allayed, when the youngest of the three martialists, seizing upon Miss Falconer's hand, exclaimed, with a laugh,

"Egad, sister Hal, we have resolved to convert you into Prince Hal, and make you Tory-taker General. Here's my friend, captain Caliver, who admires your abilities at strategy immensely; as for Brooks, why, gad's my life, he is your Grand-Vizier. But where's our dog Parker? and what news of those vagabond Hawks of the Hollow? Where's the thief, Joram, or Oram, or what d'ye call it? Ah, Captain Loring, my excellent friend! Ah, Miss Loring! ah, Miss"— —

"Brother," cried Harriet, with an energy that startled all present, "you have no time for compliments. Accident has repaired the injuries of accident, and fate has thrust him you seek into your very hands. Mount, gentlemen, mount!—Mount, all who have horses, and ride up the ravine to the witch's cottage: the volunteers, and all our friends here who are on foot, can run across the fields, and secure the road, so as to prevent retreat. The man in the red hat, and with a white horse,—the canting Poke, or the sour-mouthed Green—all is one for that; seize him, and you seize the most audacious of traitors, the most ferocious of assassins!"

"Adzooks!" cried Captain Loring, "what's all this?"

"It means, Captain, egad," said young Falconer, grinning with pure delight, "that Hal here has been hunting your famous Hawks, till she has found them; and now, egad, if we can believe her, she is about to nab them. As for the road, sister, we have that safe enough, with twenty foot, and ten picked horse, coming down from the Gap; there are two companies, also, ordered to the village; and if you want more force, why we must e'en call upon the volunteers. The end of all this, gentlemen," continued the delighted lieutenant, "is, that you have a gang of refugees among you; and that their leader, Oram or Joram Gilbert, or whatever you call him,—captain Gilbert, they call him,—a very bold, murdering fellow, has just ridden by, as Miss Falconer says, and in a red hat, egad, and on a white horse, and with some dozen names or two; and so, gentlemen, we'll mount horse, and take him."

Had a thunderbolt darted from the blue sky among the group assembled on the hill, it could not have produced a more sudden terror, than did the name of the renowned refugee, with the announcement of his proximity to the scene of celebration. The name of the outlaw was familiar to all, as an omen of fear and blood; and while many of the young men re-echoed it after the lieutenant with open dismay, it produced such a general scream from the women as made the rocks resound, and added but little to the courage of their protectors. As for the lieutenant himself, he seemed to be vastly diverted by the general explosion of fright; though he instantly waved his hand to his friends, calling upon captain Caliver to mount, and waggishly directing his brother lieutenant to 'form the women and volunteers, and march them to the scene of action;' when Hunter, leaping down from the rostrum, exclaimed,—

"This is a mistake, an absurdity; I can assure Miss Falconer that the man who rode by is no more a Hawk of the Hollow than I am; at least, I am certain he is not Green, the trader, whom I will avouch to be an honest man."

"Let Mr. Hunter first avouch that for himself," said Miss Falconer, with a glance of fire; "the question will soon be asked him.—Quick, brother, quick! haste, gentlemen, haste! and all who can do nothing better, follow me up to the road-side."

Perhaps the singular sarcasm the young lady thought fit to fling at the painter, was unheard by him,—for finding that, despite his remonstrance, the officers were running down the hill towards their horses, he uttered a sudden shout, and immediately imitated their example, bounding along at such a pace that he soon outstripped the fleetest.

In a moment, the assembly was broken up, and the revellers flying in all possible directions. Here were seen women running to conceal themselves among rocks and bushes; and there one or two prudent gentlemen, who declared themselves 'men of peace, and no fighters,' paddling across the river, to get out of harm's way, with but little regard to the beauties they left screaming after them on the shore. But the torrent of fugation, though it sent off so many irregular rills, was seen dividing into two chief currents, one of which, consisting principally of mounted men, went, like the back-water of a flood, rolling up the ravine leading to the Traveller's Rest, while the other, consisting of such volunteers as had not already broken and followed after the officers, and such worthy celebrators as had the courage to imitate the example of Miss Falconer and Captain Loring, made its way on foot towards the public road.

CHAPTER XVII

> Thorough brake, thorough brier,
> Thorough muck, thorough mier,
> Thorough water, thorough fier,
> And thus goes Puck about it.
> DRAYTON — Nymphidia.

It has been seen, that if the painter made an effort to restrain the enthusiasm of the multitude, he instantly proved that he was not without the virtue himself, so soon as he found it was really determined to pursue the suspected person. The horses of the officers had been led round the hill to the covert where the others were tied; and towards this place he directed his steps, crying out all the time, with encouraging alacrity, "Quick, gentlemen, quick!"

But the strongest proof of his zeal he gave, the moment he had reached the horses, by vaulting upon the back of the nearest, (and, in his estimation, the best,) which happened, at that moment, to be in the hands of the venerable coachman, Richard, who was leading the animal round with a degree of solicitude and attention, that were testimonials enough of its value. Herman's lodgings being so nigh at hand, he had thought it wholly superfluous to trouble himself with his own roan charger; and the present emergency was of a nature so peculiar, he did not stop a moment to consider the lawfulness of the seizure. He leaped therefore into the saddle, jerked the reins out of Richard's hand; and the wrath of the owner, who was no other than lieutenant Falconer himself, was extreme, when he beheld the audacious stranger, his own loud calls to the contrary notwithstanding, bestride the captured steed with the air of an emperor, and instantly put him to his speed.

"Harkee, halt! stop! you've mistaken your horse," cried the lieutenant. "*Who* is that impudent scoundrel? My horse, you rogue! Give me a pistol, Caliver, and I'll shoot him off."

But the anger of the soldier was unavailing; the painter swept out of sight, and while Falconer was calling on his friend Caliver, (a gentleman of a weather beaten face, very lantern-jawed, and with a red nose,) he also darted forward and vanished. Nothing remained for him but to follow the example set him by Hunter; and accordingly, he seized upon the best charger he could find, and with his brother officer and others, galloped after the two leaders.

The reader may remember that the Traveller's Rest was described as lying at the upper termination of a ravine, which swept down to the river, and just before it debouched thereon, received the waters of Hawk-Hollow Run. From the promontory so often spoken of, the cottage was plainly visible, and approachable along the bed of the river, even by horsemen, provided they were of the steeple-chase order, or were moved by any occasion so stirring as the present. The obstructions and difficulties, nevertheless, were of a nature, to call for great circumspection on the part of the riders; and accordingly the greater number of pursuers began to exercise their discretion so soon almost as they had well set out. The two leaders, however, dashed onwards with fiery zeal, and performed feats of horsemanship that gained them the applause of the laggards. It was fortunate for Herman that his spirit and address soon won him the good will of the cavalry officer, (for such was captain Caliver) at his heels. He had remarked the seizure of his friend's charger, and at first meditated a wrathful reprimand. He succeeded in coming within speaking distance, as Hunter toiled up an ascent of unusual ruggedness, and instantly hailed him:

"Harkee, my friend," said he, "you ride like a gentleman, and a little training would fit you for the army: but do you know you have mistaken your horse?"

"Faith, there is no mistake about it," cried the painter, "for my horse was not on the ground. In such an emergency, sir—but enough. Are you armed, captain? are you armed?"

"Surely my holsters are at my saddle-bow," quoth the cavalry officer, spurring up, as he reached a more level ground, on which he could display all the qualities of his charger; "and as surely you will find Harry Falconer's at his, if you know how to use them. Harkee, my friend, I will not make so bold as to consider you in a fright; but you are quite white about the lips."

"Ay, true," said the painter, clapping his hand to the holsters, and drawing forth a weapon, but taking no particular notice of the soldier's insinuation: "Captain, had you not better draw up, and wait for some of the company, while I push on, and secure the road?"

"I vow to heaven," said captain Caliver, "I would knock you off your horse, did I not know you spoke in the ignorant innocence of your heart. Draw up, and wait for company? It is not in my nature to call any man an ass, except a private; and you are here, I think, as a volunteer. So, Mr.

Gentleman-volunteer, be pleased to look upon me as commander-in-chief, and attend to my instructions.—Do you know that Oran Gilbert, when you see him?"

"How should I? The Indian trader, to be sure, I know; and you will soon find, that this fellow of the white horse is no more like him than I am."

"Very well—Fall behind, Mr. Gentleman-volunteer, and"——

"I will do no such thing," said the youth, stoutly; "I will ride, fight, and kill refugees with any man in the county; and if you show me one, I'll engage to shoot him at sixty paces,—that is, with a good pistol,—I will, by the lord!"

And so saying, the volunteer brandished his pistol with such ardour that it suddenly went off in his hand, with a report that set the whole ravine roaring, and materially expedited the march of their followers, who responded with an instant cheer.

The captain of cavalry stretched forth his hand, seized Hunter's bridle, and was about to express certain rough suspicions which this untimely explosion created in his mind, when the painter cried out, with as much apparent innocence as confusion,

"Egad, I believe 'twas a hair-trigger!"

"Spur up, and no more firing," cried the soldier; "or by the eternal Jupiter, I'll knock you off your horse. You have alarmed the wigwam; see what a hubbub you have raised in the van, as well as on the rear! the tavern is in commotion. Hah! by the eternal Jupiter, there goes Red-hat! Spur up, gentleman volunteer; or by the eternal Jupiter, the fellow will escape!"

The report of the pistol had indeed reached the Traveller's Rest, and drawn forth its two or three inmates; who could now easily behold the whole train of horsemen dashing furiously up the ravine; and the quick eye of captain Caliver was not slow in detecting a person on horseback, with a red hat, pricking hastily away from the cottage.

"The game is sprung,—the rabbit is up!" he cried, while the fire that burned on his thin nose, seemed to have raised a kindred flash in his dark gray eyes. "Gentleman-volunteer, do you see? Now you shall behold the doings of Sky-scraper, the best horse for a long race on short fodder, that was ever galled by saddle. Up the bank here, and after!"

"You are wrong, captain, you are wrong," cried the painter, eagerly. "'Tis a white horse, you know; and this is a roan, or sorrel."

There could be no truth more incontestible than this; yet captain Caliver was of too sagacious a spirit, or perhaps was warming with too much fire, to be led from his purpose by an argument not of his own devising.

"I will be uncivil to no man but a private," he cried, fixing his eye upon the fugitive, (who was for a moment's space plainly visible, as he galloped up the road,) compressing his lips, till they actually seemed to have vanished, and, at the same time, driving his spurs deep into his steed; "I say, I will be rough-spoken to none but privates, for it does not hurt their feelings; but, by the eternal Jupiter, there goes our man!—or what does he mean by wearing a red hat? and, lastly, what does he mean by beating a retreat in such a fashion? Harkee, Mr. Gentleman-volunteer, I am glad now you fired that pistol. Had we come upon the dog silently, why then I should have picked him up, rolled up in a ball, like an opossum; which is a job for a black man, and not a captain of cavalry. I say," he continued, with increasing animation, "I am glad you have roused him, and shown him a fair field; for, by the eternal Jupiter, I have not seen a race worthy to speak of for two weeks; and, by the eternal Jupiter, you shall see such a one now as will make your blood run; and, by the eternal Jupiter, I hope his horse is blooded, for, by the eternal Jupiter, I will run him, or any other respectable tory gentleman, from time temporal to time eternal, from post to pillar, from Sunday to Saturday, and from life and the dinner-table to death and"———. And here the captain of horse, who was something of a horse himself when his blood was up, ended climacterically with a most soldier-like word, which, although it may be found in any English dictionary with which the public is acquainted, will nevertheless read more agreeably in a dictionary than any where else. He added, indeed, three more words; for turning his horse's head towards the steep bank that bounded the ravine on the right hand, he twisted a lock of the charger's mane round his finger, and uttered the cabalistic ejaculation,—

"Go it, Sky-scraper!"

The words had an immediate effect; no sooner did they reach his ear than Sky-scraper, with a plunge that carried him half a length ahead of the painter, darted to the brow of the acclivity; and Herman following, he beheld the Indian trader, (for it was this identical individual they were now pursuing,) some five or six hundred paces in advance, travelling at a very unusual pace up the highway. As Hunter reached the road, he cast his eye backwards to the hovel, and beheld, riding into the oak yard, a man whom he knew at once to be the person that had first attracted Miss Falconer's notice. He rode a white horse, and there was a red covering to his head; but this latter phenomenon, as it appeared, was owing entirely to the presence of a red handkerchief drawn over the horseman's hat, doubtless to shield his eyes from the sun-beams, or from the dazzling rays reverberated from a dusty road. There was nothing at all warlike in the appearance of this individual; on the contrary, he seemed, from his dress, to belong to the community of Friends; and he paused at the entrance of the yard, looking back on the chase he had left behind, with much innocent curiosity and wonder.

"Captain," cried the painter, at the top of his voice, "wheel about. You are leaving the true man: here he is, full in view, behind us!"

The captain answered only by repeating the charm that had already nerved the limbs, and fired the spirit of his steed; and Herman, urged by feelings and inducements of his own, followed after him; and in a few moments, the fugitive and his two pursuers were alike buried in a cloud of dust, raised by the fleet chargers.

When the two leaders so suddenly left the ravine, they were beyond the sight of those who brought up the rear; and these, not doubting they had continued their original route, galloped on themselves until they reached the little inn; where the first person they saw was a tall, middle-aged, gawky quaker, the same that had been seen by Herman, sitting astride his horse, and staring on them with gaping astonishment.

"Surrender, you villain!" cried Harry Falconer, with a whoop of victory; "surrender, you bloody Hawk, or I'll blow your brains out,—or I'll make Brooks do it, that scoundrel having run away with my pistols.—Hillo-ah-ho, Caliver!—What has become of the captain?—Down, you dog, and we'll tie you!"

"'Nan!" cried the astounded Friend: "What does thee mean, young person?"

"Death and Beelzebub!" cried Brooks, "What have we here? Why, old father Broadbrim, who the devil are you? Sure, I know this horse!"

"Sure thee may, and sure thee may not," replied Broadbrim, looking wrathfully upon his captors, who were evidently nonplussed at sight of him. "He is an honest man's horse, friend foul-mouth and sauce-box with the coat of the slayer on thee back!"

"The spot's on the wrong leg!" cried Brooks, who had been inspecting the stranger's horse with a curious eye. "Hah! d'ye see the dust on the hill? Some of you guard father Broadbrim; he's suspicious: we'll examine him directly. Hillo-ho, Falconer! I'll have you! oho! oho! oho!" and away darted the young officer after his brother lieutenant, who had galloped off so soon as he discovered the course pursued by the leaders.

By this time, all the young men present had grown warm with exercise, and were now waxing valiant, as they began to understand the little danger there was in chasing, so many of them together, a single refugee, who, although desperate and dangerous enough, had shown so little inclination to face them. They began to be apprized, too, of the nature of the service in which they were rather co-operating than compulsorily engaged; and all seemed to know, that the farther they rode up the highway, the nearer they would be to an armed force, marched into the county for the express purpose of ferreting out and destroying the band of outlaws. This being the state of their feelings, there were few of them willing to accept the ignoble trust of guarding the body of the Quaker prisoner; though, having had it urged upon them by the cautious lieutenant, they were loath to discharge him without authority. It was proposed by some to lock him up in the Traveller's Rest, and entrust the ward entirely in the hands of Elsie and her little negress; while others pointed to Gilbert's Folly as a safer prison-house; and some even talked of carrying him to the woods, and tying him to a tree, until the chase they were so anxious to share in, was over. The dilemma, such as it was, was already proceeding to altercation, when Broadbrim, having understood that they were in chase of a famous tory, proposed to ride with them in pursuit; adding with a zeal that delighted, as much as it astonished them,—

"A man of war am I not, neither a slayer nor a fastener of bonds, neither a firer of pistols nor a brandisher of swords and spears; yet, friend younker whom they call Andrews, if thee is the man to show me a tory who hath broken the law, then verily am I the man that will hold him hard and fast, till the law hath spoken with him; yea, verily, I am. Ride on, therefore, with whip and with spur; only swear not, and be not awroth; and do thou, friend Andrews, ride at my side; for my horse is a horse of peace and not a horse of war, sure-footed but slow, and peradventure I may be left behind. It doth not become me to say, I hate a tory, for a tory is a man, and hate belongeth not to a fellow creature;—but, verily, I have heard of the man called Oran Gilbert, the Hawk of the Hollow; and, verily, I should not like to be summoned on the jury to try him for his manifold crimes; for, verily, it would be against my principles to judge him to death, and verily it would be against my heart and conscience to let him off with aught less than hanging. So let me detain none from the good deed of catching the wicked man; and peradventure, if this animal beneath me hath any vigour left in his legs and reins, I may stretch forth my hand afar, and take the sinner by the nape of the neck."

The manifestation of such spirit on the part of Broadbrim, who seemed well prepared, so far as strength of arm and resolution of heart were concerned, to take even a huger man than the Indian trader betwixt his finger and thumb, determined the course of his sentinels at once. They gave a loud shout, and bidding him follow, rode after the officers as hard as they could; and it was worthy of remark, that the white horse, notwithstanding the hint the prisoner had given of his slowness, began gradually to warm into mettle and fleetness, so that before the race had extended many miles, he bade fair to outstrip his attendants altogether.

CHAPTER XVIII

> If you think I come hither as a lion, it were pity of my life: no, I am no such thing; I am a man as other men are:—And there, indeed, let him name his name; and tell them plainly, he is Snug the joiner.
>
> MIDSUMMER NIGHT'S DREAM.

Meanwhile, the party of footmen, consisting of some dozen or more of the volunteers, and such revellers as were brave enough for the exploit,—followed, or rather led by the valiant Harriet, who displayed the energy of a Penthesilea, and by Captain Loring, who forgot his lameness in the ardour of the moment,—succeeded in gaining the highway just in time to catch the most favourable view of the fugitive, as he thundered up the hill upon which they were themselves rushing. Indeed, they came upon him so suddenly, that when his ears, which as well as his eyes, seemed to be fully occupied in tracing the signs of pursuit, were surprised by the sudden shout they set up, the jerk which he instinctively made at the reins, brought his steed (a goodly roan charger, which was afterwards discovered to be the property of the painter) upon his hams, and had well nigh tumbled him in the dust. At that moment, the volunteers, in an ecstasy of excitement, raised their muskets, and fired together upon horse and man; so that, had there been any better ammunition in the deadly tubes than blank-cartridges, both must have been blown to atoms.

The appearance of the trader, as he rose up in his saddle, and looked upon the throng around him, apparently as much astonished at his escape from death as he was infuriated by such a display of mortal opposition, was wild and terrific; the broad red hat had fallen back from his forehead, disclosing his whole countenance; the eye with which he glared upon his opposers, had a certain ghastliness mingled with its fury, that was infinitely appalling; the retracted lips, exposing the set teeth, seemed widened into a grin that might have become the visage of a nether imp; and his hand, with which he had snatched up, and now brandished, a huge horse-pistol, could not have appeared more dreadful, had it been dripping with fresh blood. When it is remembered, that the whole throng were now impressed with the conviction, (a conviction which their reason had no time to question,) that, in this man, they beheld the most renowned and dreaded of the Hawks of Hawk-Hollow, and perceived that he had the life of at least one individual in his power, it is not to be wondered at that their courage gave way, so soon as they perceived him unharmed by the volley. In truth, they began to shout and fly; and even the volunteers waited no longer than to see the pistol aimed towards them, before they took to their heels as hastily as the others. It was in vain that Miss Falconer cried out, "Now is the time, gentlemen! seize him!" The only individual who thought fit to obey the mandate, was Captain Loring, who, having just hobbled up to the road, sprang from a bank, and before the rover had fired, or even raised up his steed, snatched vigorously at the bridle, roaring out,

"I've nabbed you, adzooks, you rascal!—Surrender!"

To this bold summons the demi-barbarian answered by turning his weapon from the flying assailants, and clapping it instantly to the Captain's ear; when a shriek from Catherine startled, or conjured, him out of his bloody intention; and instead of shooting the veteran dead on the spot, he struck him a blow with the heavy barrel, that brought him to the earth. He then uttered a yell like the whoop of an Indian; and the roan horse, leaping over the Captain's body, bounded beyond the crest of the hill, and was in an instant concealed from view.

The next moment, and almost before the terrified rustics had plucked the unlucky veteran from the road, the thunder of hoofs again shook the hill, and the captain of cavalry, looking almost as grim and terrific as the fugitive, was seen to shoot by, pronouncing his magical war-word, "Go it, Sky-scraper!" Then, at his heels, came Herman, the painter, who, without seeming very sensible of the presence of any earthly spectators, gave forth, as he passed, a bold and stirring hurrah, that almost made Miss Falconer reject as improbable certain wild suspicions that had already crept into her brain. Then came the lieutenants and their long train of volunteer followers, bestowing as little notice upon the individuals on the road-side as the others had done; and these defeated worthies were left to themselves, busied in restoring the Captain to his senses,—a desideratum, that, to the delight of all, was soon effected; for indeed the Captain's cocked hat had done him the service his gray hairs had not; and it was soon found, that, except his being thrown into a violent passion, he was none the worse for his misfortune.

"I'll have the villain's blood!" he cried, starting up in a fury, which he expended upon all around him without much discrimination. "What are you blubbering about, Kate, you jade? Adzooks, but I'll have the blood of the rascal! Hark ye, Mr. Doctor Merribody, and you Mr. Orator Jingleum, and the rest of you, and especially *you*, you confounded cowardly volunteers! what did you mean by not rushing in upon the dog, when I had him, you puppies? Adzooks, you white-feathered hen-bantams, I had sooner trust to a regiment of suttler's wives, in a bayonet-charge, than to any such poltroonery rascals, even in the small matter of taking a tory by the ears. Adzooks, you gallimaufry what-d'ye-call-'ems, is this the way you keep the Fourth of July?"

While the veteran thus poured forth his indignant rebukes, which he continued until his daughter succeeded in pacifying him, the captain of cavalry, followed at but a little distance by Herman, still pursued the chase with untiring ardour, now catching view of the fugitive as he flashed over the brow of a hill, but oftener losing sight of him altogether, so winding and broken was the road, and so deeply embowered by forest-trees. Caliver marvelled greatly at the excellence of the roan steed bestridden by his quarry, upon whom, after riding several miles, he did not seem to have gained an inch; but, in truth, the horse was of approved speed and bottom, the rider was himself a master of the art of horsemanship, and was besides, at least, a stone and a half lighter than his pursuer. He continued, however, to follow, cheering himself with the reflection, that, by and by, the appearance of the infantry, already posted on the road, must bring the fugitive to a stand. "And then," quoth he to himself, with a grim chuckle, "he must e'en turn about; and then, by the eternal Jupiter, I will shave off the top of his poll with my sabre, or shoot him through the gizzard with my pistol, according to circumstances. Go it, Sky-scraper; and don't let it be said of you, you were ever beaten, in a fair race, by a rascally refugee!"

As for the painter, he possessed but little of the unflagging spirit of his leader; and seeing there was small prospect of gaining on the trader, he soon became tired of pursuing, and began to devise in what manner he might, without loss of honour, discontinue the pursuit. First, then, having reached a wild hollow, where a little runlet crossed the road, and was immediately lost amid a labyrinth of great rocks, trees, and brambles, he gradually slackened his pace, until the cavalry officer vanished among the windings of the road. As soon as he had lost sight of him, he came to a full halt, greatly to the dissatisfaction of his borrowed steed, whose heart was already warmed for battle. Here the painter listened a moment, as if to gather some tokens of the approach of others. A few straggling shouts came to his ear from a vast distance behind. He hesitated an instant; the cries of pursuit came nearer. He then dismounted, reversed the saddle on the horse's body, gave him a lash and a shout, and away went the liberated animal, leaving his rider standing in the middle of the highway. Here, however, he did not long remain. Another chorus of shouts, coming still nearer, reverberated through the woodland; and without waiting for a fourth, the young artist instantly deserted the road, and plunged into the wildest and deepest part of the hollow.

And now appeared the two lieutenants, rushing vociferously on, with some two or three young men who were better mounted than others, close at their heels. Then, strange to be said, came the zealous Broadbrim, the spirit of whose lank steed seemed to grow with his exertions, and who had left the rest far behind. It was the destiny of this worthy personage, like the painter, here to end the labours of the day; but with this important difference, that, whereas the painter had relinquished the pursuit, because it was his will to do so, the quaker, on the other hand, terminated his career, because it was the will of his horse he should do so. In other words, this highly republican animal, having debated in his body (for, being a horse, he had no mind,) the absurdity of the burthen being all on one side, and reflecting, that, as he himself could not ride, there was no reason why he should be ridden, now began to broach his rebellious principles in the most expressive language he could make use of,—that is, in sundry curvets and escapades; the result of which was, somewhat to the astonishment of honest Broadbrim, that the magnanimous insurgent suddenly broke his base bonds, and fled away, whinnying with the delight of freedom, while his oppressor, after admiring the print his back had made in a spot by no means dusty, now sat down pensively on the road-side, and began to ponder his misfortunes.

"'The devil damn thee black, thou cream-faced loon!'" were the first words he uttered; and he uttered them with much sincerity of indignation. "Had the gallows been close by, thou ungrateful beast, I believe thou wouldst have been just as malicious. Wilt thou never be done thy tricks, White Surrey? Out upon thee, thou ass of a horse! I have helped thee out of all manner of difficulties, and, in return, thou never missest an opportunity of flinging me into one. 'A horse, a horse, my kingdom for a horse!' Now am I in a quandary, like a fish in a net.—And suppose some one of these malapert blue-jackets should look into my saddle-bags, and pull out, one after another, first Tom Hunting-shirt, then long-tailed Nehemiah, then Will Tapes, the pedler, and then—and then, and then?—Hillo, you vagabond Hawk! you skulking tories, that have fern-seed, and walk invisible! where are ye? Now am I like a rat between six cats.—Come to me, and ye shall hear the words of grace, the comfortable and fructifying words, ye men of Belial, that hide your faces in woods and in desert places!—Hearken to me, friend Gilbert, whom men call the Hawk of the Hollow: does thee not perceive I am in great straits, and that I am thy friend in the spirit, and will hold thine enemies very fast and hard, and will peradventure strike one of them under the fifth rib, so that he die?—Out, you inhuman rascal! you captain Gilbert! come to my assistance, or,—'*paucas palabras,*'—I shall be hanged."

As the mysterious quaker proceeded in his musings, which he occasionally vented aloud, his looks, fixed mournfully on the ground, fell by chance upon a shrub-leaf close to the earth, the under surface of which was turned up, looking white and glistening among the green fronds. This he, at first, regarded with great indifference; but having observed it a second time, a thought entered his brain, which caused him to rise and advance towards it, to examine whether it had been deranged by the winds, by the foot of a beast, or by some more important agency. Its foot-stalk was broken; and divers decaying leaves beneath it were crushed into the ground. These appearances induced him to look about him with much care; and the search terminated in the discovery of several foot-marks in the damp soil, evidently impressed by a pair of moccasined feet, and that very recently. This discovery infused singular animation into his spirit, which was quickened by a sudden shout from the road behind. He sprang behind a bush, until the comer, one of his late sentinels, dashed by: then resuming the search, he found himself following a human trail, that led him into such a labyrinth of bog and bramble, as might have made him repent his presumption, had he possessed the grace to repent any thing. He persisted however with much resolution, and still made his way by the tracks, until the sudden appearance of a huge rattlesnake, bruiting under his nose, startled him out of his propriety and the path together. In a word, he soon proved himself to be no woodman; and, in the course of five or ten minutes' walk, was so completely lost and mazed among the depths of a wild swamp, as to have lost even the power of extricating himself.

"'Ay, now,'" said he, with a groan, "'I am in Arden; the more fool I; when I was at home, I was in a better place; but travellers must be content.'"

Then looking about him disconsolately, he perceived, through the trees, a little eminence, where he could rest himself, and whence, he thought, he might discover some path out of the wilderness. He proceeded towards it forthwith. It was a swell of land, on the summit very rocky, covered with beech and maple trees, and with an undergrowth of spice-wood and its fragrant sister, the sassafras. Among these he thought he heard the babbling of a little water-course; and this sound he hailed with satisfaction, for he was already tormented with thirst. As he passed up the hill, he stepped into a little nook, not above a dozen paces in circuit, enclosed by rocks and bushes, and so overshadowed by beeches as to form a thick-roofed grotto, on the floor of which sparkled a meager rill, flowing from a spring at the bottom of a rock.

An abrupt turn round a mass of protruding stone brought the wandering man of peace unexpectedly upon this scene; but before he had time to survey it, he was suddenly seized upon by an arm of iron, and hurled upon the ground. The next moment, a strong hand was at his throat, a heavy knee on his chest, and a long, bright knife gleamed like a flash of lightning before his eyes.

CHAPTER XIX

> That you are rogues,
> And infamous base rascals, (there's the point now,)
> I take it, is confess'd.— —
> May a poor huntsman, with a merry heart,
> A voice shall make the forest ring about him,
> Get leave to live amongst ye?—true as steel, boys!
>
> BEGGARS' BUSH.

"Speak—who and what are you? and what seek you here?" said the harsh voice of the conqueror.

The intruder looked up in his face with some wonder, and beheld the features of a man of middle age, very dark and fierce of aspect, with long black locks of hair hanging from his temples, wild, Indian-looking eyes, and a mouth expressive of as much inherent ferocity as was ever betrayed by the visage even of a red-man.

"Speak," repeated the apparition, impatiently, "or never speak more!"

To this the prisoner replied with less confusion of mind than difficulty of articulation,—

"Hark ye, Mr. Green, or Gray, or Black,—for a deuced black face you have!—or, if you like that better, Mr. Hawk-of-the-Hollow Gilbert, 'what is the reason that you use me thus?' 'I would be friends with you, and have your love;'—but not while I am on my back, to be sure. 'Call you this backing of your friends?' 'Slife, sir, take away your fingers, and let me up: I am Iago, the 'honest, honest' man. At any rate, be so civil as to consider, that, though your knee may find its cushion agreeable enough, my lungs do not."

"And what will they think of a knife in them?" cried the fierce captor, without relaxing his hold. "You were among the hounds that were hunting me!"

"Ay; and had they caught you, I should have been among the hunters that were hanging you,—provided they had not tucked me up first. Hark ye, friend Hawk, I should have known you better, had you stuck to the gray whig; I remember you of old, Mr. Green, the trader. I am an honest man; ask

Sir Guy Carleton else; if he don't know Ephraim Patch, who is just as honest as myself, why then ask him about one Leonidas Sterling, an old friend and correspondent of his worship at Philadelphia. 'Slife, sir, I tell you I am a true man."

"Give me some proof, and I will release you. Trifle with me, and you are a dead man."

"Put your hand into the right pocket of my vest," cried the prostrate sufferer, "and you will find it."

The conqueror did as directed, and drew forth a guinea.

"You asked for proof," said the other, with a grin, "and there you have it! Were I a rebel, you would have found naught but a roll of beggarly continentals; had there been more, I should have been an honest quaker, and neither rebel nor tory. Are you satisfied? I came here to seek you, and save my neck, which is in danger. There are men among the rebel officers that know me; and to be known, sir,—'by these pickers and stealers,' 'tis true!—'twere as good as a word to Jack Ketch, under the sign and seal of a State governor! Captain Gilbert, I come to volunteer my services under your command; and the sooner you introduce me to your rascals the better."

"Rise, and behold them!" said the refugee, leaping to his feet; and friend Ephraim Patch, or Mr. Leonidas Sterling, as he had called himself, looking up, beheld to his extreme surprise, for he knew not how they got there, two men standing hard by, in green hunting shirts, with each a hatchet in his hand, as if ready to use them, and countenances grimly forbidding.

"'The earth hath bubbles, as the water has!'" he cried,—"'Peas-blossom! Cobweb! Moth! and Mustard-seed!' 'I cry your worships' mercy!' Your hands, gentlemen: I am as honest a scoundrel as any of you, though somewhat more unfortunate."

"Honest or false," said the refugee, giving a sign with his hand, on which the two instantly stepped from the den, and were concealed among the bushes, "it signifies but little to me. You are among friends, if you speak true; otherwise, among hangmen.—Your name is Poke?"

"'That's he that was Othello'—a poor servant of the word, an expounder of the book, a sower of good seed on the way-side," said the Proteus, in the tones of the quondam Nehemiah.

"You are Tapes, the pedler, caught stealing through the American lines at Morristown, and in good hopes of dying on an oak-tree?"

"True for you, captain Gilbert!" cried the other, with a stare; "but where did you learn that? Hah! I see! the roguish refugee that assailed young

Asgill's guards, while he was riding out on parole, and would have plucked him out of the bonds of Egypt, had not the fool gripped tight to his honour, very much as a drowning man hugs a ship's anchor, at the bottom of a river, and so remained in captivity.—What, captain! was that one of *your* clap-traps?"

"You are the impudent scoundrel who has been cutting throats, and laying them at honest men's doors? cried the other, without regarding the question.

"Softly, captain—a mere matter of accident."

"And, moreover," said the refugee, sternly, "you are the masking, blundering meddler, who has twice drawn the hue and cry after myself?"

"Verily, so it appears," cried Sterling; "but now that we have met at last, we shall play no longer at cross-purposes."

"What seek you here? Why have you returned to a place where your life is in danger?"

"Zounds, sir!" cried Sterling, stoutly, "you ask questions enough to puzzle a regiment. But here is my whole story,—the history of my deeds, dangers, and desires. I am a gentlemanly scoundrel and unfortunate man, like others that shall be nameless; and after seeking my fortune in divers parts of the world, and making a grand sensation on the boards of the regimental theatre among Howe's officers at Philadelphia, I e'en consented to take service under the King, and therefore staid behind, when he ran away, and have been ever since a particular confidential correspondent of the royal generals at New York."

"That is to say, a spy?"

"Why, if you like the word better, e'en use it; the more elegant word is, correspondent. I am told, you have an excellent friend in Congress, a certain Colonel Richard Falconer"——The refugee's brow grew as black as midnight——"Well, sir, this gentleman is e'en an excellent friend of mine also; and having somewhat of the cunning of the devil in him, became busy, one morning, and entirely ruined my fortune and reputation together; in other words, he discovered and denounced me, threw me into prison, and volunteered to help me to paradise. I broke jail, concealed myself for a time; until, one night, accident drove me into his presence. I found the good-natured gray-beard alone, studying my case as hard as he could, and out of my own papers! I am quite a peaceable man, captain, 'yet have I in me something dangerous;' I became choleric, and finding a sword hanging up just at my hand, I took the liberty of thrusting it into his gizzard."

"Fool!" said the refugee, grasping him by the arm, "the throat is the only true place!—But, hark ye," he added, abating the wolfish sneer that accompanied his words, "you robbed as well as murdered?"

"Ay, 'by St. Paul,' I did," said Sterling, with infinite composure; "having declared war, I made free with the spoils of victory; and the Colonel's purse has lasted very well, all circumstances considered; though, wo's me, that say it! besides the guinea in my waistcoat pocket, there are but two more remaining, and they on the back of White Surrey. Concerning White Surrey, you must know, he is a devil born, like yourself,—I mean to say, myself; fleet of foot, untiring of spirit, and nothing against him but his ugliness and starved appearance, and, by the lord, some touch of the Marplot, especially in times of trouble. I could not think of leaving him behind me; and I was on my way to the rogue he called master, with a whole theatrical property-room on my back, when I stumbled in the dark on my friend Falconer. You must know, I had a woodman's dress on"———

"Hah!" muttered the refugee: "it was not all conscience, then?" Then changing his tone, he continued, "You have said enough. You have sought to escape, and find yourself unable?"

"Ay; and hearing the Hawks of Hawk-Hollow were out again, I even took counsel from despair, painted White Surrey's legs over again, and came hither to throw myself among them. Faith, I knew Hawk-Hollow would be the fairest place to seek them in. I volunteer, captain, I volunteer; but I hope you have a stronger force than Moth and Mustard-seed? I volunteer, and, by the lord, I am ready to go into action as soon as you order. But would to the lord I could catch White Surrey.—Harkee, captain, can you hide a man, at a moment's warning, out of the sight of a gallows?"

"Ay: there are dens hereabout deep and dark enough for a royal refugee to take his rest in."

"Hark ye, captain; give me a carbine, and I'll do you a service. I have heard," he added, with a shrug meant to be significant and confidential, "of that matter betwixt Falconer and your black-eyed"———

"Villain!" cried the refugee, seizing him by the arm, and giving him a look that curdled his blood, "you are venturing upon a subject that will bring the knife to your throat! Pho, you are a fool;" he added, checking his impetuosity, and grinning,

'A strange, uncomely, jawbone smile;'

"we are Christians here, and we forgive our enemies."

"Forgive?" cried Sterling, "come now, captain Gilbert, that's slippery. I know you better; and I know you have been wronged."

"You are deceived," said Oran Gilbert, laying his hand, with another ominous smile, on the volunteer's shoulder, "I am not an Indian, but a white man, and as you may have seen, forbearing and forgiving. They have told you, (for they have told the same to *me*,) that I am a wolf's whelp, an eater of men's flesh, and a drinker of blood; and that I never pardoned an injury, though I had grown gray thinking of it. Lies, lies all! I can walk by my father's house, and see the sons of his destroyer sitting in the doors; and yet carry myself like the best Christian of them all: I can be told, too, even by a foul-mouthed dolt like yourself, how shame and sorrow, came into the house, and afterwards death,—and yet feel no hotter for vengeance. All this I can do, because I have a bad memory for matters twenty years old, or more.—Look you," he continued, dropping his tone of irony, and adopting that of menace; "I can forgive treachery as old as that; but I remember a nave's trick a full year. If there be any deceit in you, look well to yourself during that time. You were better to have been hanged as a spy, than to come to me as one.—You shall see!"

"'Slife, sir!" cried Sterling, "you have no consideration for a man's honour!"

But while he spoke, the refugee had raised his finger to his lips, and drawn forth a low whistle; which was almost immediately answered by the appearance of the two individuals who had been in the covert before.

"Bring up the prisoner, and let the men follow," said Gilbert; and they immediately retired.

"Prisoner!" cried Sterling, in surprise, "Male or female?"

"You have volunteered your services among the royal refugees," said Gilbert, turning again to Sterling, and displaying a sardonic grin: "you shall be put on duty forthwith.—Have you ever killed a man?"

"Dozens of 'em!" replied the other, promptly; when seeing the tory stare in surprise, he fell into a laugh, saying, "That is, not in your barbarous, blood-thirsty way; but in the heroic, poetic, dramatic manner: in which mode I have also fought divers battles, from Bosworth Field to Dunsinane. No, captain, as to the real red-paint, as we call it on the boards, I have shed no more than a lamb, save in the matter of my friend, Colonel Falconer; but I am in the mood to learn: I have had a great appetite for war and glory come on me of a sudden. Hark ye, captain: my friend Falconer's son was one of the chasing party, and by and by he will be returning to the Hollow."

"Ay!" said the refugee; "what then?"

"I like that doctrine of the savages," said Sterling, with an amiable smile, "which teaches one who has a wrong to revenge, how unnecessary it is to be particular as to the individual he is to retaliate on. Now the son, I take it, is a good substitute for the father; and to my mind, it would be a pretty thing to lie behind a bush on the road-side, with a musket or pistol, as he passed by, and then,

> 'Like a rat without a tail,
> To do, to do, to do!'

Now, supposing, as my commander, you should order me to such a service, why,—'*sessa*, let the world slide,'—I should obey; that is, provided you stood by, to help me to one of those dens deep and dark enough for a refugee to take his rest in."

"If the young ape has done you a wrong," said Gilbert, coolly, "shoot him the first opportunity. You will have a chance by and by. You say, your horse is good and swift?"

"The best, were it not for his deviltry, ever bestridden by a gentleman in trouble. And then, captain, the ungrateful scoundrel (sure I might have escaped a dozen times, had it not been for my concern for him!) has all my munitions of war upon his back,—some six or seven coats and wigs of approved manufacture, a pair of pistols and a stage-dagger, a gold sword-hilt and two new tragedies in manuscript, a pair of green spectacles, and a horn pair uncoloured, a bottle of good brandy, a bible, a copy of Shakspeare, a fiddle, and my friend Falconer's two guineas."

"You must recover him," said the tory captain: "but now for duty. You shall see how treachery is rewarded by the royal refugees!"

As he spoke, there came into the den eight men attired like the two first, who were included in the number, all of them with green stuff shirts, edged and furbelowed with wolf, raccoon, and other skins, leather leggings and moccasins, and fur caps with hawks' feathers sticking in them. Each bore a thick rifle in his hand, and had a long knife in his pouch-belt, as well as a light axe suspended, quiver-wise, over his shoulder. They were dark, fierce-looking men, and perhaps an unusual degree of sternness was communicated to their features by the fearful duty they had now in hand. They led with them, or rather carried, for he was bound hand and foot, a ninth man, dressed in many respects like themselves, though he wore an old military hat, and was without leggings or moccasins. His countenance was as rude as those of the others; but instead of exhibiting the same cold and stern resolution, betrayed a look of dogged sullenness, mingled with anxiety.

As soon as he was brought into the little inclosure, he was tossed, with but little ceremony, at the feet of the tory captain, the band forming a circle around,—each, as if by previous concert, drawing the tomahawk from his back, and resting his left hand upon his rifle.

"Oho!" said Sterling, looking into the prisoner's face, "whom have we here? 'By this light, a most perfidious and drunken monster!' 'Most reverend seignior, do you know my voice?' 'Oho, my sprightly Scot of Scots, Douglas, that run'st o' horseback up a hill perpendicular!' Why this rascal was he, one John Parker, a soldier on the lines, that nabbed me, being too drunk to understand the claims of my coat to better treatment. Oh, you vagabond, I knew you would come to the gallows!"

"Raise him on his feet," said the tory leader; then turning to the volunteer, he drew from his bosom a soiled and crumpled paper, which he put into Sterling's hands, saying, with a sternness that was perhaps assumed to cover the shame he felt at his own ignorance,—

"Read it.—Our merry men here can make nothing of such pothooks. Read it aloud; and then we'll proceed to judgment."

The volunteer obeyed, and succeeded in deciphering a scrawl, of a style of composition and penmanship so similar to that Miss Falconer had shown the Captain's daughter, that, had he ever seen the latter, he could have been at no loss to identify the correspondent. It was brief, and clear, and to the following effect:

> "Honourable Madam to command—
>
> "This here is the letter what I promised to put under the bush; and I put it this night, the 3d of July, in the year of our Lord, Anno Domini as before. The rendezvous is a place called the Tarrapin Hole, a swamp on the east of the road, six or eight miles above Captain Loring's. You turn off from the road at a place where a fresh blazed beech tree grows by a rock; but the path is astonishing twistified, and not fit for horse, but can be surrounded. I had some thoughts of deserting, for I reckon some of these dogs is suspicious; but that might throw them into a panic, and so drive them to the hills, where the devil himself (begging pardon for swearing) could not find them. They say the captain (that's the Hawk) is in the village, or to be there to-morrow, when it would be easy to take him—(remember the red hat; as for the horse, there is no depending on that, for he has 'em scattered all about in depots;) and then the rest is nothing, seeing as how they are in some of a panic already, as not knowing what is

to turn up. Howsomever nevertheless, there's one thing I've found out quite astonishing; and that is, that our lieutenant, a most impudent chap as ever you saw, walks about openly, and lives at the old widow Bell's, and"— —

"Hah! enough!" cried the leader, suddenly snatching the epistle out of the volunteer's hands. "Have we more traitors than one among us? Who has forgotten orders, and told secrets to new men?"

"I, captain," said one of the men, breaking silence. "This here John Parker and myself were boys together in Monmouth; and so, for old companion's sake, I was more free about the lieutenant, and other matters, than stood in orders, not thinking there could any harm come of it. But I knock under to punishment, seeing the man has been betraying us all, and am ready to do justice on him with knife, rope, hatchet, or rifle-butt; though it goes ag'in' my conscience to take a man that's tied up like a shambled ewe."

"Cut the thongs from his legs," said Oran Gilbert, "or slack them a little. John Parker, I give you three minutes to pray. What, Tom Staples, have you never a rope here that might serve the traitor's turn?"

"I have been twisting one all the morning," said the man who had spoken, displaying a sort of cable constructed of the shreds of a blanket; "for I hoped it might be *that*, rather than knifing."

"Good Lord!" cried Sterling, shocked by the sudden preparation for such a catastrophe, "you don't mean to hang the poor devil?"

The sound of a friendly and interceding voice seemed to thrill the baffled traitor out of his apathy. He stared at the pseudo-quaker, and at once displayed the reckless hardihood of his character, though his old friend Staples was at that very moment forming a noose in the rope, by laughing and saying,

"Well done, old Tapes, is that *you?* You're no Johnny Raw, I see; but you'll come to the acorns yet! Don't go for to make a fuss about the hanging; for, you see, it's according to law, and hanging's the word; and these here raggamuffin refugees must have their way; and so let 'em hang and be d— — d! that's my notion. But look ye, Mr. Captain Gilbert, and all you tories, and you Tom Staples into the bargain, here's a notion of mine: you see, you're come to the hanging too late, for all the good it is to do; for the thing's done up so cleverly already, you're just as good as dead men, you are, damme; for I've fixed you in a hole you can't creep out of without my assistance, you can't, damme. Now, captain, here's a bargain I'll make: you'll just spare my life, and drum me out of camp in an honourable, soldierly way; and, in return, I'll show you the way out of the trap; for, damme, comrades, you're surrounded: and so we'll square matters betwixt us, and say nothing more about it."

"Peace, rogue," said Oran Gilbert; "were the whole army round us, you should have your dues. String him up to the oak tree."

"Well now, captain," said Parker, "that's what I call being unreasonable. But some of you give me a drink at a canteen, for there's no use being strung up thirsty: and, Tom Staples, give me your cuffers, in token there's no ill-will between us; and let's have a quid of tobacco to chaw on.—Hark! there captain! do you hear? The road's in a swarm, I tell you! That, I reckon, was the squeak of captain Caliver; you can hear him a mile, of a clear day; and, you may depend on it, he'll have some of you, afore I've done kicking. Won't you hear to reason?"

The coolness of the man was, to Sterling at least, astonishing. They were fitting the halter round his neck, when a faint shout from the road was heard, but whether from a new batch of pursuers, or from the old ones now returning, could not be determined. He took the opportunity afforded by the sudden surprise to beg Staples 'to be in no such fool's hurry with his blanket, and slack it off a little, for a word with the captain.'

"Harkee, captain," said he, "it's the last offer I can make. Now let's argue the case."

"Up with the babbling fool!" cried Gilbert, who had been hearkening attentively to the sounds.

"You won't?" cried the hardened desperado—"why then here's my service to you, and the devil take us all to supper together.—Hillo-ah-ho! Murder! Refugees!—in the swamp here, quick!"

He elevated his voice to a yell that caused the very leaves to shake above him; and would undoubtedly have given the alarm he intended to those on the road, had not the refugee captain snatched an axe from the nearest hand, and instantly felled him to the earth. Then, giving his orders anew, the wretch, before he had recovered his consciousness, shot up among the leaves of an oak tree; and Sterling, who watched the whole proceeding with mingled admiration and alarm, could not trace a single writhing or quivering of limb afterwards.

"'Slife!" said he, "you killed the fellow with the hatchet! But, captain, concerning that surrounding; I don't like that"——

"Peace!" said the tory; "the first duty you are to learn is, to hold your tongue—the next, to obey." He gave the wild band a signal, and they instantly betook themselves to the bushes, or to hiding-places of which Sterling was ignorant. "This man came to me as a deserter, and was therefore trusted by one who should have been wiser: he has met his fate. You I can trust, because I know you are a doomed man like myself. You must recover your horse."

"Ay, faith; but how?—'Slife! what's the matter now?" he cried, observing his companion start suddenly at what seemed to him the whistle of a wood-robin, and look eagerly from the covert. The sound was repeated once, and once again; and then the refugee, turning to him, said,—

"You must claim him. Get you quickly to the wood-side, and follow on after the others, so as to recover him before they open your saddle-bags."

"Death and the devil! you are joking! What! run my head into the lion's jaws? and just to recover a vagabond horse, that flings me whenever the humour seizes him?"

"If you lose your horse, you lose yourself. We can be burthened by no footmen."

"Footmen? why I see no horses!"

"Ay: but away with you. Seek the men you came with, and return with them to Elsie Bell's."

"God bless my soul!" said Sterling, in alarm; "that young knave Falconer will smoke me in a moment."

"Knock him on the head then."

"And then the other lieutenant, that was so curious with the spots of White Surrey's legs! a marvellous shrewd fellow, I assure you."

"Why, do the same with him then; and stay not here babbling like a helpless boy. Protect yourself. Fear not: your present coat suits you better than the parson's. Return to Elsie Bell's, secure your horse and other property, and see that you feed him well; by midnight you will be called for, and placed in safety. Keep a firm countenance, as I think you can, and you are in no danger."

"Ay; but what excuse shall I make for leaving the road, and diving into these damnable abodes of refugees and rattlesnakes?"

"Tell them any lie you will,—your horse ran away with you into the woods, and then——Or stay," he added, looking grimly up to the body of the spy; "tell them you were seized by the Hawks of Hawk-Hollow, and that you saw them hang their tool. Bring them to the spot, and let them bury the carrion: it is good they should know what value we set on traitors. And, hark ye, tell them we mustered at least a hundred strong, and that we stole off across the road, swearing vengeance upon the village. Mind you, the village: make them believe we are marching to surprise it by night. Now, get you gone—off with you. Set your face to the west—there; walk onwards five hundred paces, without looking to the right or the left, and you will find yourself on the road. Begone, and look not behind you."

The volunteer perceiving that remonstrance with such a commander might prove as dangerous as it was really unavailing, turned to depart, but not before he had seen the refugee clap his fingers to his lips, and draw forth a whistle similar to that which had attracted his own attention. There was one injunction, however, which the retreating Sterling thought it entirely superfluous to obey. He had no sooner reached a spot proper for such a proceeding, than he came to a stand, and cast his eye backward towards the den. He beheld a light figure ascending the knoll among the bushes and under the embowering trees; and just before it vanished into the greater gloom of the grot, a sunbeam, peeping through the branches, fell brightly over it, revealing to his somewhat astonished eyes the person of that identical youth whose mysterious hints had been of such service in awaking the fears and stimulating the energies of the hard-beset Nehemiah.

"Zounds!" he cried, "have we any such gentlemanly fellows in the confederacy! Oho! I recollect now," he added, conning over the words of the letter,—"'our lieutenant, a most impudent chap as ever you saw, walks about openly, lives at the Traveller's Rest, and,'—ay, faith, there was something about that old fool, Captain Loring, and a girl. Very well, young one, you will be hanged like the rest of us!"

So saying, and murmuring other expressions of a similar nature, he made his way to the roadside, almost at the very spot where a *'blazed'* beech-tree flung its silver limbs over a rock.

CHAPTER XX

> If thou long'st
> To have the story of thy infamous fortunes
> Serve for discourse in ordinaries and taverns,
> Thou art in the way; or to confound thy name,
> Keep on, thou canst not miss it;
> Keep the left hand still, it will bring thee to it.
>
> The Roaring Girl, or Moll Cut-purse.

With a better fortune than had awaited the volunteer, Herman Hunter stepped into the grot; but with much less display of heroism; for he no sooner found himself in presence of the renowned Hawk of the Hollow than he bent his eyes upon the ground, and stood silent before him.

"You are come at last!" said the refugee, giving him a piercing look, and with a voice none the less expressive of indignation for being subdued to the lowest tones, as if he feared a witness even in the dead malefactor; "you are come at last; and the son of my father comes with my enemies and hunters!"

"So I come," said the painter, raising his eyes, and speaking firmly; "I come as the friend, who, having saved you from one danger, desires to rescue you from another yet greater. I warned you last night,—nay, I sent you word long since, that you were watched: I betrayed a confidence reposed in me by one it was a double duplicity to deceive, in order that you might escape the net that was secretly closing around you. Nay, I discovered the presence and machinations of the daring spy, who but this morning was selling you into the hands of your enemies; I found his letter, and left it where you were sure to obtain it."— —

"Ay; while you were yourself playing the fool among the Independents, and leaving me to the care of a stupid ploughman and a dotish old woman!"

"It was all I could," said Herman: "I knew it was better I should be on the ground, when the officers came. Had I not been there, to join the first of the hunters, as you call them, and to fire an alarm in the hollow, neither your own cunning nor the fleetness of the roan horse could have saved you from capture."

"It was bravely done," said the refugee, with a softer voice, "and it will excuse what is passed. Where found you this dog's paper? and how?"

"Near the park-gate, under a bush, where I saw the man hide it, as I approached the place by accident. This fellow knows all your haunts: will he not bring the troops to this very spot?"

The refugee laughed, and at that moment Herman heard a noise on the bough of the oak tree, as of some animal rending away the bark; and looking up, he beheld what he had not before seen in the gloom,—the body of the dead traitor swinging with a sort of jerking, convulsive motion, as if still alive. The rope had slipped a little along the bough, and though soon arrested by some knot or other roughness, it was some moments before the motion entirely ceased. The dreadful and unexpected spectacle of a man, who, it was evident, the painter thought, had made his escape, thus hanging dead before him, filled him with horror, and he exclaimed at once,

"Oh, Oran! Oran! it is this dreadful cruelty of spirit which has made you what you are,—which has made us all what we are! For God's sake, let us cut him down, and see if he be yet alive."

"He was stiff before the rope touched his neck," said Oran, grimly; "I never struck *twice* with the hatchet. Let him hang: he died the death of a spy and betrayer. I have invited the county to his death-bed!"

"Daring, as well as cruel! Why do you linger here? It is plain, you are surrounded: before the sun sets the whole county will be out; and, to-morrow, there will not be a den of the woods, or a hollow of the hills, left unvisited."

"Why, this is what I want!" cried the fierce outlaw; "the general has tied my hands to act only on the defensive; and here are forty devils with heads of iron and fingers of fire, that are lying asleep in the woods like winter bears, for want of something to warm the blood in them. I am ready."

"Ready to die!" said Herman, solemnly; "ready to throw away your life at the bidding of a master, or the prompting of an insane passion. Fly, while you yet may: the attempt to rescue young Asgill must be now fruitless, as it is needless—even the Americans say, his life is in no danger. Fly, then, Oran, and give up your bloody designs in this fatal Hollow. Hearken to me, Oran,"——

"Hearken to *me*," said the outcast, sternly. "Has your blood turned to milk, and your heart to water? Are your wounds healed, your bones knit, your strength restored, and do you talk of leaving Hawk-Hollow at this moment? What is this they say of you? You were among the foremost of the rejoicing fools at the Hawks' Nest—have you turned American?"

"I was born upon these hills; but I will not strike the friends and countrymen of my father."

"Will you strike his foes?"

"They are in the grave with him," said the youth, sorrowfully; "and he has forgiven them."

"They are upon the earth, and his spirit is not satisfied!" cried Oran, with the wild energy, and almost in the favourite language, of an Indian orator. "Have you rested under his roof? have you sat in his flower-garden? have you walked on his path by the Run-side? have you spoken with the people that drove him in his old age from his fireside? Hyland Gilbert! they broke his heart, and then trampled him to death. Will you not do him right and vengeance?"

"Oran!"——

"Changeling!" cried the refugee, with a scowl of savage contempt; "if you have not the feelings of a man, you have at least the gewgaw brain of a boy. Look!" he continued, drawing from his bosom, and displaying with a sneering grin, a roll of written parchment, decorated with the due pomp of martialness; "you begged for the toy that would make you a servant of the king; and here it is. Take it; and for the sake of a red coat and feather, do what you would not for the name and honour of your father."

Hyland—for the assumed name of the young Gilbert must now be dropped—recoiled from the emblem of distinction as much as from the frowning eyes of the speaker, but answered firmly,—

"When I was in the Islands, it is true, I desired the king's commission; and, it is also true, I left them to obtain it; and had I reached the royal army at my first landing, no doubt I should have accepted it. But it was my fate to be cast ashore far in the south; and I esteem it no bad fortune that I obeyed a whim of adventure, and made my way through my rebel countrymen (they are *ours*, Oran,) to this spot. I have thus been made acquainted with some of the principles on which this war is contested; whereby, I thank heaven, I have been spared the shedding of innocent blood in an unjust cause."

"Do you say this to me?" cried the refugee, with a wild laugh.

"Oran!" said the young man earnestly, "your heart is not with the side you have espoused; and fierce and cruel as may be your acts, they are, they must be, at variance with your conscience. A moment of fury drove you into a cause you abhor; and if you give the bloodiest proofs of your fidelity, you are impelled to them only by remorse and despair."

"You are a philosopher!" said the renegade, with another bitter laugh; "but we will play the fool no longer. Will you have the commission? See, it has the royal mark upon it!"

"Oran," said Hyland, mournfully, "after yourself, I am the last of my father's house. You ask me to do what has brought the others to their graves—to early and ignominious graves; and what, though you have been spared, has left you the prey of shame and sorrow. Why should I strike those men, who, besides fighting against tyrannous oppression, (such it was, Oran,) are also the children of the same soil—our countrymen and brothers?"

"You are the last of the seven," said the refugee, taking both the young man's hands into his, and looking at him with mingled affection and anger; "four of your brothers were slain—one of them hanged upon a gibbet—and all by 'our countrymen and brothers!' The fifth—look you, Hyland, the fifth—the second-born and the beloved, whose name was given you, that you might never forget him, fell in battle, saving the life of one of these—my countryman and my brother!"

The face of the outcast blackened, and Hyland trembled in his glance; he stepped out of the nook, and leading the young man along, conducted him up the hill to a place where a vista through the trees, looking over the green swamp, disclosed a glimpse of the blue ridgy cliffs of the Kittatinny, to which he pointed.

"Come with me to that mountain," he said, "and when you stand upon the summit, gazing to the right and to the left, you will look upon two graves. One of them lies in the desert, among the hills: I planted a pine tree on it, and you can see its blue head afar off. Do you remember who sleeps in it?"

"I do," said Hyland, with emotion; "it is my brother."

"And do you bethink you what laid him there?"

"His humanity and his noble heart."

"He died," said Oran Gilbert—"he died that a villain might live; and you call that villain 'my countryman and brother!'"

"No," said Hyland, with some of his wild brother's spirit; "I except *him*."

"Then look to the left," continued Oran, with a glance of painful humiliation: "on the brook, and in a little bower, there is a second grave."

"It is the grave of my poor wronged sister!" cried Hyland, impetuously.

"Of your sister, and of ——. Ha, ha! Is not this a merry subject for two brothers to talk on! 'My countryman and brother' destroyed her and fled."

"May heaven pardon him," cried Hyland; "but I cannot."

"We buried her in secret, and in night, that none might look upon her shame, or upon ours," said the refugee; "and that night came into the world her brother, whom we called Hyland, that we might better remember her destroyer."

"Oran! Oran!"

"Your mother," continued the elder brother, with a cruel pertinacity, "loved the girl well, and died of sorrow for her. My 'countrymen and brothers' pointed at our shame; they visited the sins of the children upon the father, and drove him forth in his old age, a childless and ruined man."

"They did," said the youth; "he came to the island, and he died in my arms."

"My 'countrymen and brothers,'" added Oran, with a ferocious sneer, "have left the oldest and youngest to weep for the others.—Here is the commission——We will avenge them!"

For a moment Hyland seemed to share the fire of the outcast; for a moment he grasped the parchment which the other had put into his hand. His face flushed,—then turned pale; he hesitated,—faltered; the badge of honour fell to the earth; and clasping his hands together, he looked at Oran imploringly, and said,

"My father died in my arms, and charged me, with his last breath, to forget that he had been wronged."

"It was the weakness of his death-hour," said Oran.

"He bade me," continued the youth, "leave his enemies to God, and the destroyer of his peace to his fate."

"Look at his fate!" cried the refugee: "wealth surrounds him, and he is envied for his happiness; while you are ashamed of your father's name, and I am poor, and abhorred, and miserable."

"We will go to the island, and forget"— —

"Will you have the commission?" said Oran, abruptly. "You have youth, talents, education and fortune,—and will rise. This commission is to serve among the royal refugees; but if you carry it bravely at the first bout, I have the General's word you shall be transferred to the line, with a fair field for promotion."

"Look, Oran," said the youth, manfully, "I will not take the commission, nor will I trust your commander's promises. You have served him from the beginning; and none have served him better. How has he rewarded you?—You are still a captain of refugees!"

A shadow of humiliation passed over the face of the renegade; but he answered without emotion.

"I sought nothing better, nor am I fit for promotion. My station is where my habits and inclinations put me,—among the free rangers. But you have learning, youth, ambition; and are capable of training into discipline."

"I will not take the commission," said Hyland, with increasing resolution. "I have been enough with our people,—with the Americans,—to know that their cause is just, and holy, and is prevailing. Nay, you must know, that, at this moment, commissioners are deliberating over the preliminaries of negotiation, and that peace must soon be concluded."

"It is false," said the refugee, fiercely; "a trick of the ministers,—a common stratagem."

"True, or false, then, yet am I resolved to shed no blood in the quarrel; and, certainly, I will take no commission to distress the people of this neighbourhood. Oran, I am resolved; I will not fight; and I adjure you by the last wish of our poor father, and by your own hopes of future quiet, that you give up your schemes of blood, and leave this fatal valley for ever. Disband your followers; and take heed you be not suddenly deserted by your employers."

"Boy!" said the outlaw, "you are not white-livered, or you would not say these things to me! Look you, I know your folly: it is not for me,—not because you love liberty and peace,—not because you have laid to heart the dotish words of a half crazed father,—that you are so cold and shameless; but because you have set your eyes on the baby face of a girl, who will laugh at you, when the last fit of your folly is over. Hark you,—read me this knavish letter, and see what is already said of you."

"I have read it," said the young man, faltering.

"Ay, but read it again: let me know how far your madness has been talked of." And Hyland, summoning courage, took the letter and read it, though his embarrassment increased at the paragraph concerning himself, which had caused Oran to snatch it so suddenly from the hands of the volunteer. This paragraph, couched in the coarsest terms, expressed a knowledge of his affections, which had alarmed him at first excessively, though, it was probable, it was nothing more than the shrewd guess of a keen observer; and it concluded by showing how easily he might be 'nabbed, while at his gallivanting.'

"And this, then," cried the refugee, "it is that makes you so tame, so spiritless! Poor fool, could you look on none but the betrothed of a Falconer? Look you, boy, you are in a bear-trap, and the log will soon be on your back: with this baby fancy, shameful and dishonourable, you are gulling yourself into perdition."

"Oran," cried the young man, throwing himself upon the wild man's mercy, "this poor girl is betrothed against her will; and if no friend stands by her, there will be another broken heart laid by the side of Jessie. Do not scoff at me, or reproach me: she saved my life, she has treated me with a sister's kindness and trust; and if she will suffer me to aid her, I will rescue her from her misery, though I die for it."

"Do what you will," said Oran, with a gloomy frown: "though you had her heart and love, what will she say to you, when this cunning daughter of a villain, that sent yonder Parker to the rope, ferrets out your secret, and shows you to be a son of the Gilberts? Nay, what will others say to you? It is better to die as a soldier, than a spy!"

"I am no spy," said Hyland; "and when the time comes for disclosure, I will not fear to acknowledge my name."

"It will soon come," said the refugee. "Go," he added, sternly; "you are rushing upon destruction. Save yourself as you can, till midnight; and then take the commission, or be lost. Begone from this place; it will be soon full of soldiers—I have sent for them; and already they are coming.—Brother," he said, relenting, as the young man turned to depart: he strode after him and took him by the hand: "What have you or I to do with the love of woman? This is but a folly.—You have no friend or kinsman left to advise or help you.—Well, if the girl be willing to fly, why, put her upon a fleet horse, and to-morrow she shall be beyond the reach of a Falconer. It shall not be said, I deserted you, even in your folly."

How much further the wild and flinty outlaw might have been softened by the distress he saw pictured on his brother's face, cannot be told. The gentler feeling of affection beginning to yearn in his bosom, was chased away by a sudden sound like the flourish of a distant trumpet, which came trembling over the forest-leaves.

"Away," he cried hastily; "the curs are coming, and the troop with them. Dive into the swamp, and meet them on the road. To-night you shall see me."

So saying, he bounded down the hill with the activity of a mountain-buck, and was almost instantly lost to sight. The brother, crossing the swamp and brook, made his way to the road, some distance above the spot where he had dismounted.